Praise for *Mind*

"The Irish Tourist Board should reprint thousands of copies and use them as promotional material – bugger the Blarney Stone."
    Time Out

"A Corkonian Roddy Doyle, with an equally exact ear for the way people speak, but with a more subversive sense of humour . . . "
    Examiner

"A novel of brotherly love guaranteed to make readers laugh and cry embarrassingly in public . . . "
    Carl Miller, *Time Out*

"Gaye Shortland has got what it takes."
    Isabel Healy, *Examiner*

"The madness of obsession and the undying lust of the spirit are portrayed in scenes that are bound to offend. I loved it."
    Bill Hughes, Director, *Radius Television (Irish Times)*

"Outrageous characterizations abound in this hugely enjoyable first novel . . . a comic masterpiece."
    Gay Community News

Turtles all the
way down

Gaye Shortland

Turtles all the
way down

POOLBEG

Published 1997
by Poolbeg Press Ltd
123 Baldoyle Industrial Estate
Dublin 13, Ireland

The Publishers gratefully acknowledge the support of
The Arts Council.

A catalogue record for this book is available from the British Library.

ISBN 1 85371 699 5

Cover photograph by Mark Nixon
Cover design by Poolbeg Group Services Ltd
Set by Poolbeg Group Services Ltd in AGaramond 11.5/14
Printed by The Guernsey Press Ltd,
Vale, Guernsey, Channel Islands.

A Note on the Author

Born and bred in Cork, Gaye Shortland acquired a first class MA in English and taught Shakespeare at the University of Leeds. Devotion to Lawrence of Arabia and a compulsion to chase nomads led her to the Sahara where she taught TS Eliot to the appalled locals and chased the nomadic Tuareg for sixteen years with some success, acquiring three children in the process. Economic collapse forced her back to Ireland where her current husband took one look at life on the dole and, horrified, fled back to Africa. This trauma led her to imagine she was a gay man, resulting in her first novel *Mind That 'tis My Brother*.

Turtles All the Way Down is a sequel.

To Martin O'Brien –
Who isn't even a Corkman
But who gave no less than everything
For this book –
With love and thanks.

Brief Reflection on Death

Many people act
As if they hadn't been born yet.
Meanwhile, however,
William Burroughs, asked by a student
If he believed in life after death,
Replied:
– And how do you know you haven't died yet?

Miroslav Holub

1

CHAPTER ONE

So there we were on the Numbur 8, meself and Dec an Liam, the Saturday a the Octobur weekend – the Guinness Jazz Weekend. An to tell yeh the truth I was pissed off. I hate to admit it now but I was.

I know tis a bad note to start off on. I mean the last time I was talkin to yeh – aftur the funeral – aftur my funeral –

Yeah, tis me – Tony, the only survivur of AIDS unknown to modern medicine.

How're yeh doin yurself?

As I was sayin, the last time I was talkin to yeh I was on ecstasy, like yur wan – *The*-hills-*are-alive* – gallopin down that Alpine meadow. Orgasmic, in othur words.

A well-known effect a survivin yur own funeral.

But now, on the Numbur 8, I was pissed off. Isn't human nature a queer thing? You'll grant me "human nature", I hope? Dead an all as I am?

Yeh could say the honeymoon was ovur.

Yeah, I hate to admit it but – twasn't exactly Anothur Day in Paradise with Dec aftur all. We were spendin so much a our time in bed waitin for Dole Day to come round.

How bad, yeh might say, seein as how he's the love a me

3

aftur-life an I'd smothur me mothur for him. True, but believe me, yeh can spend only so much a the day havin sex when you're doin all the work an yur partnur isn't liftin so much as a fingur. I haven't the stamina for it anyway. Sometimes I get lucky an he has an erection. Mostly he reads. An y'know Dec – tis all a bit on the highbrow side. So tis Terry Pratchett an the life a Blessed Faustina Kowalska an *Interview with the Vampiyur*. I'm gettin inta it though – the readin. Honest to God.

Mindya, not bein ashes in an urun any longur, I could always get up an go out trawlin – but, well, for bettur for worse – *Yeh makes yur bed an yeh has to lie on it . . .*

Anyway: that day the streets a Cork were *jointed* with foreignurs an yeh'd a given yur two eyes out to see any one of em in his thermals – an Hallowe'en comin up in two nights' time, what's more, so the place was hoppin.

But me – I was *septic* about everythin.

Like these two young wans on the bus – one a them smokin an the othur chewin gum.

An Fag goes: "C'mere – did yeh see *Home an Away* last night?"

"I did," says Gum chewin away.

"What did yeh think?"

"God, twas stupit!"

"Ah twas! What did yeh think about Shane an Nick an the drivin test?"

"Jesus, that was stupit!"

"An Sam an the fire?"

"Stupit!"

"An Tug thought Sarah fancied him!"

"The eejit!"

"Ah, God, tis gettin very stupit all right," an Fag takes a deep drag with Gum chewin away like wintur was fast approachin an hur husband was short a pair a sealskin boots. Nothin for a while.

Then Fag looks at Gum. "So what d'yeh think about the philosophy classes? Do we have to go to any more, d'yeh think?"

"Naaah – shur we've got that all covered."

I mean *what*! An sure enough when I looked they were clutchin files an books to their chests – students! God help us all.

I swear to God – that was their conversation. Verbatim. Which it isn't – verbatim like – but I learnt the word recently (Terry Pratchett) an I fancy usin it.

I mean, do these people have any *brains* in their skulls? What is it Prince says? Somethin like *half a the staff a their brains are on vacation?*

But – yeh know what? Tis really *great* to be talkin to yeh again. Yeh havta excuse me if I'm all ovur the place. Y'see – I've no one to be listenin to me normally. Dec listens some a the time. But yeh could say we have a Communication Problem.

We should go on Oprah.

Can't blame him. He doesn't do bad, considerin. I mean, yeh can't expect livin with a Pure Spirit to be second nature, in all fairness. That's what I am now, y'know – a Pure Spirit.

No visible means a support.

Carry on Evolvin. Y'know, like that ad on the buses – there's the chimp an the gorilla an the caveman an yur man steppin up to the Hole-in-the-wall with his Passcard but there in front of em all – invisible like – is Me. Leadin the parade in the Ascent a Man.

Or not.

But eithur way I'm a pretty needy spirit these days. An I've a strong feelin I'm goin to talk yur ass off. Don't say I didn't warn yeh.

What's that? Yeh don't have any serious objections to that? Yeah, but is it goin to be like one a them rape trials? Like yeh'll let me fuck yeh an then yeh'll say I didn't ask first?

OK – I'm askin.

I wish.

Ah God, I think we bettur get back on that Numbur 8.

But – maybe we could talk about that notion latur?

Yeah?

Jesus, talk about gettin side-tracked –

Shanghaied even – back to the Numbur 8 fast before I get carried away altogethur –

Gum an Fag were sayin how stupit their philosophy lecturer was.

I moved up the bus. *Septic* now like.

I tell yeh, I'da given Hamlet a run for his money on the Numbur 8 – *Oh, how weary flat seems this world* – how does it go again? Saw him on telly a few nights ago – Mel Gibson like. Preferred him in *The Bounty*. Jesus, he was gorgeous in that. The pigtail an all. But he wasn't half bad doin Hamlet. I really liked the part where it looked like he was fuckin his mothur – I thought that was a brilliant touch. It looked so natural like.

Dec was havin a chat with a bunch a ouldies.

The Flu.

"Tis in the ayur," says a scrawny little ould wan in a purple velvet hat with a vicious-lookin hat-pin stickin outa it – Mrs Burke. "It makes no diffurence whatevur yeh takes – yeh're only coddin yurself – oh, tis a fright!"

"Yeh have ta stay away from the ayur – thas the only thing," says a decrepit ould fella next to hur, blue in the lips an thin in the nose – like somethin outa the deep freeze. "If we stayed at home we'd be safe enough."

"A better idea again, Mr Callaghan, is to stay in the pub –" says Dec.

"Batin back the pints a Guinness –" Liam.

"Oh, there's no fear for ye! With yeer pubs!" goes Mrs Burke, the voice climbin to the sky an swoopin up an down in the real Cork way like one a them rollur-coasters at the Merries. "An if ye gets a sniffle at all ye takes to the bed. Oh, ye're very bad then! Ye're desperate altogethur!"

"True for yeh, girel," goes the ould wan sittin ovurright hur, knee to knee – Mrs Mac. "There's nothin like a man for makin a mountain outa a moleskin, I always says!"

I expected a bit of a sniggur from Liam at this – but the lads got distracted at this point, lookin outa the winda. An there it was: the Smirnoff ad with the ould fella an the three blond goldy anjuls in white loincloths an Baywatch tans. Me boyos' heads swivelled while we sailed past, an Dec lookin like a goldy anjul himself with the browny-blond hair shinin an blue eyes glintin.

"Octobur," says Dec to Liam. "The month of the Guardian Anjuls."

Well, so long as he was inta anjuls I was still in the runnin.

Also Ran.

Meself, I fancied the one on the right.

"Himself, now," says Mrs Mac, tappin Mrs Burke on the knee, "himself has me pesturred. Maggie, there's a draught from under the door there – Maggie, that's a fierce draught from the winda! Well, I'm goin in now to Dunnes an I'm goin to buy him some a that terminul undurwear. An that's that. Aah, I couldn't be puttin up with that at all, day in day out!"

"Terminal undurwear? That's an excellent idea, Mrs Mac," says Dec straight-faced.

"The final solution," says Liam, grinnin behind his hand an the Luke Perry quiff. If yeh remembur, me brothur looks a bit like Luke Perry altogethur –y'know, outa *Beverly Hills* – or Luke Perry gone anorexic with a sharp Cork nose. An dark blue eyes – his best feature, as they say.

"Oh, Liam," says Mrs Burke, "wasn't I almost forgettin! I have the Petition for Tony God-rest-him here in me bag –" An she starts rootin.

"Aren't you very good!" Dec.

"Ah shur, we'd wanta be very bad not ta remembur him for the month a the Holy Souls –" says she, fishin out the usual small brown envelope with the weight a the pound coin in one cornur of it. "St Petur an Paawl's –" meanin that she wanted em to take it there for me to be put on the Novembur Dead List. For prayurs an masses like.

An I felt kinda touched an vexed at the same time – so I moved off an climbed the stairs to the uppur deck. When I say "climbed" now, yeh shouldn't see me in yur mind's eye as actually *climbin* – as if I had legs like. Which I don't. Tell yeh what – yeh can imagine me kinda swoopin around like Robin Williams in *Aladdin*. That's what it *felt* like anyway. Or the vampiyurs in the Lestat novels – Dec an meself were on the third book at that point an mad for it.

Vampiyurs? No, I haven't met any yet. I'm *hopin* to meet one. Not that I'd be his type, like. But we could always fake it.

Thing is, I haven't met *any* hunky Immortals or Highways-to-Heaven or anythin at all in that line besides meself since I died – an that's one a the things that was buggin me those days. I mean, yur average TV viewur would take it for granted that I'd be *jostlin elbows* with all a them types – like we'd be pissin against lamp-posts to mark off our territories – but no such luck.

So – uppur deck.

"Neeuv! Sit down or I'll swing yeh around the bus like a fuckin *rat!*"

Mothur an child.

Jesus.

Lowur deck.

"Jesus, let's face it – he'd be very stupit –"

But relief was in sight. There was the rivur with the Bus Station across it, the red brick a Merchants Quay, then Patrick Street with the statcha a Fathur Mathew –

The stink from Patrick's Bridge is wickit
How do Fathur Mathew stick it?
Here's up em all
Sez the Boys a Fair Hill –

an furthur along, like a slap in the eye, the grey blank side a the Opera House commonly known as The North Face a the Eigur.

The bus crossed the bridge an swung round the cornur by the Cats an Dogs – happy days – remembur? Remembur me tellin yeh about the toilets there in the old days with the hole in the wall? That yeh could function through without seein the othur fella at all?

How well yeh remembur that, now.

So, merciful relief, we were off the bus an mobile.

Not. Dec wanted to go to the jacks in the Bus Station.

So, not havin any desire to piss, jack off or voy-watcha-callit (I was jaded with that by this time) I stayed outside starin ovur the wall into the rivur. Imaginin all the crap undur the shinin surface. *Oh how weary flat . . .* somethin about *unprofitable . . .*

Did ya larn it?

Sur, the cat ate the candle.

Bend ovur –

I stared at the rivur an I felt it comin . . . an I tried to resist . . . but I knew I wouldn't . . . an then with a little whoosh a relief I opted outa it all an let me mind slide away . . .

Private Tony O'Rourke watched the sweat trickle ovur the muscled back not six inches from his face.

"Stay close behind me, boy," said Major O'Hara.

"Yes, sur!" said Private O'Rourke.

Major O'Hara looked so like Clint Eastwood – he coulda been his twin. The very head off him.

Private O'Rourke was only half-surprised to hear from somewhere close by the slow and powurful growl of a heavy metal band:

Ain't found a way to kill me yet

Eyes burn with stingin sweat

Seems every path leads me to nowhere . . .

Private O'Rourke watched the sweat form a little rivur down the strong spine now not three inches from his lips – well, four – four inches, while the machete rose an fell untiringly. The man was like a machine – untiring.

Yeh said that.

Walkin tall machine gun man
They spit on me in my home land . . .

An the bass growled makin the hairs stand up all ovur Private Tony's body an doin somethin interestin to his private parts:

Waah waah waah waah
Waah waah waah waah – waah!
Waah waah waah waaaaaaaaaaaaah!

"Those landing-gears were sure shot to hell, boy," said the Major. Between strokes.

"Only you coulda brought us down in this unpenetrable jungle – sur," said Private Tony, now tastin the salt a the perspiration dancin off the Major's skin – tanned skin – the Major's tanned skin.

"Too bad there's only you an me left, boy, and two hundred kilometres as the crow flies between us an the nearest military base," said the Major with his deltoids workin like oiled machinery. His right deltoids.

"Too bad, sur," answered Private Tony, his voice perfectly controlled. Nobody could've guessed he had a really massive hard-on undur his fatigues.

"Don't worry, son – you an me'll live to look back on this dirty little war an see it written with a small 'w'. But I think you'd better hold onto my belt, Private. A man could step a yard into this zoo – especially a cherry like you – an be lost forever. In fact, you'd better put your arm around my waist – your free arm, that is, the one not carryin the AK-47s and the M-16s and my helmet and combat jacket, the flak jackets, the Pig . . . the C-rats, grenade launcher . . ."

Damn. Too much fuckin equipment –

At that point I came to meself.

An there you have it: Major *fuckin* O'Hara. Twas drivin me spare. Twas my misfortune that Liam'd got *Platoon* out on video one night – Dec freaked an wouldn't sit through it but I was mesmerised – an I started havin heart-stoppin fantasies from that night on – about William Dafoe originally but aftur the first throes he trans-whatsited inta me old favourite, Clint Eastwood, an I was hooked. An I feel that's a really shameful thing for a spirit to havta admit. I feel like goin to Confession or somethin. A thing I nevur done while I was in the flesh – since I was a kid like – "Fathur, I get excited thinkin about men's middles" – will I evur forget it? I nearly died in that confession box.

The things that Catholics do to their childrun are unreal. Imagine sendin yur kid inta a small dark box to talk sex with a man who's three chances to one a chickun-fanciur! Jesus, the priests didn't even havta go out an cruise.

Talk about Home Delivery.

Eat In or Take-away.

I Feel like Chicken Tonight.

I was lucky that day though – he was dacent enough – three Hail Marys. He told me I'd grow out of it. Hah – the last laugh's on him, isn't it?

I'll – be – back.

Whaaaaaam! Confession box an all!

Terminatur, like.

But – to get back to Major-fuckin-O'Hara. There I was, for all I knew the only human bein evur to make it to the Pure Spirit stage, with some really heavy questions to be answered – an all I could do was waste this amazin injury-time – or whatevur it was I'd been granted – on mangy little fantasies . . .

Pathetic.

An besides, wasn't I supposed to be in love? Hadn't I been Ovur the Rainbow an back an found me Rainbow's End – Dec's like – in me own back yard?

But all that equipment? Could Private Tony be humpin all a that stuff through the jungle? Realistically like? No – he'd havta dump it. They'd havta keep the AK-47s an the M-16s – but the rest – only a wimp would wear a flak-jacket in any case, especially in that heat – but if he dumped the Pig I'd havta cut the Rambo scene – I didn't wanta cut the Rambo scene . . .

I was wrestlin with this decision when Dec's clear voice, bright and strong with layurs a laughter in it, fell on me ear.

"– the one about the GPO?"

"Jay, that was a good one all right –"

I swung round. By that I mean I stopped focusin on Major O'Hara doin Rambo an switched to Dec and Liam. It felt like swingin round.

If I'd a smile, an a face to put it on, yeh could a said me smile froze.

Dec was in his gear. His drag. His nun drag.

Shit.

Sistur Veronica rides again. The flat shoes an the nylon stockins, the silver cross an the short veil. The navy cardigan an the white blouse with the little round collar. An the navy blazur ovur the lot. I'd nevur noticed him puttin the stuff in the bag.

Oh *shit*.

Don't get me wrong now. Normally Veronica wouldn't be

13

doin anythin dramatic – well, I know, yeah, the last time yeh met hur twas a bit hair-raisin – but normally, inta Bewley's for a cuppa most likely. But, y'know, I wasn't in the mood. I nevur liked it anyway – him doin his thing. Except that it made him happy – so yeh'd let him off like.

Dec gave what yeh might call a silvury peal a laughtur.

He was thinkin a me but he was right in charactur. Twas amazin how he could do it.

"How did it go again?" says Liam an yeh could see he just wanted to hear Dec tellin it.

They were talkin about one time a German tourist was tryin to make a long-distance call from one a the boxes ovurright the GPO. He couldn't understand what this friend a mine, Jimmy, the telephone-operatur, was sayin. He kept sayin "Ja! Ja!" an doin the wrong thing. Well, y'know, the Telephone Exchange is actually upstairs *ovur* the GPO. So finally Jimmy goes "OK, just hold it, Callur!" an *runs* outa the Telephone Exchange an down the stairs to where the call-boxes are, an into the box, grabs the receivur from yur man, shoves in the money, dials the propur code, shoves the receivur back inta yur man's hand and says "Callur, you're through!"

"Callur, you're through!" said Dec. "Tony loved that one – God but you'd miss Tony!"

You'd miss Tony, how are yeh! But suddenly I felt a million times bettur. I was cheerin up anyway – we were headin down Olivur Plunkett Street an the exercise was raisin me spirits. Yeah, really. Does that surprise yeh? I'd even taken to joggin – like I'd go out an swoop around the block at night just for the hell of it. Or, if I got lucky, in the slipstream a one a them feens in slinky shorts – a type that I kinda fancy, but Dec calls "a port in a storm" an that's always said with a pityin look an sometimes with a "wouldn't yeh feel for *hur*!" – they'd be a bit scrawny for him like.

Anyway – we might a been headin for Bewley's or we might a been headin for the Imperial. Twould havta be somewhere genteel like with the cut a Dec. But anyway when we hit the GPO cornur we were hailed by an awful screech from Winthorp Street – that's the short pedestrian street with The Long Valley on it, leadin onta Pana – that's Patrick Street to you.

"Leeeeeeeeeeeeem! Deeeeeeeeeeeec!"

"Oh Jesus," says Liam.

Mad Mary, mini-skirt up to his ass, Cher wig skew-ways ovur his left earhole, hatchet-nose flyin at us like a tomahawk.

Liam kinda cringed.

I kinda cringed meself.

But Sistur Veronica stood hur ground, claspin the wrists across the stomach an lowurin the chin, an Liam kinda fell back behind hur. Like Adam an Eve aftur eatin the apple.

"Class and breeding, command and elegance," says Sistur Veronica. "Your fiancée nevur fails to astonish me, Liam, howevur often I see her."

"Jesus," says Liam.

"Tizzy waants ye," screeches Mary, grabbin holda Dec. "He's in an aawful weeaay!" An he starts draggin Dec down Winthorp Street by main force, with the scraggy muscles standin out in his scrawny legs. "An Liz's freeekin – c'maaan, c'maaan, c'maaaaaan!"

"Merciful hour," says Dec throwin the head back an rollin the eyes up like his own impression a Isabella Duncan

– y'know, that arty-farty dansur he's mad about. "Pray, good people, be civil! I am the *Protestant* whore."

What? The Protestant whore?

"C'maan! C'maan!" screeched Mary. "C'maan, Regeeeena!"

Regina – Dec's nickname like.

The *Protestant* whore – like as distinct from the *Catholic* whore?

Where in the name a God did he get that?

An the state a mind I was in, I was more worried about who the Protestant whore was than about Liz or Tizzy or why Mary was screechin like a demented hen. Mindya, Mary was always screechin like a demented hen. The original Screamin Mary. Is that a Cork one? "Screamin Mary", like?

I watched Dec an Mary tearin around Cudmore's cornur fastur than the speed a light with Liam kinda laggin behind. An I didn't feel that much inclination to go aftur em.

So I decided to take time out.

I know, I know – so Guardian Anjuls are always on the job – well, OK, so I felt guilty like. But, as they say in California, I needed my space.

What's more – I had my agenda.

So I said *fuck um* an crossed Pana an went inta Easons an started lurkin around the magazine shelves readin *Q* an *Hot Press* an the like ovur people's shouldurs. This was dead easy because a the steady stream a guys – all guys an they're tryin to tell us there's no such thing as gendur differences – doin their weekly survey a the music scene at Easons' magazine stands.

That day one a the security guards was right there next to

the stand – a smallish dark fella with a pokey nose – an I couldn't relax inta what I was doin, so I moved ovur to the bookshelves an clung meself up agin a Tom Hanks lookalike. I was goin to read ovur *his* shouldur if he was readin *Goldilocks an the Three Bayurs*.

Now, think about it. This is one experience the likes a you can nevur have – like to wrap yurself around a total stranger in a bookshop an relax inta it like inta a hot bath an have a good read at the same time. I tell yeh, I was gettin addicted.

So there I was, intrudin on Tom Hanks's personal space an lovin it until I got gobsmacked by this thing he was readin an forgot all about him – well, almost.

C'mere till I tell yeh –

A little old lady gets up at a lecture an says that the world is really a flat plate on the back of a giant turtle.

An the lecturur says "Ah, but what is the turtle standing on?" An the little old lady says "Ah, you think you're very clever, young man, very clever! But it's turtles all the way down!"

Turtles all the way down.

Well, I gave one great *scairt* a laughtur inta Tom Hanks's earhole an at the same time he goes *slam* with the book an *I* get a fright that lands me back about five yards. Me nerves.

So Tom Hanks moves off an I come back to the shelf an on the covur a the book there's a picture of a fella all teeth an glasses grinnin away in a wheelchair with a blackboard fulla mathematical symbols behind his head. An I couldn't remembur his name latur but I knew it was somethin like Puking – though hardly like. An I knew he was one a them physis-whatsits – them feens who know all about back-to-the-future an time warps an all that.

That fuckur could probably tell me if I was in a Black Hole or if I was in a kinda Virtual Reality or somethin. Or if I was just a Sweet Transvestite from Transsexual Transylvania-a-a-a.

But what was I to do now? Wait for anothur Puking fan to chance along?

The security guard was aftur movin ovur next to me. I had the urge to step ovur an goose him but I took meself upstairs instead an straight ovur to the music section. There was a foxy young fella in skinhead gear there an as I came upta him, he glanced ovur his shoulder an I saw his eyes widen a bit – greeny-blue eyes in a face peppered with freckles. Me heart gave the usual little thump – for a tiny instant y'see thinkin he was lookin at me – I couldn't get used to the fact people were lookin through me. An besides, wide greeny eyes like that lookin directly at me would make me heart thump anyway. But then I looked back an there was the security guard lampin me – Pokey-nose from downstairs.

This time me heart stopped. This fella *was* seein me.

What's more, he was goin to read me me rights –

Foxy-nob moved round the stand an with no hesitation at all the hand snaked out an a cassette-tape dived inside his bombur jacket quicker than a flash.

Wow. *I got the expertise . . .*

When he moved off I moved off with him. I kept me eyes on Pokey-nose while we were goin down but he just stood there with the arms folded starin aftur us.

I hit the bottom an there he was – Pokey-nose. Standin at the bottom with the arms still folded.

Now me nerve really failed. I swooped halfway up the down-escalatur an met him comin down.

Back to the fuckin Future. I turned round an there he was at the bottom.

Down we sailed an I was waitin for the moment when these clones would fuse togethur or else close in on me. But what happened was: they did the kinda body movements that people do when they've nothin much to say to one anothur, kinda stampin the feet like horses at a fair, an one fella says to the othur – "Jaysus, but we'd a great night – I don't rembur a thing –"

Not clones. Twins.

This was serious.

I was really crackin up.

An I had this horrific flash a meself goin mad all alone in me Black Hole. Twould be like Hell, wouldn't it?

Now I was really scarin the shit outa meself. I shoulda been considerin sendin a script to Stephen King.

I was aftur losin Foxy-nob.

So out with me an there was Liz standin on hur own outside the Savoy with hur hands in hur pockets an even from where I was I could see she was like a light gone out. Mad Mary was wrong – she wasn't "freeekin." She was just totally down in the mouth. The bouncy fairish hair was dead an the whole Shiny-Happy-People look a hur was out ta lunch. Great. We were all crackin up.

But there was Foxy-nob goin inta Merchants Quay shoppin centur.

Liz looked like she needed me.

I zipped across the road an inta Merchants Quay.

Call it cruisin if yeh like. Or call it curiosity. Anway for the next five minutes I did a Sonic the Hedgehog – y'know, *zooooooooom* – all around Roches an Dunnes an Marks an

Sparks – an I carried on zoomin till I was zippin through the
last place I'd thought a findin him an there he was: upstairs
in Roches lingerie department eyin a Wondur-bra.

Oh.

Oh?

I was waitin for it. He was havin difficulty because the
girls at the cash-point were eyin him a bit. But he wanted
that bra. Black an green it was. He took a red-an-black effort
down from its hook on this revolvin stand an looked hard at
it an put it back. Then he moved on to the next stand,
fiddled at a few things an moved off. I only knew by the
glint in his eye that he'd done it.

Well, aftur that we lifted some nylon stockins from
Dunnes an an eye-linur from Marks an Sparks an a
Hallowe'en ghoul mask from Roches. Then he called it a day
an went inta Roches supurmarket an bought all this crap:
chocolate an crisps an jam biscuits an some kinda vile-lookin
raspberry lemonade. An a Winnin Streak scratchcard from
the kiosk there in the centur. Jesus, but wasn't he mad for a
rush? I wondered whether he mightn't pull out a gun next an
we'd hold up the cash-registur in Roches in our Hallowe'en
mask. But no – he scratched the card – we didn't win – an
then he bought a cream doughnut in Kylemore an stood
eatin it listenin to the jazz band stompin out some Dixieland
stuff in their Guinness straw boaturs there in the central area
– then he chased it down with a few swigs outa the bottle a
rasa (weren't yeh supposed to dilute that stuff?) an broke
open a packet a crisps.

I was feelin a bit queasy by this time an moreth'n a bit
turned off but I still followed him out an onta a Numbur 5.

Call it cruisin if you like. Or curiosity. Or call it bein

desperate for a bit a decent music – the cassette. I'd had Dec's La Stupenda – Joan Suthurland to you – up the arse for months.

Anyway, I had to check out the girlfriend – that the bra was for.

Right?

Right.

Seriously, though – about the music – at that time I'd a *died* for – oh, I can't say that – I'd a sold me soul for – jay, I can't say that eithur. All that I *had* was me soul – like good ould Tracy's momma – an like hur I'd learned that the hard way.

But, an this one goes out to all the REM fans I've left behind, there's one thing I *can* say: a passion for REM outlasts death. An I'd a given me two eyes out at that time for a copy a *Monstur.*

So I was lookin Foxy-nob up an down trying to figure out what he'd go for. Not ska or punk – I hoped. He didn't look like yur fanatical skin. Didn't have a real crop – it was longur even than a numbur five – more a crew-cut. He'd probably just go for techno-crap. Anyway, I knew his cassette wouldn't be *Monstur* – I couldn't be that lucky. I wasn't. But hang on a while. Wait'n I tell yeh.

He got out on College Road an walked back to a shabby-lookin house – a big old-fashioned one in a terrace – Minerva Terrace – I checked out the name. I thought maybe he was a student – like a first-year maybe – because a lot a them houses are let to students now but when we went in I got the feelin twas a family house. An sure enough a foxy girl with high-heeled boots an black leggins on hur came clatterin down the stairs an we goin up.

21

"Mam's gone out," says she an hur voice floatin back up the stairs to us. "She left the dinnur in the oven but it's flippin awful . . ."

"When'll yeh be back?" calls Foxy-nob aftur hur in a nice light kinda voice.

"I dunno – tonight –" an the front door banged.

For the first time I saw him smile. An he had a gap between his two front teeth. An me heart gave anothur little thump like a rabbit in a hutch.

His room was fierce macho altogethur with combat posturs an combat figures an comics lyin round like *X-men* – *Tank Girl* was there an *Judge Dredd* – an even kids' wans like *Bustur* an *Whizzur*. An a big pile a stuff like *True Detective* an – I forget the names but yeh know the kinda thing – *Serial Killurs Today*. There were airplane models an actionmen an Trekkie stuff all ovur the shop – an, aah, I spotted his cassettes so I skeetered ovur an had a gandur. Holy Hour! *What!* Haydn's *Creation* an Handel's ninth an Bach's sixth an Vivaldi's twenty-seventh an a half – *what*? Jesus, what was this stuff doin in a room where yeh thought he might take down a few hat-boxes an set up his display a severed heads – or worse – along the mantelpiece?

I should be so lucky. He slaps the cassette inta his hi-fi an turns up the volume –

I crossed me fingurs an held me breath – so to speak . . . Ah, shit, it meant nothin to me. A snappy guitarry intro an then this feen with his voice crackin like a thirteen-year-old:

We call them cool
Those hearts that have no scars to show . . .

But hang on – I'd heard it before all right –

We call them fools
Who have to dance within the flame –
The full horror didn't dawn on me yet.
But then –
Standing outside the fire
Standing outside the fire –
Oh *Jeeesus*!
Garth fuckin *Brooks*!
Oh *Gaaawd*.

Yur man meanwhile was strippin off his gear an jivin away (line-dancin?) to the music, so I tried to ignore the nausea brought on by Garth because this was worth seein – y'know, bombur jacket, braces, Union Shirt, Fred Perry – an then he was naked to the waist in those short jeans fit to do yur balls in when they're hitched up with the braces – with button-flies an the braces trailin ovur his ass an the laced-up boots a'course – DMs cherry red. He had that luminous kinda skin red-heads have with a kind of a blush to it – an the icin on the cake was these little tattoos he had, like SHARP (Skinheads against Racial Prejudice to you) around his navel an that neat Trojan just below his collarbone. An though he'd looked thin in his gear, he was very nicely muscled because a'course these skins go in for that – the bettur to be able to murdur each othur.

I'd found meself a beauty.

The boots came off with me seriously admirin the way his ass pushed against his jeans when he hitched his leg up to undo the laces.

I was beginnin to feel this where it mattered – all ovur. Because, like I told yeh before, once I'd crossed ovur an no longur actually had the equipment for the job, I'd become this kinda walkin prick – it's like me whole soul goes inta erection –

An, yeah, tis every bit as painful as it sounds.

But at this stage twas still pure pleasure, like gettin inta a hot bath.

But when he reached inside his wardrobe I kinda cringed. I was really confused by this time, expectin him to be gettin out his shouldur-holstur an 44 Magnum to do a Taxi Man – y'know, put in a spot a practice in fronta the mirror for assassinatin the Taoiseach – or the Tánaiste – or Big Bird –

But what came out was bright an pink an satiny an flouncy – yur deb's dress kinda thing. A ball-gown.

And a'course from the Wondur-bra stage I'd clicked that this was where it was at, but in me confusion an what with the severe shock a Garth Brooks (he was singin at this point about his Daddy an blood comin outa his mouth an nose – *The blood came from my mouth and nose but the tears came from his eyes*) the deb's dress floored me when it actually happened.

Twas the shock that done it – that an him whippin off his pants an undurpants an startin to do peculiar things to his dick – but suddenly I was past the hot bath stage an dealin with a very nasty hard-on. This really amazed me. I've nevur been inta TVs like – to put it in a nutshell I've no time for these trannies who don't want yeh to touch their dicks – an Dec gettin inta his gear doesn't do a thing for me. But I dunno why – watchin him go through his routine, posturin around in the green-an-black Wondur-bra an puttin this glittur-shadow on his eyes an gettin into the dress – well, Foxy-nob got to me that day. An at the same time I was angry. I was angry because me skinhead beauty was bein turned inta this kinda monstrosity before me eyes.

And he, Foxy-nob, was doin it.

I coulda killed him.

Garth an his old man were gettin down to basics – He said *"Son, it's gonna hurt me more than it hurts you"* – we've all heard that one – *but somehow I couldn't help but have my doubts* – as well you might, Garth boy –

I tried to chill out. I mean I didn't wanta admit I'd bitten off more than I could chew. I sat down on the bed – mentally like – an pretended I was his boyfriend an he was doin all this for me. That was even a worse turn-on.

I knew I must get up an go. This wasn't on. I tell yeh what I was afraid of – I was afraid that I'd get so much outa control that I'd go ovur an latch onta him an start jackin off against him like one a them pathetic dogs yeh see ruttin against people's legs.

I broke out in a sweat at the thought. I'd be barred from the Union.

Not on. Not on. This wasn't on.

Garth was singin a bluesy kinda song about kickin an screamin –

Ain't it funny how we come in kickin giddyup
And go out hollerin whoa –

I'm thinkin: problem solved – I'm just goin to come in my pants right now – if I had pants like – when yur man gives a final twitch to the carroty wig an a final wiggle a the bum an then he turns an fixes me with a smoulderin look. The hand with the inch-long pink false nails spreads out against the skirt an he vamps ovur an sits next to me on the bed. The false eyelashes sweep the blushered cheeks an he puts his hand on me crotch.

"Garth honey," says he in a swoonin voice. "Make love to me . . ."

Well, every atom in me went into a kind of a tailspin an the room went dark in fronta me eyes an I don't know if I left that house by the stairs or the winda or through the roof but when I came to meself I was tearin back to town like The Flash himself. An I hit St Finbarre's Cathedral before I wound down an stopped an leant up agin the wall, shakin an swearin, starin up at the Goldy Anjul waitin up there for the Last Day with his double-barrelled trumpet.

An some trick a the light made me think he was *glarin* down at me.

Talk about guilt.

I looked away, not wantin to meet his eye. *He* was doin his job. He wasn't fartin around an slopin off for a quick one.

Jesus! He put his hand right on me crotch! Well, where me crotch would be if I had one. How could he know where it *was*? Was he *seein* me? No, no *way* –

An to be taken for *Garth Brooks*! Without so much as a stetson on me – or a fat ass squeezed inta tight pants for that mattur –

Serve me right. What did I expect? Desertin me post. Jesus, I thought, but I should stick to me last. Turtles or no turtles I had a job to do an people to take care of.

So with this thought an enough guilt to wallpapur a room with, I pulled me scattered atoms togethur an navigated inta town. Private Tony AWOL – reportin for duty. Sur.

CHAPTER TWO

So we've somethin goin like? You an me? I mean the stuff I d'be tellin yeh – well, I wouldn't be tellin everyone. I'd be mortified. So? D'yeh think we should take it a bit furthur? Not rushin yeh like . . . *I've got all the time in the wor-rold* –

I think.

Tizzy was AWOL when I got back an they were tearin in an outa shops an pubs demented lookin for him. I found em – with Liz – batin their way through the crowd in fronta Roches. Twas murdur there – y'see, Cork people have a habit a meetin on the pavement in fronta Roches for no good reason at all – well, except it's near where the buses stop at The Statcha –

What? The Statcha – oh, right, The Sta*tue* – of Father Mathew, The Apostle a Temperance, that is – y'know, the guy who tried ta stop us drinkin ourselves inta the grave.

As I was sayin before I was so rudely interrupted – what? No, I'm only messin – that's just a joke – Jesus, are yeh gettin all sensitive on me now or what? Isn't it always the way? As soon as sex rears its ugly head, the best a relationships start gettin dodgy . . .

Joke.

Joke!

Jaysis, will yeh let me get on with the story! Look – look – I didn't *mind* bein interrupted – you're entitled to interrupt me if yeh don't undurstand what I'm sayin – aren't I always tellin yeh to call here to me? OK? Can we move on now? OK.

In any case, yeh know I don't think sex has an ugly head – not any a the ones I've seen –

As I was saying: Roches' pavement – an the whole a Pana – was jointed.

But meself, I could cut through a crowd like a knife through buttur an I got the ould antennas up an found Tizzy no trouble at all an hustled the rest of em along to him easily enough.

So there he was – in fronta the goldy shrine to the Mothur a Good Counsel in Saint Augustine's – on his knees (his favourite position but prayin on this occasion) – a picture a distress an innocence. He coulda been a young saint a the Middle Ages or somethin, with the pale face uplifted an the gorgeous lips tremblin an the puddin-basin hair. Tizzy's a hairdressur, if yeh remembur, an twas wonderful the way the candlelight was pickin out the honey streaks an highlights – Zeffurelli now coulda done somethin with him, like with a few sparras thrown in or wolves an strappy sandals in the snow. Even the bitten fingurnails looked the part.

Dec touched him on the shouldur an he nearly collapsed.

"*Jesus* Mary an Josuph!"

"Take it easy, boy!" whispered Liam. "C'man out in the porch –"

"No, no, no!" Tizzy was freakin out, grabbin Liam's arm.

"Dey'll be lookin for me! Dey'll be checkin out De Odhur Place for me!"

So who was "dey"? I still hadn't a clue what was goin on.

No way could they get Tizzy outa the church. "No, no! De Odhur Place'll be swarmin with bluebottles –"

The *guards*? Jesus, what'd he done? The Othur Place – y'know, the cafe an Gay Centur next door to St Augustine's – yeah, they'd be casin it if he'd done somethin outa line. But what? Tizzy was *always* the victim, always gettin beaten up, mugged, robbed, raped – you name it, someone had done it to Tizzy – an then come back an had anothur bash for good measure.

They hadta give up on tryin to shift him outa the church an they done a tour a the Chalky Gods instead – Olivur Plunkett, Rita (Dec's favourite) an so on – talkin in stage whispurs that echoed all ovur the church an had the few decrepit charactur there givin us looks.

So there they were – all starin up at the picture a Rita, Patron a Hopeless Cases, with hur cat a nine tails at hur feet an she lookin all orgasmic at a crucifix that's hittin hur in the forehead with somethin like a lasur-beam – *Star Trek* again but yeh can't get away from it can yeh? Where was I? Oh yeah, there they all were pretendin to be transfixed, except poor Tizzy who was beyond keepin up appearances.

An Mary who was checkin his wig for split ends.

"So what *happened*, Tizzy?" whispurs Liam.

Tizzy had one hand clasped on the back of his neck kinda draggin at the roots of his hair an he spoke in a breathless voice without lookin anybody in the face. "Wan a de Fathur Rock boys soured on me – he hadta really because we trampled on his cakes –"

"God grant us patience —" Sistur Veronica with the eyes turned up. "*What* did *you* do to *him*?"

"I toldyah —" cackles Mary.

"Shut up, Mary!" says Liam.

"Tizzy —" Liz tryin to get a word in.

"I was just foolin around," Tizzy blushed. "I din't ask him for money or anythin —"

"But *what* did yeh *do*?" Liam in a fierce whispur.

"He shagged him, dint he, I toldyah," says Mary with a horse's whinny that bounced off the rafturs.

"Shut *up*, Mary!" Mary was goin to get a clattur from Liam if he didn't belt up. "Look, Tizzy, we know what yeh *didn't* do —"

Tizzy has only the one ball, remembur — so they knew he'd hardly be up to shaggin anybody up agin the wall in broad daylight — well, early mornin or whatevur.

"So we're askin yeh: what *did* yeh do?"

Tizzy started wringin his hands togethur in that way he has. "I only gave him a gobble-job . . ." an he squinched his face up like he was suckin a lemon.

"Well, we can thank God he was old enough for *that*!" Dec.

"Where?" Liam wanted to know.

Tizzy looked up at Liam kinda puzzled an I swear for a minute he was goin to say "His cock, where else?" but then he copped on an said "Ovur in de lane behind Whippins an Lashins —" The Irish Girl Guides to you.

"When?"

"Yesturday mornin — he was on his run — dat's how he had his tray with him — an I swear I nevur meant it — I just stepped on de cakes by accident — what happened was —"

"*Fuck* the cakes," Liam snarled in a whispur, doin severe damage to his larynx judgin by the way he clutched at his throat afturwards. Try it yurself some time.

I should fill yeh in here: Fathur Rock is a big Franciscan with a berd – beard – who's set up workshops an drug-abuse centurs an trained all these young fellas to make cakes an the like – you'd see em all round town with their big trays a cakes with check cloth ovur um an the lads in their white coats an check trousers with them cute little hats – y'know the ones – like papur boats upside down. Most of um young fellas in their early teens. Some of um right appealin.

They haven't got round to accusin him – Fathur Rock – a sexual abuse yet. An it'll be a fuckin tragedy when they do because the whole a Cork has fantastic respect for him. Don't get me wrong now – I've nevur heard anythin against the man unless yeh count lashin the lads' bums with his Franciscan cord – playfully like – an cuttin one fella's hair off with a garden-shears as a joke –

The only odd thing – *I* think – is that the social workurs an volunteers – girls now like – keep fallin in love with the oldur lads an runnin off with them to the States an Sweden an suchlike. But that's not Fathur Rock's fault. I suppose.

The lads were aftur movin down to the back a the church an they stopped outside the Chalky God shop that appeared there like an ovurnight mushroom at one stage – in the right-hand cornur – *inside* the church like.

"Tizzy, yeh *moron* –"

"He'd nevur a soured on me if it weren't for de cakes – dey were cream wans, y'see an –"

"Jesus!"

"Yeh stupit *muppet*, Tizzy –"

"Yeh know him, Leem – with de foxy hayur –"

"*Him!* That young fella! Shur that little fuckur d'be upta all kinds a craic!"

I saw hur before any a them. A sour-faced ould wan with glasses – y'know, the tight perm an the nylons an the dead-even dentures – glarin at em from the door a the shop.

"Excuse me," says she lookin daggurs. "Is there a problem, Sistur?"

"Yes, there is," says Dec without missin a beat an I heard Liam suck in his breath.

There was goin to be a *fuckin outrage*.

Dec had this kinda bright-eyed look like Maggie Thatchur usedta have before reachin out to grab the Cabinet by the balls. "I don't know how long it is since you read your New Testament," says he, soundin almost chatty, "but I'd advise you to check out your Gospel according to Matthew –"

I twigged where he was comin from. Or goin to. Oh Christ. Yur wan was lookin stupid at him.

An next thing Dec was hittin high doh: *"Then Jesus went into the temple of God, and drove out all those who bought or sold there –"*

There was a click a dentures – yur wan's mouth was aftur fallin open.

We were all bug-eyed.

The arm went out an pointed at the shop – *"It is written, my house shall be a house of prayer, but you have made it into a den of thieves!"* Or words to that effect.

She's still gapin at him.

An Liz an Liam were freeze-framed in this Crucifixion pose like Mary an John, with their hands to their hearts, an

Mad Mary makin a grand Mary Magdalen tearin at hur wig behind em.

But when he drew breath for anothur round they were galvanised inta action an he was grabbed an frog-marched out to the porch where he started straightenin the veil in a fierce huff – like a nun that'd just been raped an was real put out about it.

"I enjoyed that," says he once he'd recovered. "Righteous angur. Nothing like it."

"Oh, great goin," says Liam, snortin. "Low profile – that's you. Yur wan is bound to call someone."

"Yeh should've had a whip though," says Liz, chucklin away to hurself. "To scattur hur with."

"Run back there, Tizzy," says Dec. "And see if she's got a cat o' nine tails for sale –"

Tizzy looked amazed. "A cat?" says he uncertainly.

"For Chrissake –" says Liam.

"The Ships' Chandlurs near the Cats and Dogs would be the suppliers for that kinda thing –" says Liz with the mischief dancin outa hur eyes.

"A casss! A casss!" screeched Mary. "Whacha wanss a casss for?"

"Holy Hour," says Liam.

"A cat?" says Tizzy again.

"But, Liz," says Dec. "The Roman House is nearur and they must have them – for supplying the convents, you know – self-flagellation –"

"Holy Hour," says Liam. He looked fit to be tied.

"De Cats an Daaogs," screamed Mary. "Dey aalweeays has streeays dere –"

"Jesus Christ!" Liam. "Will ye shut *up*!"

They did. Dec smirkin. Liz bitin the lip to keep serious. Tizzy bitin the nails. An Mary – well, nevur mind about Mary.

A lot a heavy breathin from Liam. "What'll we do about Tizzy?"

"I'll teeake him houm ta me mam!" screeches Mary.

"Mary, you haven't a brain," says Dec. "They're sure to check all our places –"

"No, no," says Liam. "Hould yur horses – that's not true – shur they haven't a clue about Mary –"

Mary bein permanently incognito like. I didn't know his propur name meself.

"What about Fawlty?" asked Liz. Fawlty Towurs bein the guard who had the Brief Encountur with Mary on Oscurs night there last year or whenevur it was – when I was still ashes in the urun. "Does he know where you live, Mary?"

"Naaaaw!"

"But they'll check Denis's flat for him," says Dec.

If yeh remembur, Mary was half-livin there till Denis managed to get all those Jackson belts off our Mike (Fort Knox like) an moved in – I mean moved him in.

"We can warn Denis about that," says Liam.

So twas settled – almost.

Liz had a funny little look on hur face – there was no way she could draw Tizzy an his rape charges on hur family in middle-class Douglas an she was feelin bad about it. An Dec was lookin huffy again. He didn't like the idea a this drama bein taken outa his hands. I could almost hear his brain spinnin inta top gear. "But don't you think, Liam, that there is something providential about us being here? In the church?"

Liam bristled. He could smell trouble. "Whatchamean?"

"I think he should seek sanctuary. In the sacristy."

"Sanctuary? *Sacristy?*" says Liam pop-eyed.

"But it's providential, Liam," says Dec gettin all bright-eyed an bushy-tailed about this notion. "His own instinct brought him here to the church –"

"No fuckin way," said Liam.

"Nowah fuckin weeay," screeched Mary – I suppose that was the first thing he could twig – an, in support a Liam, he dug his claws into Dec's veil like he was inta abusin nuns every day a the week. So there was a bit of a scattur in the porch an Dec did get the veil torn off but in the end anyway they managed to get Tizzy outa the church an onta the Numbur 8.

So: back to Maryfield. Real fancy, isn't it? The name, I mean. A fierce facelift altogethur. The old name in Irish is *Baile na mBocht* – Poortown to you – an I'm a bit vague now like but I think in the old days twas a small little bit of a country village an then they shifted all a the paupurs outa the centur a the city because they were dyin like flies a TB an settled em there. The locals musta felt like twas *War a the Worlds.*

Well, if they wanted to give the consumptives a bit a fresh air they done the right thing – tis so high up the buses can't climb the hill up from the city in the wintur if there's sleet or ice. An at the top a Lotamore at certain times yeh can see the housewives flappin off their own clothes-lines the wind is so strong.

Y'see, the centur a Cork city is a marsh that they built ovur. That's what the name means – *corcach* – a bog. An every wintur the watur comes up an floods all the shops down Olivur Plunkett Street an people are wadin around in two feet a watur for days. Yeh think I'm makin that up, don't yeh? Watch the news.

So: Liam was still rantin an rarin an railin at Dec even when we got off the bus. "You an your *sanctuary*! Jesus, that's your style all right! You'd have us all in sanctuary next! D'yeh know what you remind me of?"

"What?" Sistur Veronica was tight-lipped.

"D'yeh remember that story we had in school about Tom Sawyur?"

"I do. I fail to see the relevance."

But Liz was grinnin away.

"D'yeh remember how him an Huckulberry get the black fella Jim outa prison? D'yeh remember – Tom gets Jim to dig a tunnel to escape an the door a the shed is actually open all the time or somethin like that – an he gets Jim outa the shed an makes him carry stuff *back* inta it to dig the tunnel – d'yeh remember? An he wants to saw Jim's leg off instead a liftin up the leg of the bed an slippin the chain off – d'yeh remember?"

"I do. I still fail to see the connection. Enlighten me."

"The connection? The *connection*?" Liam was aftur workin himself inta one a his rages. He'd be dancin up an down in no time now. "Have yeh forgotten yur shenanigans about Tony's funeral – when all he wanted was to be quietly scattered on Little Nellie's grave an we end up with RTE an all? Oh Jesus, when you get the bit between yur teeth we misewell all run for covur! Sanctuary? No fuckin way."

"Nowah fuckin weeay!" screeches Mary.

An off with Liam, stridin away with Mary staggerin aftur him – the heels like – an Tizzy bringin up the rear wringin the hands.

We were takin the short cut that led to the steps at the top a Shaggin Wank – as the inhabitants a the two neighbourin parks below us – Shannon Bank an Lagan Walk – called their housin area.

We reached the steps behind the othurs an me an Dec an Liz stood there lookin down at the roofs a the houses in the little valley an the smoke from the chimneys blurrin the air an the lovely view a the illegal rubbish-dump beyond, home of a thousand vermin – though havin said that, in all fairity I havta mention the green hills beyond that again almost close enough to reach out an touch, with furze an cows on em, an away in the far distance, just about visible to the naked eye through the haze an the smog, the mountains a North Cork.

We had a bird's eye view – like the Goldy Anjul – the one with the trumpets. Dizzy Gillespie. He had plenty to be lookin at. Still an all, I thought, bird's eye view or not, he must be bored stiff.

Twas a bit pathetic – he was like one a them Japanese soldiers they find left behind in some jungle still fightin World War II. I mean, who gives a fuck about the Last Judgement these days? He was supposed to blow that trumpet three days before the Last Day to warn the citizens a Cork. But the way things are goin, when he eventually *does*, the citizens a Cork are likely to say "Fuck aawff, baoy!" an show him the fingur. But, be that as it may be, he was one a them stand-an-wait types that Dec was always quotin about – the ones that Also Serve. Y'know – anjuls in fronta the throne a God. Jesus, that was pathetic – Also Serve. Twas like Also Ran.

Mindya, accordin to Wacko Jacko, those same anjuls are singin an spinnin all the time an the harmonies are brilliant but the beat is simple – march-time mostly. Well, I know tisn't the *coolest* thing to be quotin Michael Jackson but . . . Besides Dec tells me that the feen that wrote about them stand-an-wait types was a right bastard who made his daughter read for hours to him in Latin an Greek when she didn't understand a word of it – an a Puritan with it, one a Cromwell's crowd that slaughtered all the women an childrun a Wexford around the cross in the marketplace. So what would the likes a him know about anjuls? I think I'll go with MJ an those singin spinnin ones – I mean, the worst anyone can say about him is that he was seduced by a thirteen-year-old. An I mean, weren't we all?

But me – was I a kinda anjul meself? An if I was, was I supposed to stand an wait or sing an spin?

Stick or twist?

I turned to Dec to ask him to quote me the bit about the stand-an-waits –

"Dec," says Liz. "I'm pregnant."

Dec gave a little start an the blue eyes widened an then a whole littur a expressions ran across his face. He looked for all the world like someone shufflin through a hand a cards to see if he has any decent card at all worth playin.

Stick or twist . . .

He settled on a card. He did this camp kinda pullin down a the lips at the cornurs that goes with pullin in the chin an a very slight little jiggin a the head. "Well, aren't you the eejit! Admit it! You nevur even put the diaphragm in, did you?"

Liz looked off an up to heaven an there's a word that describes how she looked an sounded – but I can't remembur it – no, not that one – tis like bein sorry but a bit amused at the same time – "The statistics for the diaphragm must be away out . . ."

This was mega now. The Bonny Boy – Niall Ryan, the boyfriend – was still at school. Sixteen, he was – no, seventeen now. Legal, like – but only just. They'd been doin a line for a while but behind their parents' backs. Now she was really left holding the baby – if there was a baby. An she with no job nor nothin, bein a student.

Social Studies.

She was inclined to put a lot inta hur work.

"Are you sure? How late are you?" His voice sounded shaky now – like he was feelin the cold.

"Oh, I've done the test. And I'm nauseous an all that."

"Oh!" His hand flew up to his mouth. "Poor Uncle Nick – an Auntie Eileen! Did you tell them?" Hur parents.

"No. Not yet."

"Does Niall know?"

"Yeah."

"And?"

"He told his parents."

"And?"

"They won't let him have anything to do with me –" She broke off. She was going to cry.

"Well! Well!" Dec's eyes were sparkin. "It's just as well marriage is out of the question! He's just a snivelling little cafflur – I don't know what you see in him! But that's you, isn't it? You're always turned on by these scrawny little scuts!"

Liz's face flushed. There were tears standin in hur eyes but now she looked angry. "Excuse me now! There's nothing scrawny about him and if he's such a pizawn why are you always comin on to him?"

"Well, I do – I don't deny it – I mean he has the *makings* of a good-lookin man but –"

"In any case, you don't have to worry," said she, stickin the hands in hur jacket pockets an soundin real bittur – for hur. Heart a gold, has Liz. "His Daddy won't let him."

"There's nothing else for it," said Dec. "I'll have to marry you myself."

She looked at him for a long moment an then she took the hands outa hur pockets an put the arms around him. She made a kinda noise that was half a chuckle an half a sob.

"No wonder I love you," she said.

An me whole world lurched like as if some a them turtles were collapsin undur the strain.

We'd been here before. But this was it, this time. I was goin to lose him heart an soul. Oh *God* – just because she wasn't afraid to put her arms around him an say she loved him.

But then he put his foot in it. "Well, you'll have to give the child a name an forget about Ryan."

Liz stopped huggin him an stared.

The turtles were teeterin around but hang on – they might find their balance yet.

"A name." Hur voice was heavy with annoyance.

"I know you think that's not important!" said Dec. "But it is! I've no time for these newfangled ideas about disposable fathers!" Says he – an him with an absentee fathur himself who luckily disposed of himself ovur – in England like – an stopped comin home plaguin the family. "Liz, you know you'll need help – I mean, I mean –" He was aftur thinkin a somethin. "Liz – you're not considering *abortion* are you? God, I'll take the baby!"

She gave a little impatient shake a the shouldurs. "Come on," she said startin down the steps. "I'm frozen."

"Hang on a sec – hang on."

She looked back.

"Are yeh going to think about it? About marrying me?"

She looked away.

This looked very weird – Dec bein still in his nun drag an all.

It was more than weird. It was sick. To me, like.

"Liz, you know it worked when we shared the flat! That was really like a marriage. Even the money thing – I mean what money I had we had and all that. An vice versa. An I'd *love* takin care of you – you know that. I swear you'd want for nothing –"

"I know, I know, Dec. You'd be terrific I know –"

"An like I told you before, we could do our own thing sex-wise – or – or I could *try* – I suppose I could *try* – I mean it's not that I *can't* manage with a woman –"

Oh God. I was goin to throw up if he kept on –

"Dec –"

"The only thing is twould be a bit like incest between us but maybe we could get ovur that –"

"Dec!"

"Yes?"

"I'll think about it."

"You'll think about it?"

"I will."

Jesus! How could they even talk about it? The whole idea was gross. To me. I mean what I was feelin was not just jealousy. To me it really was like incest an it made me flesh crawl. So to speak.

41

Anyway – when she said "I will" I expected him to do a Veronica on it – like dance a little jig an go "Goodyyy!" – but he bent down an grabbed a fistful a grass an dirt from beside the steps. The fist was raised to the darkening sky an I knew what was comin.

"*As God is my witness* they're not goin to lick us!"

Oh, for fuck's sake!

"We're goin to live through this – as God is my witness!"

Oh, leave it out, Dec –

"And you and the chile will never go hungry – no – nor any of our folk –"

Oh, do Princess-fuckin-*Di* – do Sharon-fuckin-*Stone* even –

"If I have to lie, steal, cheat or kill! An the Ryuns can eat shit!"

Jesus! Between him an Tizzy I was aftur havin *Gone with the Wind* up the arse so many times – an couldn't he stick to one role at a time – or two – or three – I did a quick count: Veronica, Scarlett, Isadora, Regina, Expectant Fathur – the Protestant Whore –

But the beauty of it was that Liz was grinnin again. I shoved aside the disgust an the jealousy an the impatience. Dec's notion was mad anyway – it wouldn't come to anythin.

"Come on Scarlett," said Liz with the giggle back in hur voice. "They've got the band out for us!"

An sure enough there was a burst a activity from one a the houses across the park below with streamurs an balloons an the like an kids runnin in an out.

"Huh! Dat uppity niggah too shiftless t'do a day's work – him an dat no 'count wife o' his –" Scarlett was still in full flight, tossin the head an swingin the crinoline. Then suddenly – "But c'mere – we'd better get down there while there's anything left –" He could smell the drink even at that distance an all concerns were forgotten at the prospect a gettin outside a six-pack.

Y'see, the drink was always his first love.

The othurs were already clutchin cans by the time we got down – sittin on the garden wall if yeh could call the patch a grass a garden like.

"Hello Susannah," said Liz to a kid who was kneelin on the path with her smallur sistur on hur lap – the two of um all decked out in ribbons an flounces an the small wan wearin a witch's hat. "Whose birthday is it?"

"Mine! I'm ten! I got a Rollur-Blade Barbie," says the kid. "An we had a Barum Brack for a birthday cake an I got de ring!" An she stretches out a hand with a bit of a nervous tremor to it to show us the goldy ring.

"Oh you'll be married before your Confirmation in that case," says Dec smartly without a smile.

"Listen now – I'm teachin Tanya. Tanya, say fuckur."

An Tanya goes "Fuck-ur."

"Good *girl*, Tanya! Tanya, say langur."

"Lang-ur."

"Good girl! Say fuckur-langur."

"Fuck-ur-lang-ur."

"Dat's a good *girl,* Tanya! I'll get you a sweet at de shop in de minute."

"Lovely!" goes Dec.

An with that intro to the festivities, in we went.

I'd nevur actually been to Mary's house before thang-god an I expected the worst. I wasn't disappointed.

43

The Americans don't *know* the meanin a the word dysfunctional. Roseanne, how are yeh.

The first thing that hit us – well, you'll think I'm aftur liftin a page from Roddy Doyle now when I tell yeh – but the King's the King an not only in Ballymun. An he was pourin outa the hi-fi like Golden Syrup. Connie, Mary's fathur, was standin in the kitchen swayin around with the can an the cigarette an the eyes closed an the strains a *It's Now or Nevur* lappin round him – lookin like Johnny Travolta aftur a forty-day hungur-strike. A cartoon version at that. Like yeh started with a good-lookin man an distorted him every which way but loose. The arms were too long an the hands were too big an the forehead an jaw were juttin out too much. An I thought that if I was the cartoonist I'd a finished him off with a massive great langur an a couple a outsize balls. An I was bang on if I did but know it at the time.

He opened the eyes an peered through the cigarette-smoke an the shock a grey-black hair fallin ovur his forehead an spotted Dec in fronta him. An swayed towards him – cock first like – singin – *"Is now ur nevurr – Come hold me tight* – oh, Jaysis, sorry Sistur – sorry Sistur – shur I nevur – Sistur –"* An he stood there grinnin an shakin the head an pointin at Dec with the hand with the fag in it.

An I should explain to yeh that if *you* were listenin to him talkin all you'd hear would be "rargh-rargh-rargh-rargh-rargh-rargh-rargh", so I'm kinda cleanin up his act here an interpretin for yeh.

Anyway, whatevur look he gave, he saw Liz behind Dec an the eyes opened in a kinda cartoon surprise an he lurched past Dec at hur – "I dunno now would a student – ah, a

student now wouldn't have any *meas* on de likes a me –"
Shakin the head an smilin away all charm. An, with the
cigarette hand to the chest, he sings –

"When I first saw you
With chur smile so tendur
My hart was capchurred
My soul surrendurred –"

an he drags hur out to dance. So there he is latched onta hur
an Liz gigglin an puttin up with it outa Christian charity –
hur bit a social work for the day like. An Connie likewise
gettin off on the fact she's a student – so they're well
matched. Except that she has a fierce struggle keepin him
from jackin off on hur.

So Sistur Veronica settles down with a nice tolerant prissy
smile on hur face an starts downin the beer fast.

Oh no, Dec, I thought. An with a sinkin feelin I knew I
was facin anothur endless night an him in a drunken stupor.
Twas hardly worth the effort a tryin to fight it.

"Dec, boy," says I –

An the door a the extension bangs open an the next thing
Mary's mothur, Florrie, this massive woman with a big head
a foxy hair, comes lumberin in with a cigarette in hur hand
an comes right upta Liam without let or pause an kinda
clings him up agin the wall. "Liam, de ambulance is aftur
just goin," she breathes inta his face without a trace a
expression. The eyes were like big glassy-alleys.

"The ambulance?" says Liam.

"Roberto."

Yeah. Roberto. Mary's brothur, named aftur one a the
heroes in a Mills an Boon. A scrawny young fella – well,
maybe about twenty but he didn't look it.

"Roberto?" says Liam.

"Shifted."

"Shifted?" said Liam.

"Shifted," said she.

Liam had a whack at movin the conversation forward a bit.

"Oh God, Mrs Casey, did he get bad again?" says he with the eyes dartin around lookin for eithur an escape or a beer, I dunno which.

It's now or nevurr – goes Liz an yur man.

An Mary's mothur looks ovur hur shouldur an smiles a big lippy good-natured smile at the carry-on – like yeh would when a favourite child sings a song at a party – an then she shifts from one foot to the othur but give Liam no leeway or loophole at all. In fact she moves in anothur bit an the two massive tits on hur trap Liam between em an kinda pin him to the wall. "Very bad," says she. "He took very bad aftur de business last week."

"The business?" says Liam. Dec was aftur shovin anothur can in Liam's hand an he hadta kinda prop it up on hur right – no, left – tit to drink it.

"De brush-handle," says she.

"Brush-handle?" goes Liam like an echo.

"Couldn't get it out," says she, openin the mouth very wide, half-speakin an half-mouthin.

The King changed pace –

Love me tender, love me sweet

Never let me go –

"Outa where?" asks Liam lookin at hur stupid.

For answer she kinda mouthed somethin an the hand with the fag went behind hur back an made a kinda movement.

46

"What's that?" says Liam.

She mouthed again with hur big teeth workin away an the hand made a movement behind hur again for all the world like a cow tryin to swish flies away from hur arse.

"Up de –" says she, openin the mouth very wide on the last word an comin down like she was bitin inta a Big Mac.

"The – the –" says Liam with the eyebrows shootin up inta his hair. "The –"

Anothur big slow-motion snap a the jaws.

"The – the – *ass*?" says Liam. "Is that what you're sayin? Up the – *ass*?"

Love me tender love me long

Take me to your heart – goes the King like Golden Syrup.

She nodded. No expression at all.

"Godilmighty, Mrs Casey, who did that to him? Who'd do a thing like that?"

"Himself. Shur dere was no wan else heeyur."

"*Himself?* But what did he do that to himself for? What made him take a notion like that?"

All my dreams fulfil–

"I dunno shur. His fadhur found him. He hadta get de saw to it."

Liam winced an went white in the face. He was havin fierce trouble breathin, but whethur twas the thought a the brush-handle or the saw or the pressure she was puttin on his lungs I don't know. "The *saw*? Didn't he – didn't he try some – some – vaseline – or oil or somethin?"

"Vaseline an buthur an bicycle-oil." The fag was burned down to hur fingurs but there wasn't a twitch outa hur.

"No good?"

"No."

For it's there that I belong
And we'll never part – Elvis like hot porridge on a wintur's mornin.

"No?" says Liam. "So what did he do?"

"He hadta put a raincoat on him an call de ambulance."

"Yeh mean he – he – hadta leave it in? But what was the saw for?" Anothur thought struck him. "Jesus, how did he get a raincoat on him?"

"Sawed it off at de ass an put de raincoat on him. De raincoat Roberto uses for de odhur business –"

"The othur business?" goes Liam an then he musta decided he didn't wanta *know* because he rushed on – "God, that's terrible, Mrs Casey – he's a sore trial to yeh. An did they keep him in?"

"No. Outpatients. Emurgency. De worst case dey'd evur seen, dey said. But den when he got back home we had de doctur an Fadhur Murphy an de guards an de teachur an de social workur –"

"Ah, God, no wondur he got bad with all that lot tormentin him. Wouldn't it be fittur for them to leave him alone? About a thing he done in private?"

"Yes shur," says she, an the glassy eyes bulged even more. "Wouldn't it be fittur for dem to be doin sometin about de knackurs livin across de park – an dey not fit ta live beside dacent people with deir dirt an deir scrap an deir drink. I'm not goin ta rest till de Corporation gives me a transfur outa dis place. Shur today didn't I see some a de kids with a dead cat in a shoppin trolley playin with it like twas a doll –"

"A dead cat," says Liam lookin faintur than evur, his voice labourin. "That's terrible – a dead cat –" He looked like he was goin to pass out. He jerked the beer-can towards the pair on the floor, spillin some beer on hur tit. "Will yeh look at himself –"

Diversionary tactic.

She half-turned but left one tit pinnin Liam. But that was enough for him. One push an he was staggerin free. I dunno why but it reminded me of a TV commercial – like *He's-had-his-Weetabix* or somethin – like this wimp stuck behind those tits an then someone shoves a packet a Weetabix inta his hand –

Anyway – Connie comes lurchin ovur wavin the cigarette an singin. *"Are you lonesome tonight? Do you miss me tonight?"* An I saw Liz behind him grabbin a can an makin hur escape out the hall. Connie was swayin ovur Dec an peerin into his face. *"When I kissed chou an called chou sweetaart* – Sistur – Sistur – d'yeh know sometin? I'm goin to tell yeh sometin now. Hurself – hurself ovur theyur –" Hand with the fag does a big demonstration. "Hurself gives me a terrible time – shur she has me barred from de bed. I'm barred from de bed – dere are nights I dunno what ta do with it –"

"Oh, my dear man," says Sistur Veronica rockin back to avoid the fag that was weavin around in fronta hur – that an the fumes. "Patience – you must possess yourself in patience. *No Cross, No Crown – More to Suffur, More to Offur –*"

"Suffur? Suffur? Heartbreak Hotel, Sistur – dis is Heartbreak Hotel – barred from de bed – I dunno what ta do with it – *shhh, shhhhh,*" an the fingur was raised an the eyes closed. Elvis was startin inta the camp spoken part. *"I wondur if you're lonesome tonight?"* goes Connie, swayin away lost to the world. *"You seemed to cheange, You acted streange, Why I'll nevur know –"* He stopped an took a hungry drag outa the cigarette. Exhaled all ovur the place. *"Honey, you lied when you said chou loved me* – Sistur, no word of a lie – I dunno what ta do with it – wan a dese nights I'm goin downstairs an I'm goin stickin it in de lettur-box –"

I saw Liam clenchin his teeth an curlin the lips like he was aftur takin a swig a vinegar.

"The letter-box?" goes Veronica in a kind of a yelp. She sits up straightur an pushes hur knees tightur togethur. "My dear man, you mustn't dream of doing that – you might do yourself an injury – surely there's some othur solution?"

"Sholution? Shur de priest – she went up ta de priest – de priest – he's de wan should tell me what ta do with it – he's de wan dat won't let hur take de Pill –"

"But the letter-box, Mr Casey – I imagine that would be very painful – surely you could find something more – er – appropriate than that –"

"I dunno *what* ta do with it – shhh – shhhhh – *Now the steage is bare, An I'm standin dere, With emptiness all around –"* An his chest started heavin an his mouth twisted an next thing he was bawlin his eyes out.

"Oh, good grief, my poor man, you mustn't – oh Mr Casey – it's pointless 'having monsoon' – *if tears could build a stairwell, we could all ascend to Heaven –"* Sistur Veronica was lookin very distressed – hur eyes were runnin ovur the stacks a six-packs. Things were gettin outa hand an Dec had the fear a God on him that we'd have ta leave before he could get enough inside him.

"Dec," muttered Liam, three corn-beef sandwiches in one hand an a beer an a sandwich in the othur – he musta bein feelin a bit bettur. "I havta go." Meanin home.

"The loo's upstairs –"

Liam looked daggurs at him. "I'm *outa* here," says he through his teeth. "But we've gotta arrange somethin for Tizzy first."

"Oh, calm down," says Dec. "The night is young. And it's arranged, isn't it? He's staying here. And look at the condition of poor Mr Casey —"

Liam looked at the condition a poor Mr Casey. Then he gave a blackur scowl, took a savage bite outa the sandwiches, an stalked out the hall leavin em to it. I went aftur him. The othurs were still outside on the wall with their cans. Twas gettin dark.

"Oh God, are there sandwiches?" said Liz.

Liam shoved two a his bitten ones inta Liz's hand.

"Givus a sangwich, Leeem!" goes Mary.

Liz takes a big bite an says – not very clearly – "Mary's had a brain-wave about Tizzy."

An Liam kinda squinched up his face. The notion a any kinda activity at all goin on in Mary's brain was too much for him. But he let it pass.

"C'maan an I'll show yah," says Mary, dead pleased with himself, an he swung his legs ovur the wall tearin the backs a the two stockins an not takin the blindest bit a notice.

"Wait an I g'win an get some sangwiches," says Tizzy.

"Jesus, c'*man*," says Liam an catches him by the scruff a the neck an shoves him ovur the wall.

There was plywood ovur the windas a the empty house next door an when Mary pushed at the door it swung open. In they went an blundered around bumpin inta each other because the light was fadin fast. Up the stairs with them makin a fierce racket on the bare boards.

I stood in the small hall tryin to get a feel a the place. An empty house. A handy place for any stray vampiyurs or the like. This might be my lucky day – night.

Hello, boys.

Jesus, what was the mattur with me? Even live humans could sense somethin from empty houses –

I could hear Mary cacklin upstairs. Yeah, not much chance a tunin in with Mary disturbin the airwaves.

I went up. Mary was stretched out on a single bed with a mattress an all. I could just make out a big postur a Elvis on the wall. So this was where Connie was spendin the nights he was barred from the bed. *Now the stage is bare, And I'm standin there, With emptiness all around* – Jesus, he knew what he was talkin about. Heartbreak Hotel wasn't in it.

Liam was flickin a small little torch around the place – one a them disposable ones he was aftur gettin free with Walkman batteries. An, whethur by accident or what, it focused on Mary's crotch – or, I should say, it passed ovur Mary's crotch an then it gave a jerk an came back again. Mary had his legs thrown open an one a his feet up on the metal bedstead an in the small circle a light we had a view a the scrawny thighs above the stockins an the white knickurs he was wearin – white with little red hearts – an, in the interests a ver-whatsit, I gotta tell yeh at the risk a turnin yur stomach, half a one hairy ball hangin out one side. A revoltin sight for anyone with normal sexual instincts.

But – me brothur Liam. Liam suddenly wasn't so interested in leavin. I could feel a kind of a concentrated silence from him like someone prayin or choosin their Lotto numburs. What can I say? Me brothur Liam is a cool guy – sharp an funny – an loyal. An a little bit butch even. He'd be inta leathur now – that kinda thing – given a choice. He'd really go for the macho thing. Bikes. But – Mary – I dunno what it was about Mary – there were times I thought he was just sorry for hur –

But othur times – an this was one of em –

The torch cut off an Liam moved ovur to the bed. I heard the clank a his can hittin the floor.

"Fuck aaaafff, baaoy!" goes Mary – automatic, like puttin a penny in the slot.

An immediately – automatic, like a showur a coins when yeh hit the jackpot – I heard Tizzy an Liz fallin down the stairs an swearin like Walt Disney rats desertin a sinkin ship. They had the right idea. Jesus. I'd seen Liam an Mary in action before an twould turn yeh off sex, I tell yeh. If you have any notion that sex has anythin to do with – with *communication*, yeh should come an watch Liam an Mary at it. Unnatural. No othur word for it. If a – a – an alligator took a notion to shag a ferrut now, yeh might get somethin of the same result. Or if the fox in the yarn decided to shag the Gingurbread Man just for the heck of it –

I was leavin. I wasn't stuck in some fuckin urun any more an no way was I goin to have me world vision twisted by the sight or sound a me brothur shaggin that creature.

Well. Yeh've heard a the fryin-pan an the fiyur? (An I'm not referrin to the ones the tenants a Shaggin Wank are in the habit a leavin on their gas-cookurs in the hopes the house'll burn down an they'll get a transfur from the Corporation. Those'd be chip-pans anyway.)

Wait till I tell yeh.

Twas high time we went home, so I started tryin to put pressure on Dec – well, d'yeh know the yarn about "the pig won't get ovur the stile an I'll nevur get home tonight?"

Y'know – *"dog, dog, bite the pig"* an somethin about the rat bitin the cat or the cat bitin the rat? Well, no way could I get Dec ovur that shaggin stile. Everyone got narky – at least one of em was leavin all the time but they could nevur get it togethur. I set Liz on Liam an Liam on Dec but Elvis kept warblin an the beer kept gurglin an then Liam would get fed up an go back for anothur bout with Mary. Liz got the last bus back to Douglas by hurself in the end which wasn't great because she was lookin a bit green. An the rest of us stayed there.

Sistur Veronica was langurs by the time Liz left. *Locked.*

When I saw hur goin out back with Connie to look at the ferruts – well, me first instinct was ta try that Spontaneous Combustion crack – failin that, to go back to the fuckin jungle.

An Major O'Hara.

Private O'Rourke. Reportin for duty. Sur.

But I hadta know the worst. See the worst. Bettur than imaginin it. Mindya, I was tremblin like a leaf – but I followed em out back to the little shed.

The stars were doin their thing.

The ferruts were doing their thing, barin their teeth an weavin about like they might devour themselves from the arse up in their little caged worlds. Inside the shed the caged birds were doin their thing in their little wooden cages – bein caged birds like, a full-time job. Down among the sacks a grain the mousetraps were doin their thing – hangin onta mangled mice for dear life.

An Dec was doin his thing – givin Connie a blow-job.

Sistur Veronica was way outa line an away outa charactur. An yet – an yet it looked like she'd been doin it all hur life.

She was on hur knees, a'course, which looked very natural. An there was somethin to cut yeh to the soul in the efficient way the hand went back an flicked the short veil outa the way.

Mindya, she had hur work cut out for hur. Connie was hangin like Christ Crucified outa two bird-cages, one on eithur side a the shed, raisin the head an droppin it on his chest – gyratin like mad to his rendurin a *Heartbreak Hotel* an Elvis the Pelvis wasn't in it. With Veronica hangin onta his cartoon langur an lookin in danjur a bein whipped about the shed with it.

An yeh could only pity the man – no wondur he didn't know what ta do with it – Jesus, if he stuck *that* in the lettur-box they'd havta call the Fire Brigade. Florrie would be in hur element. I could just hear hur: *de worst case dey'd evur seen, dey said.*

So not only was Veronica havin a *major* problem tryin to get hur mouth around this monstrosity but *Heartbreak Hotel* was the wrong choice altogethur – for a blow like. They needed a bit a in-yur-face cock-rock with a good hard riff. Yeh might think *Heartbreak Hotel* is smoothur than a new piston but just try ta wank to it –

No, I can't wait till yeh root out yur old Elvis vinyls – but the thing is like a surf-ride with all kinda jerky changes a pace an direction – believe me –

An Connie was still more interested in deliverin Elvis than anythin else in the universe, so his langur was beatin the air like a lazy helicoptur-blade one minute when Elvis was doin this kinda warblin loop *Oh Baby – well life is so lonely baby, well I'm so lonely, well I'm so lonely I could die* an doin deep throat on Veronica the next "We-e-*ell*! Since *my baby* left *me* da da!" But when the lonely caught up with the deep throat he did this kinda mixin the Christmas puddin in Veronica's gullet that nearly left hur for dead every time. She soldiered on – a real troopur – gettin slapped about the face an throttled by turns. Twas hard to see what she was gettin outa it.

An when the big one came an Connie at long last rode that long curve a surf, she lost it an went undur good an propur an drowned – splutturin an gaggin an gaspin enough to need the Kiss a Life.

I didn't wait around to see if Connie obliged.

Besides: he mighta thought of a song for it.

Outside the stars were still doin their thing. I stared up at em an thought to meself: Dec will laugh when I tell him about Veronica an Connie in the shed. Or more likely he'll be disgusted. Grossed out. Maybe I bettur not tell him . . . keep it to meself . . .

I felt like I was cryin but – *there's no cryin in baseball* – an the painful pressure that was grippin me an shakin me had to be somethin else.

I went back to the empty house.

Major O'Hara, where the fuck are yeh? He was off playin golf.

But the house wasn't empty any more – the othurs were aftur turnin in for the night. There was a small night-light glowin in one a the little red-domed Sacred Heart containurs that are comin back inta vogue an I could just about see Mary's wig an all his gear on the floor. An I could hear him whisperin to Liam – I didn't know he *could* whispur – with the red glow a Liam's roll-yur-own comin an goin in the dark.

Dec came staggerin in not too long aftur that – coughin – an collapsed alongside Tizzy on the extra mattress Mary was aftur bringin up there. Needless to say, no way was I goin near him.

Here comes that awful feeling again – twas a long, painful miserable night. Jesus, I'd a listened to Garth Brooks an been glad a it.

Wondered whethur Foxy-nob was up in Minerva Terrace sittin in Garth's lap. Or down town workin his aggro off, beatin the shit outa someone in steel-capped bovvur boots.

And at one point I had a kinda wakin dream where that Puking guy in the wheelchair was sayin "And now we come to the case of Tony O'Rourke –" An he started writin all these mathematical symbols on the blackboard explainin everythin about me an life aftur death, an Arnold Schwarzenegger was takin notes. Arnie kept noddin away like light was dawnin by the minute but I couldn't understand a fuckin thing.

CHAPTER THREE

The next mornin was the worst kind of a mornin for a Pure Spirit – the mornin aftur the night before. When everyone is brainless an gutless an lyin there for endless hours without a twitch out of em. The only bit a light relief at all – an not much to me taste at that – was when Liam woke up at the crack an without even botherin to wake Mary assaulted him without mercy for about one minute by the clock an then fell back inta a stupor again. *Love me tendur.* Not a twitch outa Mary. Well, he did open an eye long enough to verify that twas Liam doin the shaggin an then he went back to sleep again. *Love me true.*

At long last Mary got up, all scrawny an pathetic an peculiar-lookin naked without his gear – like one a them naked little birds in a nest – an he got half dressed an went out next door to his own house.

An aftur an Eternity I heard his mad squawk at the front door an I peeped out through a gap in the plywood an saw a suit goin up the path. Twas Sunday an people with umburellas were goin to Mass. It'd rained cats an dogs most a the night an twas still lashin.

In comes Mary in a pink quilted housecoat an fluffy

slippurs all mucky from the rain an a ribbon in hur hair, delighted with hurself, carryin a tray loaded with cups a tea an toast for the lads an sloppin it all ovur the place. "Wan a de neighburs taaought I was me sistur!" Cacklin like mad. "He wants ta know when we're havin a house-warmin!"

"He must be *guzz*-eyed," says Liam yawnin away. "Jesus *Christ*, Mary!" Mary had lobbed half a cup a tea inta his lap.

That woke him up, an not long aftur when it stopped rainin Dec an himself staggered inta town for a cure, leavin poor Tizzy lookin very miserable but busy bitin his nails an Mary gettin busy with a sweepin-brush that looked a bit short in the handle –

Dec was still in the nun gear.

Jay, for me that nun drag was a right turn-off. Even if I was inta drag that cold hard synthetic look a the habit was a dampur. I felt the same about priests. But that's by the way. Habits were far from me mind that mornin.

Not.

Inta the Imperial. Which is a big classy hotel a the old-fashioned sort – mirrors an chandeliers an all that.

"Was Mary's sistur supposed to move into the house or what?" says Dec an they up at the bar – the Captain's Bar. "I mean that neighbour seemed to take it for granted."

"Oh – yeah," says Liam. "Florrie was aftur wanglin a promise a the house from the Corporation because the sistur was gettin married – the banns were up an all but she took off ta London – I don't know what the story is – a row with Connie ovur somethin –" An he had half his pint gone before they sat down at all.

Dec had a vodka an white (twould look bettur like) an he

was sittin there with the ankles crossed an the back straight an a little nun-like smirk on his lips.

I drifted back out inta the hall – an floated up to the massive mirrors on the walls. I was kinda mesmerised by mirrors – I'd go right up to the surface an stare. An that blank space where I knew I was would stare back at me. I'd stare till I was dizzy sometimes, just willin meself to appear.

An I had the notion I should be able to step inta the mirror an that if I did I'd become visible. Or I'd look back an see meself on the othur side.

There was somethin about vampiyurs an mirrors – I couldn't remembur – they couldn't see themselves eithur? Or they looked different in mirrors – like the picture a Dorian Gray? What if I was aftur agein at the speed a light an one day I'd look in a mirror an I'd see meself all decrepit an bloated?

Jesus, I was scarin the shit outa meself again.

I spoke to the space that was me in the blank mirror.

Pull yurself togethur, boy. Ashes to ashes an dust to dust. You don't have a body any more, yeh muppet, to get decrepit an bloated. You're safe from that forevur.

Fastened to a dying animal – that was yur man Yeats that I'd "larned" or not larned in school – somethin about his soul bein fastened to a dyin animal.

Nevur again for me –

Been There.

Done That.

Got the T-shirt.

I was driftin back to the lads on that note when anothur bit of a line came inta me head – *soul clap its hands and sing* – fuckit – from yur mano Yeats ta Wacko Jacko they were all at it –

An really is that what *I* should be at? Clappin an singin an spinnin like yur Baptist convert? Madonna – *Like a Prayur*. Would that do the job?

I spun me way back into the Captain's Bar.

Hallelujah, Brothur!

I had company.

The Caucasus Dixieland Band.

Swingin Soviets would yeh believe. From Georgia near the Black Sea. In embroidered pyjamas. Two with beards an all with moustaches an grins as wide as the formur USSR.

"I dunno why but I've nevur been into sexual fantasies much . . ." Dec was sayin in a soft kinda girlish voice, the faraway look in the eye, the head at a bit of an angle. All soul.

"More's the pity," says Liam, gapin ovur his shoulder at the Caucasuses – their trumpet man was blastin inta a mad jazz version a some Russian folk-song. "At least yeh could do that in yur own time – yeh wouldn't havta drag me inta um. Tis yur othur fantasies I can't deal with." He slid around to Dec's side a the table.

"I only fantasise about someone I'm actually in love with. So my fantasies are more about happiness – being with someone like."

Being with someone like. I liked that. If he did but know. I began to feel a kinda pressure as if I was turnin inside out. I suppose it's what people feel when they say their heart turned ovur.

"That's a bit of a handicap on the game like, isn't it?"

Liam had started rollin his own – did I tell yeh he was inta that? Cheapur like. An I knew he was goin to make a hames a it on accounta why he wasn't concentratin – he was makin eyes at Igor.

"You mean when guys want me to take part in their fantasies? That was worse when I was youngur. I can't do it – I laugh or sniggur or giggle. There was one guy – there was some programme on TV – it was a re-run actually of something from way back. This guy had two sons and they lived in this fantastic dormobile, with motorbikes on the back –"

"Leathur?" Liam looked up an all the tobacca slid off the papur. "Shit!" He checked whethur Igor was aftur seein. Igor grinned. Liam grinned – delighted.

"No, no – all denim-clad – the two sons were all-American boys, like you know blonde, tanned . . . anyway I had no interest in them because they were too young and I wanted an oldur man like. But this guy who used to pick me up was really into this thing. I nevur figured out if he'd been abused as a child or what. I hope to Christ he nevur got married and had kids of his own anyway. I couldn't get inta this thing . . . with him. You know, he'd be the fathur. I have to give it to him: there was plenty of scope for the imagination. Anothur problem was that he was into discipline like and I wasn't. But anyway – it didn't shock me. It just wasn't me." With his nun's face all nostalgia.

"Run that by me again –" With an eye on Igor an the tongue poised to lick the papur. "*You're* not inta discipline?" He caught Igor's eye an licked – slowly. "What d'yeh call hair-shirts? An thorns down yur back? An the chain around yur waist when you were a kid –" He was goin where anjuls fear ta tread – pissin in Dec's tray, in othur words. He should a known bettur. But then he had an eye on Igor.

"*Liam,*" with the eyes sparkin. "Do you *really* see no difference between the *spiritual* discipline of the nun in her cell and being *flayed* by some tarty dominatrix you pay to attack your *dick* with a cheese gratur!"

"Aaaw, Gawd, *Dec*!" Liam started squirmin around violently an kinda grabbin at his Luke Perry quiff.

But Dec had started smirkin an next thing he made a kinda genteel little wave across the bar. Liam stopped squirmin an stared. A nun was crossin the bar to our table.

"Breeda!" says Liam, delighted but lookin a bit – that thing – that word I was tryin to think of about Liz an the diaphragm – kinda regretful but good-humoured about it. He knew he'd havta stop oglin Igor.

Breeda was peerin a bit uncertainly, so twasn't until she got right up on us that she started to laugh.

"It is you, Declan, isn't it? Well, honest to God!" says she, sittin down.

This was a bit awkward – not least Dec was wearin hur veil – he'd snaffled it from hur.

I forget if I described hur to yeh before. Remembur Breeda? She spoke at me funeral. Anyway, yeh'll havta forgive me for repeatin meself. *There's joy in repetition* – Prince. An talkin a Prince –

Ah, come on now – yeh know yeh can't hope to get away with a Prince-free ride – this is *me* yeh're talkin to –

No – if yeh *don't* wanta hear about Prince yeh can go fuck yurself –

An yeh can forget about us makin a *date* like . . .

Talkin about Prince – I was readin the othur day about some Japanese scientist who was aftur translatin a mouse's genes inta music –

What? No, I don't know how he done that.

But the mouse's genes sounded just like a lively waltz-

tune – very like a certain one a yur man Chopin's waltzes –
an when yeh think about it, why should that be surprisin?
Like a bird-song has a pattern an a tune – so why can't a
mouse's genes? So d'yeh know what I think? I think
somethin like Prince's *Joy in Repetition* is written inta our
genes an that's why –

What? Oh – Breeda. Oh all right – *rewind*. I left hur
crossin the Volga with Jelly Roll Morton – no, she was
already sittin down. Oh yeah, I was goin to tell yeh what she
looks like. How the fuck did I get on to Prince an mouse's
genes? Mindya, Breeda looks like *hur* genes might be in
lively waltz-time too. She's a small brown-haired youngish
smilin person with bright, bright eyes – blue. She always
looks totally wide-awake. Always sittin up with hur back
straight. With hur eyes wide open always.

She sat up straight now with her hands crossed on her lap
an hurself an Dec were like mirrur-images except for him
bein blond and blue-eyed an a bit heftier – like he says
himself, he's past his willowy days.

"What're you doing, tell me?" says she. "Is it a fancy-dress?"

Cute out. She knew damn well what he was doin.

"You might say that," said Dec. "A performance at the
club. I'm rehearsing." An he gave a blast a "*The* hills *are
alive*!"

"No better man to do it," said Breeda eyin the veil. "But
I can't get over yeh!" Takin in the nylons an all. "You look
better than I do!"

"Well, I can put a veil on bettur than you can anyway!
D'yeh mind if I fix yours for you? It's adrift."

"Go ahead!" She was always charmed with him. She
thought he was great gas.

He started foolin around with hair-clips an things, singin – *"Anything you can wear I can wear bettur – In what you wear I look bettur than you . . ."* Then a big sigh. "God, wouldn't you look beautiful in the old habit! Aren't you sorry tis gone!"

"Is it jokin you are?" said Breeda. "You and your old habit! Heavy and hot and cumbersome and you couldn't work in it! Shur, weren't we all stinking! How often could we wash the things? You *couldn't* dry em! And we had no deodorant! That was considered perfume! Nothing but carbolic soap! And the starched wimples like horses' blinkers – I wonder how *you'd* feel after a day in one of em!"

On ecstasy, if she meant Dec. He was aftur arrangin the veil an now he was fixin hur fringe, flickin it across hur forehead.

"Listen, lads," says she. "I'm over there with Jer Buckley – we're comin from the Sunday Art Class –"

"Oh God it's Sunday!" said Dec. He'd forgotten Mass.

Breeda gave him a bad-boy look for fun and went on: "The thing is, Jer says he needs to go over to the Simon Community to meet someone. Ye'd never be able to take him over there for me, would ye? We've been here a while and he's had a few and –"

"Say no more," said Liam.

"Bless you – I didn't want to leave him – but listen, before I go – tis providential I met you now –" An she started tellin us about this priest, this Fathur Twomey, who was comin to give a lecture at UCC that very night an he was goin to squeeze in a talk for gay men at The Othur Place first.

Dec was fierce interested an asked loads a questions about

yur man an wasn't he the one who married separated people an nuns an priests an all that kinda thing?

An Breeda was goin on about how liberal yur mano was when Liam reached out an touched hur on the arm. There was a peculiar expression on his face. He nodded – indicatin somethin across the bar –

Breeda swung round an stared.

An there was Jur Buckley, thinnur again than when I'd last seen him, cowboy hat an fringed jacket an all, in his wheelchair wrestlin with a piana.

Wrestlin with a piana that had St Vitus's dance an a Caucusus attached.

Crocodile Dundee wasn't in it.

The wheelchair was one a them motorised things an he somehow was aftur aimin wrong an gettin stuck in the leg a the piana. He was kinda chewin on his moustache an grinnin away like mad.

Breeda rushed to help him. "Lord, Jer –"

"No, no, lemme alone, I'm grand," says he grinnin away.

Plastered. He musta been on spirits. Trebles. "Everythin's in control . . ."

The barman came ovur at a trot. "Can I help you, sur?"

"No, no, lemme do it meself – lemme do it meself!"

But the trouble was the whole piana was movin. Twas a great big heavy piana like – but those wheelchairs are fierce powerful things an the piana an Jur an the wheelchair an Boris were all jerkin back an forth togethur.

Twasn't clear why Boris kept tryin. I suppose them Soviets are usedta havin it tough. Food queues an all that. So he soldiered on at a jazzy version a *I'm Always Chasin Rainbows*.

"Ride em, cowbaoy!" shouted some smart-ass across the bar.

"Could you revurse, sur?" The barman was in a state.

"I'm revursin," says Jur. "Can't yeh see I'm backin back!"

An the piana lurches backwards.

An Boris misses his aim an comes down on one atrocious chord an he starts laughin an shakin his head an gives up an stands up with a big shrug in his buddie's direction.

"I'm backin back," goes Jur. An he bursts inta song. *"I'm al-ways cha-sin rain-bows! Waa-chin clouds driftin by!"*

The rest a the Caucasues were thrown off their stride by this caturwaulin an the loss a the piana – an their ace trumpet man was startin to sound a little bit less than ace.

"Jer!" says Breeda almost cryin. "Stop the motor! Just stop it an we'll get yeh out!"

Outa the cornur a me eye I saw Dec an Liam hangin onta each othur – their faces crucified with the effort a tryin not to laugh.

"*My schemes are jus-like-*all-*my-dreams* – outa me way now – I'm backin back!"

"Jer!" Poor Breeda had hur fingurs bitten off.

The wavur in the Caucasuses' swing was enough now to put yur teeth on edge.

"Lemme alone! I'm backin back!"

"Godilmighty, sur!" shouted the barman. "Will yeh *stap*!"

"End-in in the sky!"

The manajur arrived in time to see the wheelchair free itself with a terrible wrench leavin the leg kinda hangin skew-ways an all the Caucasuses makin for the bar.

"There now," says Jur, dead pleased with himself, grinnin away like a ferrut aftur a blood-bath.

I don't havta tell yeh we made a quick exit from the hotel – the manajur was doin a Basil Fawlty.

Jur took off down the South Mall so we followed him on the trot an I'd say for once Breeda wasn't sorry to see the back of us.

The Simon House was goin to be a haven a peace an sanity aftur that.

"I havta see a man about a dog," said Jur when we got to Simon. The fresh air was aftur soberin him up an he was lookin every bit as sharp as usual.

"The loo?" said Liam. "Oh, we'll give yeh a hand with that –"

"What kind of an eejit d'ye think I am? Ye can keep yeer hands to yeerselves. Twill be a while yet before pullin down an i-zip is beyond me strength – ye can be lookin forward to that. But anyway I'm not talkin about takin a leak."

"Oh?"

"I havta see a man about a dog."

Liam's ears pricked up. "Drugs?" says he with the dollar signs flashin in his eyes.

"A dog."

"A dog?"

"Are yeh thick or what? A dog!"

"Yeh mean a *real* dog?"

"*Yeah* – a dog. A greyhound."

"Oh."

In we went.

I wasn't lookin forward to this venture at all. I always found the place real depressin an I nevur went there when I was in the flesh except with Liam or Dec when I was short a dosh an not upta floggin me arse around town. The ould fellas were pathetic an they were always dyin an that.

But me two buckos were mad for it. The last time we were there an ould fella called Barry was dyin – his heart – an he took the notion that Liam was his son – some bastard that was aftur throwin him outa his farm down in West Cork – an nothin would do Liam but to hold his hand all night. Like he did for me.

Y'see, they coulda called the ambulance but they knew he was scared shitless a goin to the hospital – the ould fellas only go there to die or be dried out – an Dec figured he wouldn't make it anyway. An Dec has a lot a experience – workin in hospitals an homes an that. Mad for that kinda thing.

Ould Barry didn't make it. Or maybe we should say ould Barry did make it.

To tell yeh the truth, I was dreadin that he was goin to cross ovur an join me on the othur side – a fate worse than death – for me I mean. Imagine strugglin through Eternity trailin this wino aftur yeh. Jesus. Anyway there's been no sign a him. Maybe because I missed the big moment – I went down with Dec to take a leak an when we came back he was gone.

Anyway. This day with Jur twas in an out more or less – a real quickie – to me relief.

So we're able to fast forward here.

Or *ff.*

An we're walkin down the South Mall with Jur in the wheelchair haulin this miserable-lookin greyhound aftur him on a piece a string.

An Liam is sayin: "What I don't understand is – if she's as good as yeh say she is why doesn't she have a decent lead or muzzle an that? An why is yur man destitute down in

Simon? An why d'yeh want to get rid a hur aftur payin for hur an all?"

"Look – yur man has a problem with the gamblin – that's the story – she's a winnur but he blows the money – an it got to the point he sold the lead an that an now he can't afford to keep the dog –"

"Isn't she very small?"

"A flier – she's a flier. Small an light, y'see – no weight to carry – an a fierce fast trappur –"

"So why can't yeh keep hur yurself?"

"Jaysis, I can't exercise hur, Liam – this fuckin MS has me banjaxed –"

Which is true – yeh shoulda seen him before, with his football an his huntin an his cross-country runnin. An the exercise he got liftin pints.

"Y'see, I wanted to help the ould fella out an Jesus, she's a terrific bargain – I tell yeh now, this is yur lucky day – she's yours for a tennur –" An he's chewin the moustache an I know that means he's chancin his arm. "I'll be along to yeh with hur papurs when I get em from yur man."

Sure.

ff past the row Dec has with Liam about the greyhound.

I didn't stay for it anyway because a funny thing happened – I was lookin back up the South Mall while they were squabblin an for the first time in me life I noticed the sun shinin on Dizzy Gillespie on the roof a St Finbarre's an I was amazed that yeh could see him from there. A thought struck me an I scooted down the South Mall, keepin an eye on him all the way. I lost sight a him behind the branches a the trees with their dry autumn leaves when I got towards the end a the Mall, but when I hit the docks – *Statio bene fide carinis* – I turned on Devil Éire Bridge an looked back. An there the buggur was, shinin brightly in the sun, lookin clean down the Mall from a mile's distance. Tis hard to explain to yeh why this is so extraordinary – I mean a hundred yards down the road from St Finbarre's he's already outa sight, hidden behind buildins an houses – an y'see he's not right up on top a the Cathedral – he's on a lowur roof farthur down –

Tis especially hard to explain it to yeh when you're still tryin to figure out what *Statio bene fide carinis* means an you're not listenin to me at all – and no, I'm not goin to tell yeh. Tis the motto a Cork, yes –

Well, *I* don't know who the Protestant Whore is, do I, an *I* havta put up with that –

Forget it – serve yeh right for not knowin any Latin or forgettin what yeh evur knew –

So that was the day I realised the Goldy Anjul had been keepin a weathur-eye on us for years durin all our shenanigans down on the docks. A thought I didn't welcome at all.

ff – tough, I'm not tellin ya – *ff* up to Denis's with this fuckin awful-lookin animal, a blackish speckledy-lookin thing, an yeh didn't havta be a spirit or a psycho to know what the odds were on *hur* winnin a race.

So up to Denis's flat – to tell him about Tizzy.

Up the stairs draggin the greyhound. Who wasn't keen.

But I was keen. I always got a lift outa seein Denis an Mike an I usedta be mystified about this kinda yella glow there always was around em – if I'd a been in the flesh I'd a thought me eyes were goin funny – until I was readin about this *aura* business in *Woman's Way* one day an I realised that was what it was. They had an aura. An I'd be baskin in the aura an rememburin all the trouble we took to get em togethur – the pathetic berks. What's more, they always had some half-decent music, though I missed Cohen since Mothur gave him up with the drink when Wacko Jacko became the soundtrack for their Grand Passion.

An the lads had nice expectant looks on their faces that said somethin about wine an spaghetti bolognese an whiskey. *They* hadn't given up the drink.

An we knew he was in – because we could hear the hi-fi playin –

Everybody knows that the dice are loaded
Everybody rolls with their fingers crossed –

Liam stopped. Dec stopped. The greyhound stopped half-strangled. Everybody's mouth dropped open, includin the greyhound's, like they were puppets on a single string.

Cohen.

Me heart stopped.

Dec an Liam closed their mouths an stared at each othur. The greyhound snapped hur mouth shut too.

Everybody knows that the boat is leaking
Everybody knows that the captain lied –

No, this'd got to be wrong –

They staggered up the last steps with the dog whinin.

Dec raised his hand an knocked.

Everybody got this broken feeling
Like their father or their dog just died –

The door opened an there stood Mothur – Denis, that is – with a glass a whiskey in his hand. An Jesus, did he look rough! The cheeks were hollow an the bit a short beard longur than usual. The eyes were bloodshot an the fairish hair was greasy an grey-lookin. He wasn't wearin his rings. An he sure as hell wasn't wearin an aura.

"Benedicite," said Dec. Rewind. Or rew. The Benedictine Rule, Chaptur 63: *Whenever the brethren meet, let the junior ask the senior for a blessing.*

Mothur rallied. That's the word, isn't it? Rallied?

Like he pulled himself togethur?

"Ah, *daaaahlings*! Declan! Liam! Come in, come in! Believe me, you're a sight for sore eyes!" An he staggered back into his livin-room, wavin them on like Westward Ho the Wagons.

Jesus. Yeh should have seen the cut a the place! I mean tis normally a bit of a mess what with his artist's materials an all that crap – an Dec had stopped cleanin for him since Mike moved in.

But now. Half-full bottles a soured milk an empty wine-bottles in the fireplace. Banana Bubbles in the goldfish bowl – I mean like a whole small sample packet, carton an all. Mansize Tissues in shreds an lumps right left an centur – I saw Liam toein one an peerin at it an grimacin. Bits a toast an dirty socks embracin each othur on the table. I could go on. I think yeh get the picture? Mothur saw us takin it all in. He kinda shrugged. The mouth an the eyebrows twisted. "Trash on the floor," says he.

"From weeks before – just gets deeper by the day –"

The lads stood there – what's that grand word? Aghast. They were *aghast*. That's what they were.

If aghast means what I think it does.

Aghast.

But not at the Mansize Tissues or the sour milk. They were starin at the wall above the mantlepiece where this massive postur was rent from top to bottom. Half a it was streelin down inta the fireplace so Denis's wall was now decorated with a larger than life-size picture a one long greasy black lock trailin ovur a peachy soft-focus male chest.

We knew what it was – or what it shoulda been – Michael Jackson in the throes a the Panthur sequence in that video that got banned. Y'know, where he does all this really gross wankin while dancin on top of a car –

And so the question arose: where the fuck was *Mike*?

Mothur was aftur throwin himself into an armchair.

He waved his glass around, sloppin the whiskey. "My life! My life!" cries Mothur. "Ruined! Ruined!" An he lets a hollow groan outa him. I nevur heard a hollow groan before but I read about em, an it definitely was a hollow groan that Mothur left outa him that day. The first a many.

"There's no point in *moaning*," says Dec – very severe. "A sighing heart nevur breaks, as the Bon Secours say – so you misewell leave off the hollow groans –"

Twas forevur happenin. He was aftur catchin my thought.

"Where's Mike?" says Liam. Evur a one to get to the point.

"He's left me!" Massive groan.

Me two boys started breathin fast.

"When did that happen?" says Liam.

"Oh, I don't know daahlin," says Mothur lookin around him kinda vaguely. "Some time ago –"

"Four bottles of whiskey, five bottles of wine and two bottles of sour milk ago," said Dec. "Sometime yesturday, I would say."

"He's left me –" groaned Mothur.

"The fuck he has!" Liam was suddenly furious. "The *fuck* he has! If he thinks he's left yeh he's got anothur think comin! *We* didn't suffur months a you whinin an pinin about him an then go to all the trouble a gettin ye married – more or less – just for him to up an leave yeh without so much as by yur leave!"

"Did he give you back the ring?" Dec.

"*Threw* it at me!"

"Classic," says Dec.

"*Fuck*," said Liam. "That's serious."

Mothur gave a hollow groan. "Get yourselves some glasses daahlings –"

They did. An found somethin to put in em. Which was easy because if yeh stretched out a hand at all you'd knock a half-empty bottle ovur.

"What is that thing?" Mothur was aftur noticin the dog for the first time an he craned his neck towards it from the depths a the armchair where he was crumpled.

"Tis a greyhound," said Liam.

"Oh. Then I take it that it is *real*?"

"Unfortunately yes," said Dec.

"I thought, you know, it was a *cat* –"

Dec gave Liam an "I toldcha so" look, pullin the chin in.

"A cat," he repeated – very distinct on the "t".

"But I *thought*, you know, it was a *figment* of my imagination – a creature from the twilight zone of my subconscious –"

Dec's head swivelled to Denis, chin in an all. Then back to Liam. "Jesus, he d'be very bad," says he.

Liam sniggered. Then he kinda wiped the sniggur away with his hand, a bit ashamed a himself. He gave a cough that meant he was goin to get serious. "So what happened, Denis? Did ye fight about Jackson again or what?"

"No, my dear boy, though I have no doubt but that is at the root of it all. Hence my cowardly assault on the poster. But no –"

Y'see – Mike an Denis'd been goin through a real rough patch since Wacko Jacko's frolickin with Free Willy hit the headlines. Accordin to Mike, twas all because Denis had put a curse on Wacko. I know that sounds off the wall but Mike's barely clingin onta that wall with his fingurnails at the best a times. An it can't be denied that Denis – I told yeh before – had the habit a writin mockiyah headlines *Wacko Jacko Fucks Dolphin to Death in Florida Hotel Pool* on bits a papur – like doodlin –

All right, all right – *rew.* Back to way before Free Willy dawned on Jacko's horizon when our Denis nearly expired rampant because Mike was aftur takin a vow a chastity on accounta why he thought Jacko didn't have a sex life. An Denis always prayin that Jacko would be the centur of a huge sex scandal – an even givin money to Dec to light candles an do novenas an Denis a Protestant – because he figured that would be his only hope with our Mike.

The Mothur a Good Counsel, Dec says, nevur lets yeh down. An eventually Free Willy's fathur sued Jacko an the rest is History. (Though by that time Denis was already aftur bustin Fort Knox.) Mindya, normally Dec'd have scruples about doin novenas wishin ill on somebody. But Denis was payin him. So he found his way around that one. Somehow. So yeh could say our Mike had a case.

Right. *ff.*

"And I was *so* looking forward to the Jazz weekend –

Geno Washington is at the Country Club – and Mike and I intended to *lock* up the flat and devote the *entire* four days to it – it would have been such a *learning* experience for him –"

"Denis!" says Liam. "What did ye fall out about?"

Big sigh. "Aah, well, it was about takin him to Georgia –"

"Georgia? In Russia? We're just aftur seein a band from Georgia!" Liam's eyes lit up. "You're goin to *Russia*?"

Liam was off.

"No, no, dear boy – in the United States – that Georgia. I believe there is another Georgia also – an island in the Pacific if I'm not mistaken – named by a Captain John Shortland after his fiancée –but I'm not quite certain of my facts here – I seem to remember – now *who* told me about it?"

"At a guess – one of the Shortlands," said Dec, real tart.

"Oh, yes, of course, yes, indeed – yes, if I remember correctly, he certainly named the Shortland Islands, part of the Solomon group – you know, *Bali Hai* my special island and wasn't Rossano Brazzi to *die for* in that? *That* voice. Like rough treacle. You know, now in my darkest moments it helps me to imagine him singing *This Nearly was Mine* clinging onto that aircraft in his tuxedo – though I must say the love affair between young Lootenant Cable and that native girl was most titillating – *Younger than Springtime* – ah yes – pity it wasn't a boy –"

"Denis –"

"She *looked* like a boy in that little white shirt and black trousers –"

"Denis –"

"And those little bare feet –"

"Denis –"

"It *should* have been a boy –"

"Denis!"

"I'm *sure* it *must* have been a boy in the original version –"

"Denis!"

Denis stopped.

"You're *rambling,* Denis," said Dec. "Could we get back to our original query?"

"Oh – sorry – I do ramble – yes, of course – well, I'm not sure whether it was he or his father – who was also a John Shortland – and apparently a curious situation arose in 1947 when a stamp intended to commemorate the finding of coal in Newcastle – Newcastle Australia that is – *not* Newcastle-on-Tyne which oddly enough is also associated with coal as witness the saying 'bringing coals to Newcastle' –"

"Denis –"

"A stamp as I say issued in commemoration of the finding of coal by Shortland Junior mistakenly bore a portrait of Shortland Senior – that is, his father, who like his son was an officer of the First Fleet – that is, the first ship bearing convicts for the colonisation of Australia –"

"*Good God,* Denis!" An Liam slammed his forearm down on the table an set all the glasses an the bottles an the goldfish bowl hoppin.

"Whatever is the matter, Liam? It really is quite extraordinary that such a mistake should be –"

"*Who the fuck cares?*" Liam to the ceilin.

"Why, the *Admiralty* does for a start –" says Mothur amazed.

"The *Admiralty*," says Dec. "The *Admiralty*. A lot the *Admiralty* evur done for us that we should be listenin to your rawmayshing!" He turns to Liam. "Liam, does he be on some medication he forgets to take?"

"*Mike,* Denis – we were talkin about Mike –" says Liam.

Hollow groan. "I know it – I know it – but it pains me to think about him – my brain goes skippin away –" Huge slug at his empty glass. "Oh –" More whiskey sloshed in.

"Something about Georgia –" says Liam promptin him.

"Ah yes . . ." Huge sigh. Huge slug outa the glass.

"He asked me if I would take him to Georgia. And I said no. An he wanted to know why not. He was very hurt."

"But why did he want to go to Georgia?" The lads were lost.

"Well, he didn't – in particular. It was the fact I refused, you see, that upset him so dreadfully."

"Wait a minute now," says Liam. "Just outa the blue – like that – like one mornin ovur Banana Bubbles – Mike says 'I want yeh to take me to Georgia' –" Liam was tryin hard.

"No, no – the question was: *if* I were going to Georgia *would* I take him?"

"And you said?"

"Well, I thought about it – I gave it full consideration – and then I said: no, *if* I were taking the train to Georgia –"

"*Ten minutes before the train,*" said Dec – but I'm not stoppin now to remind yeh what he meant – rew yurself.

Liam waved at Dec to shut up. He was starin at Mothur.

"*Train* – but, Denis – yeh can't get a train to Georgia from *Cork* –"

"Liam, you are missing the *point* – the point was: *if* I were taking the train to Georgia *would* I take him with me? And I said no. *If hypothetically* I were taking the train and *if hypothetically* I were a black homosexual failed entertainer on a one-way ticket, no, I would *not* take him with me!"

I clicked.

The lads didn't.

"What in Jesus's name are yeh talking about?" says Liam amazed.

"I told yeh he was on something," said Dec.

Denis ignored them. Lost in the past. Like, yesturday.

"So he asked me why not? And I said: what would my old black mammy say? And what would I *do* with him there? Put him out picking *cotton*? Can you *imagine* Mike doing that? I thought it a ridiculous idea. Well, he'd look the part perhaps being so dark-skinned – I daresay his father probably *came* from Georgia if we did but know it but *temperamentally –*"

Liam stared. "Denis! Denis!" says he like in absolute astonishment an he clutched his quiff. "Are you talkin about the *midnight* train to Georgia?"

"Well, yes, of course, dear boy –"

"The song?"

"Yes, of course –"

"What!" Dec's blue eyes were nearly fallin inta his whiskey glass. "What!"

Twas a historic moment – Dec was lost for words.

Mothur looked peeved. "I don't see why –"

"Holy Hour, Denis," says Dec. "You should have the boy assessed –"

"No, no, Declan, I told you –"

"And yourself while you're at it – consorting with him has obviously affected your brain –"

"No, Declan, you don't understand –" He stopped an stared at Liam who was aftur gettin up an startin this kinda turnin round in circles act, hands to the head, that he did sometimes when words failed him.

He was doin it more an more these days.

"Let me get this straight – he – asked – you – to take him – on the Midnight Train to Georgia –"

"No, Liam – heavens, the boy has some intelligence – he merely asked *if* I were *hypothetically* taking –"

"He-asked-you-if-you-would-take-him-on-the-Midnight-fuckin-Train-to-Georgia – and *you* said *no*! But Denis, *why* didn't you just say *yes*?"

Denis looked at Liam an gave a huge sigh. "I see that now, Liam. It would have been so easy to say yes. I thought I was being honest with him. But of course I was lying – to him and to myself. He told me so – he said – through his tears poor boy: 'You're a fucking liar'. He was right. And I was wrong. Of *course* I would take him with me and *fuck* my cotton-pickin mammy – the boy is my heart and my soul, you know that – *if* I were about to board –"

"Enough," says Dec tearin off his veil. Things were gettin serious. "In God's Holy Name – enough. The whole situation is – is insane. I refuse to spend anothur moment thinking about it. Liam and I will now clean your goldfish bowl."

"But Declan!"

"Why are you feeding them on Banana Bubbles?"

"Declan –"

"And why expect them to consume the carton too? After all those were cut-price surplus samples and this is carrying Protestant thrift too far –" Fishin out the carton.

"Please Declan!"

"I mean *we've* been through the famine while *your* lot were living off the fat of the land and taking the pigs out of our childrun's mouths for rent and shipping them to

England but even in those days we would've told ye what to do with yeer surplus Banana Bubbles if ye started shipping them back to us –"

"We wouldn't have fed em to our *goldfish*!" Liam stuck his oar in.

"Shur what goldfish did *we* have?"

"Liam! Declan! Have pity on me!" Mothur was crumpled even furthur inta his armchair. "I'm sorry about the famine – truly I am –"

Dec turned at the kitchen door with his goldfish-bowl. Big camp sigh. "Well, all right so."

"*Thank* you – *thank* you –"

"Say no more, say no more," said Liam. Fishin the sour milk-bottles outa the fireplace. "We'll talk to Mike."

"And little enough time we'll have to do it – what with the wedding coming up next week –" came Dec's voice from the kitchen ovur the sound a runnin watur.

"Wedding? A wedding!" Denis perked up a bit. "Oh who's getting married?"

"What wedding?" Liam calls out. He was stickin empty bottles in his jacket pockets to carry them inta the kitchen.

Dec appeared at the doorway with his sleeves rolled up.

"You'll be amazed when you hear," says he with a little smirk. "But right now tis a secret. At the convent – a private affair – but you're invited – bring your own trade."

At the word "convent" Liam's eyebrows came togethur an lines ran up an down an across his forehead like the San Andreas fault on a bad day. No way was he goin for a repeat performance of the kinda shambles Dec "organised" at the convent for me funeral. But before he could get his teeth inta this Dec'd gone back to the goldfish an he let it pass.

Maybe he thought by ignorin it twould go away. He shoulda known bettur.

Maybe his mind's eye was still on Igor.

But mine wasn't – an I suddenly felt like I had a hangman's noose around me neck.

So when the goldfish were swimmin around all perky in clear watur, Dec an Denis got off on anothur tack. Denis half-hearted an with many a groan for a while but then he lightened up a bit an got inta it. They'd told Mandy L'Amour they'd do a duet for the Hallowe'en performance at the club so they decided on Nelson Eddy an Jeanette MacDonald – the Golden Couple.

Dec knew he could do a great Jeanette. He'd trained himself against all odds, taking Joan Suthurland as his role model – a great lump of a girl who became a glamorous Diva an who pushed hurself to go up anothur 5 notes when she was already hittin high doh (actually twas hur husband pushed hur but anyway). Personally, I have me doubts about the glamour an we usedta argue about it when I was in the flesh. I mean, Jesus, yeh should see hur singin hur swansong with Pavarotti at Covent Garden – he looked like a midget next to hur an yeh know what a great mound a pasta *he* is – an she lookin like a great greengage jelly in a green net frock with a chin on hur like a hatchet.

I suppose you're wonderin how I know so much about Sutherland? Shur didn't I have years of it from Dec an he doin the ironin of a Sunday mornin – listenin to *Oldies an Irish* or whatevur tis called on the radio. An Liz would be there an the boy sopranos would come on an Dec'd be "this is for you now, Liz."

Anyway, Dec knew he could *look* the very spit a Jeanette

as well as sound like hur so they settled for that an started arguin about which song. So Liam said he was the ref an he decided on *Sweet Mystury of Life* – sorry, no – *Ah! Sweet Mystury of Life* – on the strength a the *aaaaaaaaah*!

   "*Aaaaaaaaaaaaaah! Sweet Mystury of Life at last I found you! Aaaaaaaaaaaaaaah! At last I know the secret of it all! Aaaaaaaaaaaaaaaaaaah!* . . ."

Dec sang falsetto an Mothur did the baritone (is it?) an I dunno which of em felt the strain more but the two of em seemed to be in agony anyway. Thing is, it sounded grand but it looked fuckin hilarious because they hadta go inta all sorts a contortions to get the soprano an baritone (I think) out. Y'know, hangin onta the backs a chairs an the like. An they practised moves – like the one they copied from the record sleeve with Dec in fronta Denis, backed up agin him with his head back on his shouldur. An real sick expressions – Dec usin what Suthurland usedta call GP or GPE – General Pained Expression – the all-purpose sick expression she used for all a hur operas.

So then they got inta fixin up costumes an rehearsin an, by the time they'd finished, Mothur hadta make lemon an honey drinks to ease their throats that were torn ragged. An a'course that wouldn't do eithur of em without a ferocious amount a whiskey lobbed in.

So by the time we left the lads were more than merry but Mothur was aftur turnin fierce maudlin.

He stood at the door – a picture a misury in his Nelson Eddy military coat (one a Mike's Jackson jackets). "Leave me that poor animal, I beg of you – that *cat*-thing." An "*cat*-thing" was said with a kinda jerk a the whole body. "We could be such a comfort to each other –"

"The dog can't survive on whiskey, Denis, even if you can," said Dec. "You're in no fit state to look aftur an animal – look what you did to Michael Jackson –" The postur. He had money in his pocket from Denis to buy a new one. An, by the way, Dec was back in his jeans an jacket thang-god – his own propur self, the way I liked him.

"About Mike," says Liam. "He's in the bag – we'll talk sense inta him if we havta beat it inta him – yeh'll get him back if we havta drag him here an tie him down –"

"No, Liam – I know this is the end. The truth of the matter is: even if I requisition the whole *fucking* Midnight Train he will *never* forgive me for putting a curse on Jackson. No – I've had my brief moment of happiness – and, you know, somehow I've always thought of it as a parting gift from Anthony – it came to me with his death and funeral –"

He meant me like. Ant'ny, as we say in Cork.

"Well, pray to St Anthony then," said Dec. "The Findur of Things Lost or Stolen –"

"No – no – this aching is not supposed to ease. I embrace my loneliness – I want to *liberate* it, to *ravage* the land – to embrace everything with my loneliness –"

This sounded great. An Denis was at his most pound-note-ish. Except that he was quotin Leonard Cohen. Verbatim.

"Oh God help us all if you start embracin everythin with yur loneliness," says Liam. "We've been there before."

Dec did the lips thing. "Don't forget to feed the fish."

"Mind the horses, children," goes poor Mothur – a pathetic attempt at humour, like.

Dec started down an then Liam swung round at the top a the stairs an tripped ovur the dog an nearly went flyin.

"C'mere to me!" says he to Denis. "*Did* yeh put a curse on Jacko?"

"Well – evidently I did." Misury.

Down the stairs with us. Dec stopped at the bottom a the stairs an raised a fingur. The two of em – three of em – pricked up their ears.

This nearly was mine
One love to be living for –

"Well, at least tis a bit cheerier than that Cohen ghoul," said Dec. "But d'yeh think he's safe? Should we leave him the dog – for company?"

"Jesus, no – the poor animal might commit suicide. She might make a suicide pact with the fish. C'man."

An I had a sudden flash a the dog flippin the fish outa the goldfish bowl an plungin hur head in like a Gary Larson cartoon. I was gigglin at this headin down Bridge Street when Liam joined in.

"Whasupitcha, girel?" said Dec.

"I was just thinkin – imagine you're a failed black entertainur an you're just boardin the Midnight Train to Georgia on yur way back to yur mammy an just when yeh're gettin on the train there's Mike there on the platform in his make-up an his streelin hair an his red plastic *Beat It* jacket an his white socks an his *Billie Jean* hat an he says 'I'm comin with yeh' – can yeh imagine –" An then he was bent double.

"I get your point," says Dec – very dry. "I wouldn't take him eithur."

CHAPTER FOUR

Too much fuckin equipment. I couldn't sort it out. I thought he could just dump it, but then I remembered that those guys in *Platoon* or any a them films were always just *laden* with stuff. Festooned – festooned – that's the word isn't it? For Christmas trees? They were festooned like walkin Christmas trees – with yur grenades an yur canteens an yur machete an yur harness an yur butt-pack an yur ammo pouches an yur field dressin pack an yur pistol an yur bandoliers an yur knife an yur rifle an yur extra bandoliers for the Pig draped around yeh –

Gee, sarge, it's gettin heavy –

Shit, son, we ain't even started yet –

an yur C-rations an yur ALICE with hur metal frame an yur flares inside an yur radio batteries an yur rope an yur cleaning kit an yur mosquito repellent an yur wet weathur jacket an pants an yur poncho an yur steel pot an yur flashlight an yur diggin-in tools an yur anti-tank weapons an yur shavin gear –

An yur tin-openur. An yur socks. An yur fags. An those branches for camouflage. An yur condums.

Jesus. No wondur they lost the war.

Guerilla warfare, how are yeh.

Michael Collins could teach em a thing or two.

An I nevur saw them throw anythin away – except the helmets – William Dafoe with his head band – like groovy, man. Unless they had a base camp – which me two boyos didn't. But how the fuck was Private Tony goin to feel up Major O'Hara if he didn't even have a free hand?

Yeah, yeah, I heard that – very funny. But seriously, I thought a that – but if he got on his knees with all that crap on his back he'd nevur rise again.

But Private Tony's need was kinda pressin. He was cross-eyed with lust by this time. An I'd bettur do somethin about it.

No.

Let Private Tony go fuck himself. I'd more important things to do –

Like keepin an eye on the crowd a maniacs I called me friends – seein Tizzy through –

An that – unfinished business with Foxy-nob –

An I hadta find out who the Protestant Whore was, didn't I?

An get back to visit Puking an them turtles – now *that* was pressin business. Fuck Private Tony's hard-on . . . I dunno . . . he'd just *havta* carry the stuff. In the interests a ver-whatsit. All that gear was kinda sexy anyway.

But in the interests a gettin a grip on the Major's manly membur . . .

Oh Christ – there was that heavy metal band again . . . ridin in on a powurful bass loop . . . oh fuck . . . oh yeah . . .

Walkin tall machine-gun man
They spit on me in my home land
Gloria sent me pictures of my boy –

"A mean place to fight, boy," said Major O'Hara wipin the sweat from his brow with a powurful forearm. "If I die here, bury me face down so this fuckin country can kiss my ass. You think this is bad? This is a picnic, son – this is no search-and-destroy – you shoulda been with my unit last tour – leeches, ants and cobras, festering insect bites. We burned the leeches off with cigarettes – you get a leech feedin off your privates, Private, an see how you like that – we watched the festering rot creep up our legs and thought our balls would fall off. Step on a punji-stake smeared with excrement an you were lucky if your foot didn't drop off – eventually. Uniforms rotting on our bodies, everything slick with sweat – the enemy could smell soap a mile off so we couldn't use it – watch it there, boy! That branch nearly had the pin outa your grenade."

"Sorry, sur – thank you, sur."

"My luck to get stuck with a cherry like you. Let's move on. Looks like we can make progress without the machete. Keep close behind me boy –"

Jesus – what a butt – it – *it oughta be in jail*

It's on the verge a bein obscene –

Get the fuck outa this fantasy, Prince –

"Move real cautiously, son. This is no place for diddy-boppin. Keep an eye peeled for dead vegetation. Could mean a punji-stake trap or just a nice little toe-popper. Or some tanglefoot or an ambush up ahead. And watch for any one of the 133 species of snakes – 131 of which are poisonous, the most poisonous being the most common –" The Major looked back. "Boy, do you know what to do if my ass gets hit by a cobra or a krait? Did they teach yuh that in boot camp? Or did they fail to mention it?"

"Eh – I'm not sure, sur –"

"You better be sure." The Major halted an drew his knife from his belt. "Look here, boy. So you remember good. First you lay me down –"

I only wanna lay ya . . . down . . .

"You gotta keep me still – stop the poison travelling too fast – tie me down if necessary –"

"You can count on me, sur."

"Then a H-shaped cut in the wound –" The blood sprang to the surface as he cut the neat little H in his forearm. "And you suck out as much poison as possible –"

D'yeh want me to practise that now, sur?

"Like this –" He sucked at his arm, the steel-blue eyes fixed on Private Tony's face with a curious expression. Private Tony was feelin faint. But he knew that if he collapsed undur all that gear he'd nevur rise again. So he swayed heavily against the Major's chest instead. A naked arm went round his neck. "You all right, boy?"

And Private Tony felt like he was choking on the blood pounding through the body against him and the hammering of the powerful heart.

"Boy! You all right?"

"Fine, sur –" gasped Private Tony. "Just give me a minute, sur." Wondurin why the Major wasn't takin a tack a notice of the slow beat of the heavy metal band that suddenly seemed to be drummin in his ears . . .

Yeah they come to snuff the rooster
Yeah here come the rooster
You know he ain't gonna die –

This is unreal, thought Private Tony, watching outa the cornur of his eye the bright blood flowin from the arm around

TURTLES ALL THE WAY DOWN

his neck in a tiny trickle down across his collarbone and onta his chest undur his drab shirt. An seein as it was unreal anyway an it didn't mattur what he done he moved his head an clamped his lips ovur the little wound in the naked arm.

"Christ!" The arm was pulled away roughly an Private Tony was lookin inta the Major's startled face. "What the fuck you tryin to do, boy?"

He couldn't speak.

For a long moment Major O'Hara looked confused rathur than angry. Then the steely eyes narrowed.

"I – I – sorry, sur. You were bleedin on my fatigues." His voice came dry as a whispur.

The Major stared and his lips tightened. There was a long silence. "You've got blood on your mouth –"

"I – sorry. Sur." He didn't have a free hand to wipe it away so he licked his lips.

The Major looked away – his mouth twisted an he spat inta the vegetation. "Now we're goin to attract every mosquito in this damn zoo –" he muttered. Frowning, he swung round and strode off. Cautiously.

He didn't say "Keep close behind me, boy" thought Private Tony with a kinda despair so deep and unexpected it made him feel sick. His mouth tasted bitter and his sight blurred. And suddenly, in that moment, he saw an felt it all – the hope an the excitement an the pain – and the defeat that must come – that always would come. An he stood there shivering like a dog out in the rain – outside a door that would nevur open. To him.

Holy *Christ*!
What!

91

What in Jesus' name was goin on? I came outa the fantasy like a deep-sea divur comin up too fast.

There's no cryin in baseball! How the *fuck* did I let Private Tony get inta such a state? Drippin blood an tears all ovur the shop? Major O'Hara was supposed to be me R & R – me rest and recreation like, for Chrissake.

Jesus, I misewell be watchin *Twin Peaks* for all the light relief this was givin me.

The heart I didn't have was hammerin. I'd a loved a cigarette. Even though I was aftur givin em up.

I was standin on Patrick's Bridge – by meself – without the lads. I couldn't remembur where they were. I couldn't remembur how I even got there.

No – sur. Won't happen again – sur.

Major O'Hara was goin to do me head in. I stared into the rivur, tryin to pull meself togethur.

There was something really putrid about the whole thing. A Pure Spirit havin a mangy little fantasy – about a crapulous *war* – I could see it down the road – Dizzy Gillespie on top a St Finbarre's would nevur stand for it – I'd be barred – I'd be barred from the Union, no doubt about it.

In a kind of a panic I started goin through me agenda again – Puking, Protestant Whore, Tizzy, Foxy-nob, Liz, Dec – not necessarily in that ordur.

Jesus – what if this was some kinda test? For all I knew those turtles were gearin up to blast me inta extinction. As a failed experiment like.

On the othur hand maybe they didn't give a fuck. Maybe they were too shaggin busy tryin to keep their balance. On the othur hand (the third hand like) maybe they were bent double – convulsed laughin at me efforts – like the pair a aliens in Bart Simpson.

But the notion that they didn't give a fuck or that they were bent double only skeetered through me brain that day like flashurs at a football match. I felt a kinda pressure an panic on me. I felt it only made sense I was some kinda experiment. Like an easily assembled somethin-or-othur that came without the instructions.

Anothur thought struck me an put the kybosh on it. It hit me like a bolt a lightnin – *that's why* there were no Hunky Immortals or Highways-to-Heaven around – they were all Failed Experiments. All rejects.

Christ! That made sense. That's why there was only me.

New Improved Ultra Tony.

But, Holy Jesus, why me?

Maybe twas somethin to do with the AIDS. I mean that was the only thing about me that was different.

I was a new breed. Something new an unexpected squirmin around at the bottom a the testtube.

Like the mullet squirmin around in the shadow a the bridge. Suspended – wavin a bit against the flow a the watur. Facin upstream.

They hadn't a shaggin clue I was up here lookin down at them. They hadn't a shaggin clue air even existed. Or they mighta leapt inta it a few times like astronauts walkin in space.

An there probably was some flithurin *newt* swimmin around in the mullet's bloodstream who thought *that* was the universe.

Layurs an layurs. Blood – watur – air – space – what else beyond that?

Turtles all the fuckin way down . . .

I was lookin down at the mullet. An the turtles – Teenage Mutant Ninja Turtles for all I knew – were lookin down at me.

Or God was. The original Mad Scientist – the boyo who'd thought up a nice little number like AIDS in a spare moment. I know you're up there, yeh bastard –

Have yeh the *faintest fuckin* notion a tellin me what the *fuck* I'm supposed to be doin here?

Divil a word.

God was out playing golf.

You're demoted, says I to God. I'm puttin the Teenage Mutant Ninja Turtles in charge. They'd make a bettur job a runnin this circus.

Suddenly I wanted to be back in Dec's room with me head on his chest listenin to that heartbeat that said "I'm alive you're alive, I'm alive you're alive –"

But where was Dec? Probably gone back up to that squat to keep Tizzy away from the long arm a the law.

I faced upstream – away from the rivur – up Pana – towards the bookshops. Puking was definitely on the agenda.

Twas Sunday but Waturstones were often open odd hours an besides, what with the Jazz Festival, twas business as usual in a lot a places.

So I was on me way when I spotted Dec an Liam – an the greyhound – comin out onta Pana past the bronzy statcha a the Echo-boy (newspaper-boy to you), an they stridin along all business. Me heart warmed at the sight. "Hey, sham!" I called out like yur real Corkman an they crossed an we turned down French Church Street.

94

They were arguin about somethin. What else is new.

"Rectus-a-um," says Dec very firmly.

"Oh God, Dec, that isn't a reasonable name for a dog – hur name will be on hur papers anyway when Jur brings em – but if yeh must name hur how about The Bishop a Cork aftur that one on Glenroe – or was it Fair City?"

"Rectus-a-um," said Dec.

"An no wan's goin to twig tis supposed to be Latin so yeh're wastin yur time with yur a-um –"

"Keep them guessing," said Dec. "That will make the name stick in the puntur's head – Rectus-a-um is perfect from that point of view. No one's goin to forget a dog called Rectus-a-um in a hurry –"

"Ah, Gawd, Dec –"

"Rectus-a-um. In memory of the Christian Brothurs an all their efforts to educate the youth of Cork ovur the decades: *Rectus-a-um – did yeh larn it? Bend ovur.*"

"Hey! Will yeh look at yur wan –"

An there was Cliona standin outside Quinnsworth – twas open for some afternoon hours because a the Jazz Festival – in the smallish square known as the Red Square, with a collection box in hur hands.

That's Cork for yeh – tis all right in yur hand like *Cheers* on a larger scale: everybody knows yur name. An that's got its own kinda kick an comfort. Even though yeh know that on any given night the most excitin thing that's happenin is that up in Grawn such-an-such a fella is jerkin off – still it's nice to know if yeh drop inta Loafurs yeh're goin to meet the fella yeh nailed last night sittin there at the bar – an yeh thought twas a one-night-stand an *Jesus* I musta been *scutturred* he's a *dog* an can I pretend I'm me own twin –

So, we bumped into Cliona.

I braced meself.

There she was with hur long streelin hair an a big long purple streelin scarf around hur neck – one a them crochet ones fulla holes – an a big long purple streelin skirt an a big long fawny cardigan an Doc boots.

There she was with the horse's mouth on hur open an the Boy Scouts' collection-can an badges in hur hands. An I felt that familiur sinkin feelin.

Next thing she claps hur eyes on Dec an Liam an *hollurs* out across the square in hur actor's voice – y'know, all projection across the footlights: *"Scandal rocks the hospital – I'm innocent, says Nancy!"*

An the whole square gapes at hur – an the drunk outside the Simon shop who's singin an atrocious version a *What a Wonderful World* in honour a the Jazz Weekend shuts up like his throat was aftur bein slit.

"Tie me up and bind me, Robin, says Batman," Dec comes back at hur falsetto.

Oh, Jaysis, they were off! I knew this one of old. They'd go on forevur now tryin to outdo each othur.

Oh Godilmighty! I hated this stuff! Fuck the woman!

"I don't know nuthin bout birthin no babies, says Jemima!"

The trumpet an sax doin Dizzy Gillespie's *Afro-Paris* opposite Bracken's café stuck their heads round the cornur to check out the opposition.

"Presentation is everything to the TB patient, says Sister Finackapan –" Dec.

An now they're togethur an hangin outa each othur an givin each othur digs an they're in hysterics at this crap.

An Liam has one eyebrow lifted so one side a his face is grinnin an the othur is lookin cynical.

"Course I loves ya – don't I buy ya chips an screw ya of a Friday night, says Aggrieved Husband –" Cliona.

"My husband and I would like to wish you a Verray Merray Christmas –"

An they changed pace.

"Yur hair is lovely – is it yur own?" goes Cliona.

"No, tis me mothur's," goes Dec.

"Tis a lovely shade!"

"Frivolous Fawn," goes Dec preenin himself.

An this brainless crap could a gone on forevur – well, I know tisn't *brainless* really – I mean, let's face it, Cliona's brilliant that way – but –

Jesus, I hate the woman.

But anyway, as luck would have it, just as she opened hur mouth to make some smart crack about the greyhound (Rectus-a-um?) a Squad Car came crawlin up Paul Street behind Waturstones.

"Regina, hold me fag, you can keep it if he shifts me," goes that daft bitch without missin a beat an she shoves the collection-can an badges inta Dec's hands an *runs* across the square an *straight* at the Squad Car. Then she stops dead an claps hur hands to hur head. *"Tis the Vice Squad!"* she screams an whirls round an makes for Carey's Lane. An whatevur happens Liam gets in hur way an she grabs him by the arm an, with Liam an Rectus-a-um hangin outa hur, she *tears* off down the lane. An a'course a guard jumps outa the Squad Car – we're in a pedestrian area an the car can't get in – an tears down the lane aftur em an the Squad Car goes screechin up Peter an Paul Street – to cut em off at the othur end on Pana.

Leavin us standin there like eejits with our collection-can

– a roundy effort strapped up with green tape with a picture of a grinnin Cub on it – a real cutey. An the sticky badges all with Cubs on em.

An people start puttin money in.

A couple a minutes latur Liam an Rectus-a-um come pantin outa Carey's lane. "Jesus," says Liam. "What was that about? I was halfway down the lane when I aked meself what I was running for!"

"Where's Cliona?"

"They got hur – they sangwiched hur between em in the lane an she had a field day screamin an runnin up an down an cowerin on the ground an all that. They're aftur takin hur away in the Squad Car."

"They let you go?"

Liam was fumblin with his tobacca an papers. Rectus jerkin at hur string wasn't makin a tricky job any easiur. "Naaaw," says he. "I just stopped an yur man went right past me!"

"She's always doing that," said Dec. "For no reason but a chase. She'll wangle her way outa that now, no bother to her! Oh, thanks a million!" A woman was puttin a pound in the box. "Thanks! They won't even search her – shur she knows them all! They know she's an informur! She'll be spinnin em yarns now to beat the band!"

"God! She's unreal! Maybe we should go up to the Bridewell an see what's happened to hur? Just for the craic?"

"We can't – you're forgetting about Tizzy –"

"Oh God yes –"

An I remembur somethin – they're aftur forgettin altogethur to tell Mothur about Tizzy. Oh Christ – if Fawlty called to Mothur lookin for Mary . . .

"Oh – thank you, sir!"

"Shur we're always happy to help the Scouts – they do great work with the youth – is the dog sick?"

"Eh, no, she's fine – she's just thin," says Liam an he lookin mortified.

"I wondur how Cliona got into this collection thing," says Dec. "And y'know, I'm *amazed* – why wasn't she dressed up as a Scout? *There's* a lost opportunity! Something for the Scouts? Something for the Scouts please?" Dec started rattlin the can. "There's a fair amount in this. Something for the Scouts please?"

"I'll see ye on the way out," says a woman with a bunch a kids – fierce apologetic like she owed us somethin.

"Something for the Boy Scouts! Boy Scouts!"

"Gimme a go," says Liam grabbin the can. "Move ovur here closur to the door so they havta walk ovur us."

"Oh God, we should be puttin these little badges on people – I'll do that."

"We'll take turns – if you think I'm goin to pass up the chance a glawmin some a these types –" Liam bounced the money in the can. "Scouts, scouts! If you're not in, yeh can't win!"

"Oh, is it a raffle?" goes a little ould wan, all shoppin bags an she starts wrestlin with hur outsize handbag.

"Yes," says Liam. "We're rafflin a Boy Scout."

"Oh, very nice," says she puttin in a twenty-pence piece.

Liam grinned at Dec. "Right. Boy Scout to be raffled – if you're not in, yeh can't win!"

"Boy Scout to be raffled – oh, thank you, sir. First prize a Boy Scout. Ticket for a Boy Scout. Thanks a million – oh you're great –" Dec.

"Ah well, we have to give the Scouts something – I was in the Scouts myself –"

"Thank you, sir – your badge, sir – let me do it there! Whoops! Oh, wait – there!"

"Boy Scout to be raffled," Liam with the eyebrow up. "Something for the Scouts please! Badges here, Dec," an a whole family queued up to be branded.

"It's like givin flu vaccine," said Dec. "Acquired immunity. Against furthur harassment."

"Harassment? Not at all," said Liam. "These people are mad to give their money away – tis amazin – there's no stoppin em – thank you, ma'am."

"Are you the *Catholic* Boy Scouts?" a middle-aged man – the wife on the arm – wanted to know.

"Eh –" Liam took a gandur at the can.

"Yes, of course," said Dec.

"Well, I don't approve. You're encouraging discrimination."

"Oh, we're non-denominational," says Dec.

"So what's the point – what's wrong with the SAI?"

"Nothing at all," said Dec. An I could hear him thinkin – what in God's name is the SAI?

"What's the SAI?" says Liam. Couldn't restrain himself. Me brothur the reportur.

"Ye don't know what the SAI is? Well, that's disgraceful!" This was gettin sticky.

"Personally," said Dec. "I'm canvassing for full amalgamation with the SAI. It's only a mattur of time."

"And *about* time," said yur man an he shuffled on with his ould wan, mutturin somethin about Devil Éire. Sorry, De Valera.

Oh – so that put the Catholic Boy Scouts dancin at the crossroads with the Legion a Mary an the Pro-Lifurs an the Anti-Information an the Pro-Censorship an the Anti-this an the Pro-that. And isn't it a wondur that they don't choke on all their Pros and Antis? That they don't stick in their craw an choke them? Can yeh imagine what twould be like tryin to get a Pro or an Anti down yur gullet? Twould be like tryin to swallow coat-hangurs. There they'd be at the crossroad droppin like flies to the tune a good clean nationalist music –

Meself, I'd call that progress.

"Can't win em all," says Liam. "But I must remembur to find out what the SAI is – Boy Scout up for raffle! If you're not in, yeh can't win! Boy Scout – yur very own Boy Scout – yur personal Boy Scout –"

A handicapped guy on crutches came lurchin up.

"Oh, don't trouble yourself, sir," says Dec.

"Tis there in me hand," says yur man, jerkin his eyes down to indicate his left hand that was clutchin the crutch. "Take it outa me hand."

Dec took the pound outa his hand an put it in the box.

"You're very good – thanks a million."

"God, aren't people great all the same?" says Liam. "I nevur knew people were givin away money like this –"

"I wouldn't support that at all," says a tall man in a sportscoat passin by. "They're dangerous," says he ovur his shouldur.

"Dangerous? What d'yeh mean?" said Liam.

But yur man walked on.

"What do you mean, sir, they're dangerous?" Dec called aftur him.

Yur man kept on walkin. "They get led astray," says he ovur his shouldur an he goin in through the automatic doors.

Dec made a face. "*There* goes a man with a story –"

An at that point inta the square troops a showur a young fellas all about twelve years old, cute as hell, in knitted hats – with a fella with a berd an a cloth cap. An they all with music sheets in their hands. An collection boxes. An before we knew where we were, they'd started singin an ruined our trade. Collectin for childrun's holidays. A right bunch a little chansurs now by the look of em in their hats with Man United on em an Chicago Bulls an LA Dodjurs an Póg mo Thón –

Think Global, Shop Local –

Póg mo Thón? Kiss my ass.

Right little cafflurs now – we're not talkin Trapp Family here – but they delivered the goods with a lot a punch an a heart-an-a-half an sounded grand. An bags a passursby stopped an stood around grinnin an enjoyin them.

Fair dues to yur mano – the teachur. Soonur him than me tryin to whip that lot inta shape.

I hoped they wouldn't accuse him a sexual abuse before Christmas so they'd get through the Christmas carol season at least.

Dec an Liam gave up against this opposition an took off an I made to follow but then the young fellas started singin a Cork song I nevur heard before, to a kinda calypso rhythm, an I lingered because the chorus took me fancy –

Oh, I'm Cark city bor-un an I'm Cark city bred
An when I die I'll be Cark city dead
Dey'll build a little statcha in town
In me-mo-ry of me –"

I hadta laugh. At the thought of it.

An I set off aftur Dec an Liam in great form.

Twould be a long time before they'd build a little statcha a me. *But*, all the same, a town that builds a little statcha of an Echo-boy with his bronzy mouth open goin *Echooooooaah* –well, yeh nevur know . . .

Now that I was a VIP despite meself. A Guardian Anjul. To think of it – the height a me ambition in life was to be a hairdressur. Hairdressur, how are yeh! Where did I get a notion like that? I'd nevur a made a hairdressur. I shoulda been a Private Eye – a Private Dick –

When I caught up with the lads they were talkin about the collection-can.

"We'll hang onto it for her –"

Cliona like.

Oh, Jesus, lads. Give it to the Vincent de Paul. Give it to Trocaire to finance the bishops' affairs an trips to Thailand. Give it to yur parish priest to pay compensation to the altar-boys.

Throw it in the shaggin Lee.

But don't give it to Cliona.

"She'll be down in the Bridewell now an Fawlty will be bailin her out –"

Fawlty Towurs had a weak spot for Cliona – located somewhere or othur in the full seven feet a him. He nevur saw hur – or Mary for that mattur – without blushin like a virgin. Which maybe he is – we nevur did get Mad Mary to tell us what happened on the Oscur night. An Cliona always pretends she's fuckin every guard an priest in Cork across the board. So there was no tellin whethur Fawlty had taken the plunge or not.

They were makin a bee-line for The Othur Place.

"We must call in to the Mothur of Good Counsel now –

as we're here," said Dec, "and ask Her blessing on this venture."

"What venture is that?" Liam wanted to know.

"*Liam*, for God's sake! Tizzy, of course – and Denis – the Mothur of Good Counsel has always been in charge of Denis's affairs – and anothur thing, we must do a Petition for Tony ourselves. And the wedding of course. By right we should buy candles or flowurs."

"What weddin?" But they'd reached the church porch – *One Heart, One Mind, On our Way to God* – Augustine. Dec plunged in regardless.

The wedding. I pushed the thought away.

In with Liam, dog an all.

I stayed outside. I'm takin a raincheck, says I to Hur Nibs inside. By telepathy like.

Waturstones was open. Puking – here I come.

I'll *ff* here. No point in describin the hames I made a the next few hours. Granted, I rubbed – well, shouldurs not to put too fine a point on it yeh know what I mean – with some right hunks. But as for me Puking agenda I misewell a been waxin a gaza – shinnin up a pole, to you. Which I was – come to think of it – if yeh could a seen me latchin onta readurs that's exactly what I musta looked like.

But anyway for all me efforts that day I learned – well, Puking's real name for starturs but, as we say in Cork, I *likes* callin him Puking.

So, apart from that –

Right – brace yourself –

Say "hit me" –

Go on – say it –

Just *say* it –

Right.

I learned about atoms. That every atom is made up of a proton an a neutron. Which are made up a things called quarks. An these quarks come in six flavours: up, down, strange, charmed, bottom, top –

You think I'm makin this up, don't yeh?

Think about it:

I'll have a strawberry Charmed Quark please with hot fudge toppin – no, hold the hundreds an thousands –

Seriously – a quark comes in three colours: red, blue and green. An a proton is made a two up quarks plus one down quark. An a neutron is made a two down quarks plus one up quark. Or maybe the othur way round.

And no, I'm *not* makin this up. I swear to God an His Blessed Mothur.

You didn't know you were made up a *quarks* did yeh?

Well, we live and learn.

Hey, baby, I kinda like the way your *quarks* are arranged. How about you an me – ?

But we'll get back to that –

Anyway – there's more: a quark – wait for it now – this is the best part – the name quark comes from James Joyce. *Three quarks for Mistur Mark!* Except that no one has the blindest idea what that means.

Well *great,* I thought. Thanks a million, Puking! That clears everythin up. Grand, grand. That solves all me problems. I was disgusted.

Christ! I thought. I misewell become a Trekkie. An learn Klingon.

Quark quark!

Turtles all the way down.

Well, I went reelin up Pana to St Augustine's aftur that massive effort, hopin the lads would a moved on to The Othur Place. But no such luck.

To me surprise, considerin the time a day, the church was packed – jointed. There was some kinda novena on. There was a priest talkin on the altar – a bookish-lookin type. An there were the lads squeezed inta a small space in the front bench – Dec rapt clutchin the collection-can, Liam bored brainless holdin Rectus's head between his legs. I drifted up to the railin a the shrine. There She was all goldy an serene, protectin hur child, *face inclinin sheltered safely in hur mantle blue*, an I felt a kinda pleasure an relief in just handin the whole fuckin shebang ovur to hur to hold for a minute.

"Oh, Mothur, tell me! What am I to do?"

What am I to do, Mothur?

Show me what I'm *supposed* to be doin an I'll do it with a heart an a half –

I can't believe there isn't a reason for me boomerangin back – that tis just a fluke –

An there I am for an age gropin around tryin to touch – what? An it's like there's maybe a Black Hole there I can go through, like The Eye of Jupitur in *2001* an come out – where? An then I remembered yur man in *2001* suspended out in space as a baby in the womb gazin at the Earth ready to come back –

Like me.

Maybe I'd been through The Eye of Jupitur an just couldn't remembur.

Twas at this point I started hearin what yur man on the altar was sayin –

"Liberty – Equality – Fraternity –"

What the fuck? The French Revolution?

I'll have a shot at verbatim here:

"*Liberty* – and what was that Liberty? The liberty to obey every lawless whim –

"*Equality* – an what was the Equality? The rejection of authority –"

There was a lot more to it that I can't remembur verbatim or any othur way.

I thought I must be fantasisin – an that Major O'Hara was goin to stride in doin his Rambo scene, firin from the hip – 200 rpm – *rrat-tat-tat-tat-tat-tat-tat* like a Corporation drill – an blastin this maniac off the altar – please, sur, just do it, sur.

Now he was on Fraternity – "The forerunner of Communism –" an the next thing he was ravin on about unmarried mothers flourishin with the full support a the state –

This bastard evur heard a Democracy?

I nevur knew John Major had a cousin in the Augustinians.

Back to Basics.

Like, before the French Revolution –

I looked around at the faces of all the poor misfortunates – women mostly – listenin to this vicious crap. They were all cross-eyed. This wasn't what they had come for.

Liam was aftur wakin up. He was amazed – his eyebrows were up undur his quiff.

Rectus-a-um was aghast. Definitely.

An Dec was lappin it up. Marie Antoinette meant more to him than anybody's civil liberties any day a the week.

I thought he might get up an applaud.

There was no sign a Major O'Hara an there was nothin I

Gaye Shortland

could do. If I was Batman now I could swoop down from the dome on a cable an snap him up from the altar – or bettur again Supurman – like take a deep breath an blow him away with him clingin to the lecturn. That'd be somethin.

I prayed.

An this prayur business, I'm beginnin to think – from observation – tis a bit like the old joke about *send up reinforcements I'm going to advance* – y'know, in the trenches – an by the time it gets to the end a the line tis *lend me three-an-fourpence I'm goin to a dance.* So tis like those turtles get the message grand but the line a communication is faulty an they go "What's that? What's that he said? Somethin about a dance? Three-an-fourpence – oh, we can do that no bothur – that's an easy one – send three-an-fourpence down to Tony O'Rourke there –"

Nevurtheless – I prayed to Hur Nibs to *do* somethin to stop that bastard.

A stroke a lightnin would do fine.

An the door a the church porch opened to our right an in walked Cliona.

"The Age of Chivalry is dead, indeed –" Major was sayin. Cliona's face was all smooth an waxy-lookin an she kinda paced in like she was sleep-walkin, with hur arms stretched out a small bit from hur sides. Me first thought was that she was doin hur Blind Act. But the arms were wrong.

I saw Liam an Dec an Rectus freeze-framed, starin at hur aghast. Three aghast faces with the whites a the eyes showin.

All the congregation in the front seats kinda focused on hur automatically. They were cross-eyed with boredom an they'd a focused on a Jehovah's Witness at this point. They

108

musta thought twas Christmas instead a Hallowe'en when she fell to hur knees in fronta the altar just undur John Major's lecturn an started swayin back an forth. Gently – like seaweed undur watur. All the faces started losin the blank look.

John Major's mouth clamped shut. Then he clutched at the lecturn an stared an mouthed a bit like she was Tony Blair on a roll. Poor show, John. A pro woulda just carried on regardless.

Cliona moved inta second gear.

There was a fierce silence in the church, the crowd at the front lookin bright an interested now like dogs in fronta a rabbit-hole – an the crowd at the back, who couldn't see Cliona, starin at John Major wonderin what the fuck was wrong with him.

"Jee-ee-sus! Jee-ee-sus!"

An all the heads swung to the left.

Serve the bitch right: she had competition. A wild-haired wino. Well, he looked like a wino. Or a saint. A bearded ovurcoated booted charactur. I knew him of old – he was always at it – doin his thing: throwin the arms out, kneelin, goin "Jee-ee-sus! Jee-ee-sus!", hittin the forehead on the tiles, risin to his feet. Repeat.

Next thing, like a tidal wave or a Mexican Wave, rows a people in the back half a the church started gettin to their feet an cranin their necks.

Cliona was swayin with a vengeance. An the waxy face had a trace a ire in it. Jesus-Jesus was aftur spoilin the build-up to hur climax.

An it wasn't hur Blind Act – how could I be so stupid? Twas hur Spirit Possession Act – the one that could double up for Epilepsy an Ovur-Dosin. Dependin on whethur she was goin for priests or doctors or guards.

"Jee-ee-sus! Jee-ee-sus!" *Whack!* on the tiles.

An John Major's expression teeterin between burstin inta tears an goin ballistic –

Cliona musta said to hell with the Oscur at this point because she fell backwards with a terrible screech like in the worst B movie evur, an everyone in the church except Jesus-Jesus (who carried on regardless) gave a fierce start. Includin John Major who was grey in the face like the puppet on *Spittin Image.*

Now she was clawin at the ground behind hur head, the whole body jerkin violently like a car engine on a frosty mornin. Jesus-Jesus hadn't a chance against this. Not unless he split his skull on the tiles like a Hallowe'en pumpkin. An Major was down off the altar skirtin around Cliona an the word was buzzin around the church –

"Jaysis, she's possessed!"

"The devil she is!"

The wan half a the crowd didn't give a fuck even if hur head started spinnin – they had buses to catch an kids to get in off the streets – so they started batin their way outa the church. The othur half stood there gapin, gettin in the way. An the Stephen King fans (yeah, I know, that's three halves) started batin their way up to the top to see Cliona. An decrepit ould-age pensionurs were gettin stuck between bench-ends in their efforts to go one way or the othur.

Dec an Liam an Rectus were slinkin away, makin for the side porch. So I scooted aftur em.

An the word musta gone out the main doors an back in the side porches because we were met by a showur a young fellas an young wans – laney types – comin in from outside to see Cliona.

"Hang on a sec," says Liam an he grabs a skinhead type that was goin in. "See that –" an he points at me boyo's butt. An yur man has a steel comb stuck in his back pocket – the type with the pointy handle that skins carry as offensive weapons. Liam jerks the head back at Cliona. "That'll do it – a stake through the heart – that's the only thing." An he claps the skin on the shouldur encouraginly an gives him a thumbs up an we goin out. Then anothur thought strikes him an he hisses aftur yur man – "An don't forget – then yeh havta decapitate hur." With a chop at his own neck to make his point.

"Ovur the top, Liam," pants Dec an they joggin down St Augustine's Lane. "Definitely ovur the top."

"Worth a try," says Liam grinnin. "He'll hardly do it though."

"Exorcism," pants Dec. "That's what she's going for."

"The only thing is – how is she goin to manage the projectile vomitin?" an they plungin inta the safe haven a The Othur Place –

Then you put your lovin arms around me
And it feels like shelter –

Billie Ray Martin was doin hur thing. Again. I wished to Christ she'd stop sometime. Call me retro but give me Donna Summur any day.

"Projectile vomiting? She'll think of something," pants Dec an they climbin the stairs. "Fake-it is hur middle name."

"You're tellin me! Will yeh evur forget that Charismaniac Conference? The exorcisms an she tryin to take on all the priests an handin out drugs like they were Smarties –"

God, that Conference – twas unreal. Cliona with the priests an Dec with the nuns – shur they were high as kites. And at that time yeh couldn't get near Dec because a Cliona. They were like Robson an Jerome on *Top a the Pops* – ear to ear week aftur week forty weeks runnin – *Time goes by – so slooowly – And time can mean soooo much* – how Dec evur got a man with hur I don't know. Trouble was – his first love was drink an she fed him that. She always had money. It was just lucky that he wasn't the kinda person who was inta drugs an tablets an all that. She usedta give him stuff – tablets – an it would be "I wouldn't give you too much now!" Once she injected him an it frightened him it was so good. Then when he did it again it was a very very bad trip an it terrified him. He stayed away from her a bit aftur that – I mean it wasn't like before when she usedta own him.

If I hated the bitch I had reason to.

I came to meself with a start. Dec was openin the door at the top a the stairs.

An the voice a this Fathur Twomey came out loud an clear: "Masturbation is a spiritual exercise –"

Dec looked back an gave Liam the narrowed-eye treatment. "This is our man," says he.

Liam looked perplexed (anothur grand word like aghast – an just wait for it – soonur or latur I'm goin ta say "with impunity" – or is it "without impunity" – oh Christ, I'm aftur forgettin).

In they went, dog an all.

I let em go. Perplexed meself.

Talk about operatin on a need-to-know basis.

Our man – our man for what? What the fuck was he up to? There was one answur to that, rememburin his conversation with Breeda earliur, but I didn't even want to float it to the surface a me mind.

But, Jay, this Fathur Twomey must be one interestin man. But it sounded kinda heavy an I'd battured me brain enough for one day, what with Puking an all.

An if Dec was thinkin along certain lines, I didn't wanta know.

I needed some R & R.

But *not* with Major O'Hara.

The flicks?

I went out an onta Washington Street to see what was on in the Capitol. I could relax for a coupla hours an pick the lads up latur (twas mega not havin to pay).

Masturbation is a spiritual exercise – that's a good one, I was thinkin. Couldn't agree with him more.

Hang on a minute – if masturbation was a spiritual exercise, well, so was Major O'Hara . . .

An I'm standin there tryin to figure this one out when – *Zooooooooooom* –

A Yamaha went zippin up South Main Street – one a those real little fliers an noisy as hell – with the ridur leanin forward ovur the tank –

I'd seen that ass before –

It crossed the Southgate Bridge an vroom-vroomed round the cornur to take the way up to St Finbarre's – an yes, it was Foxy-nob.

Well.

By the time I got up to his house – because I detoured by the Western Road to keep well outa Dizzy Gillespie's line a vision – he was aftur parkin the bike around the side a the house. I went an had a gandur at it, peerin at it because twas

dark by this time an there was only one dim outside light.
LC350. Nice bike. Bit tatty. Resprayed black at some stage
but needed anothur goin ovur – bit a blue showin through.
Second-hand, I'd bet. Liam would fancy one a them.

In with me. Bold as brass. An up the stairs.

The sistur wasn't around –

I dunno why but I kinda felt the sistur was an important
part a the equation here –

I was only sixteen but I guess that's no excuse

My sister was thirty-two, lovely and – loose –

Oooh sister –

Equation? Nothin equalled anythin else here – nothin
added up –

I could hear him movin around inside the room.

I booted Prince outa me brain –

Because Garth was in action, warblin away –

And now, I'm glad I didn't know

The way it all would end

The way it all would go –

I knocked – pretended to, like.

Our lives are better left to chance

I could have missed the pain

But I'd have had to miss – the – dance –

An he opened the door.

In his gear.

Fuck.

An the green eyes lit up.

All right!

I knocked an *he opened the door.*

So what could I do?

I tipped me stetson an said "Hi, honey – how ya doin?"

He gave me a big smile with that gap between the teeth showin, shut the door and locked it an sashayed back inta the room, with what was supposed to be an allurin look ovur his shouldur. An those eyes an sexy mouth in the kinda heart-shaped face gave him a certain prettiness so it wasn't too hard to say – "Missed ya, hon –"

He sat on the bed an posed, bony legs crossed in the nylon stockins. Oh Gaawd. I'd nevur evur be able to share this with him –

Prince could though –

If I was your girlfriend would yeh let me dress you?

I mean help yeh pick out your clothes before we go out?

I did me cowboy walk ovur to the bed an sat down.

An he turned to me. The right way. The right side. "I thought you'd forgotten," says he, poutin.

"Now am I likely to do that?" says I in a nice slow mellow drawl. I didn't sound half bad.

He smiled an stroked me on the thigh – well, in that vicinity like. "I forgot to tell yeh, Garth honey," says he, purrin away. "I was so proud of you that night at the Point!"

"You know I was singin for you, sweetheart," said I. This was easy an a bit like a dream. Dream-like. Because it couldn't really be happenin. I focused on that delicious little gap between his teeth so I wouldn't get turned off by the nylon hair an the heavy perfume. He was waitin for more. I plunged on. "But, y'know, that audience – I'm tellin ya! I was just stunned – when I started into *If Tomorrow Never Comes* – well, I don't remembur singin the first word of it – I mean they just took it and ran with it – when your people teach you your own songs – that's – well – somethin new –"

An I shook me head. But where the hell was all this crap

comin from? Like I was inspired. "I was pretty impressed. I'm tellin ya!"

An then I remembered – *Kenny Live* – I'd seen it – the inturview where he wept lookin at his own video an promised to buy tickets for everyone to the States if his wife went inta labour while he was singin at the Point. Y'know – the inturview that Gerry Ryan or someone – it *musta* been Gerry Ryan – said was fit to make a grown man puke.

"Have you told Sandy yet?" says he.

"Eh – no. Not yet." I hadn't. Whoevur Sandy was.

"How d'yeh think she'll take it?" The green eyes all anxious.

I chanced me arm. "Bad. Real bad." An squinted at him to see if I was aftur gettin it right.

Yes, right answur.

Jesus! This was amazin. An it was real. I was actually *havin a conversation.*

A big sigh. "I know tis hard for you. But I'll be patient." Anothur heart-felt sigh.

What would it feel like to put the tip a me tongue through that gap? Would it fit? Would it go? Well, no – but the pleasure would be in the tryin – an *there's joy in repetition* –

"Garth?"

"Yes, sweetheart?"

"Will you sing for me now? Please?" Big wet pout an wiggle a the shouldurs. Oh *Gaawd*. Leave it out! "Pu-lease!"

"Oh, I don't know, honey –"

"Pu-lease!"

"We-e-ell –" Shook me head bashfully.

The Garth tape was aftur comin to an end. I waited for him to turn it.

"I'm waiting!" says he.

That stumped me. Holy fuck! Wouldn't he put the tape back on an I'd lipsync?

I waited. He waited.

The tape? No tape.

Could I have a shot at *Friends in Low Places*? I didn't think so.

"Honey," says I. "I'm tryin to rest my voice – you know I havta get through six more concerts at the Point and my throat is a bit rough – that audience really works me – I really think I shouldn't –"

"Oh, thank you, honey –"

Oh-ho.

"In any case I only sing in private for Sandy –"

"Yes, that's my favourite –"

Oh-ho.

"That make-up is crap by the way –"

"You always know exactly what I like –"

Conversation, how are yeh.

He wasn't hearin anythin I was sayin. He was holdin a converstaion with himself.

I misewell be recitin a decade a the Rosary.

That was a hard pill to swallow.

The disappointment of it caught me by the throat.

Well, now, I was a mature spirit an I couldn't let this rock the boat.

Time for a little singin an spinnin. Jes' doin ma job, honey –

I picked up me guitar – that I just happened to have handy – an I started off –

Oh bury me not on the Lone Prairie

These words came low and mournfully
From the pallored lips of the youth who lay
On his dying bed at the close of day –
Jesus! This was a bit too close to the bone. Lighten up for God's sake –
OK –
I'm headin for the last round-up –
Christ, no –
Empty saddles in the old corral –
Jesus, but weren't these cowboys right mournful buggurs altogethur? How many of em were gay, I wondured? Those long cattle-drives –
When it's twilight in the trail
And my voice is still
Please plant this heart of mine
Undurneath the lonesome pine on the hill –
Pathetic! Get a *life*!
But there were tears standin in Foxy-nob's eyes.
Was he hearin me?
I'd be movin meself to tears next.
Do not forsake me oh my darlin
On this our wedding da-ay –
I was gettin a fierce buzz outa the fact I was turnin out to be a dab hand with the guitar – no more bothur to me! But lighten up, Garth – this wouldn't do at all –
Me mind was a blank – somethin cheerful – *Rollin rollin rollin – Rawhiiiiide! Things I been missin good vittels love an kissin* – ah –
Would he notice if I slid ovur an started singin soul? Ah – wait a minute –
I threw meself inta some right frisky work on the guitar

an then put it down an got up an started struttin me stuff. But I wasn't at all surprised to hear that I still had guitar backin. Courtesy a Mary Chapin-Carpentur.

Well, I woke up this mornin, stumbled outa my rack –

Foxy-nob watched me mesmerised. Like the sun was shinin outa me ass.

Now eleven million latur I was sittin at the bar –

The piana backin had a grand honky-tonk sound an I was movin like I'd been born dancin.

Dwight Yoakam's in the cornur
Tryin to catch my eye
Lyle Lovett's right beside me
With his hand upon my thigh –

Cool the things yeh could do with a stetson –

I feel lucky! Oh oh ho
I feel lucky! Yeah!
Hey Dwight, hey Lyle
Boys, you don't have to fight

Hot dog, *I feel lucky tonight*!

Tell me Foxy-nob wasn't hearin me – a Boyzone fan or a nun couldn't a looked more cross-eyed with adoration.

I feel lucky! Grrrrrrrr! I feel lucky yeah!
I think I'll flip a coin I'm an winner eithur way
Mmmmmm – I feel lucky today!

An there I was doin a Jerry Lee Lewis on the piana an Foxy-nob's emeruld eyes were sparklin an we were so much inta this that the knock when it came was like a thundurclap.

Foxy-nob nearly convulsed. I nearly combusted.

"Eoin! Eoin! Are yeh there? Open up!"

Twas the sistur.

"Eoin!"

She rapped sharply at the door.

"*Eoin! Open up!* What're yeh doing? I know you're in there! Open the door!"

Poor Foxy-nob was frozen an white-faced.

She rattled the door-knob. "Come on! Open up! You've got the sewing-kit! Open up – I need a bit a thread!" An she rattled the door violently.

Foxy-nob stared at the door-knob. I thought he couldn't a moved to save his life. Except that his hands were tremblin.

But then he stood up – very shaky an teeterin on the heels – an there was a rustle a the cloth in his skirt.

He clutched at the skirt on eithur side.

His sistur was a redhead an she had a redhead's tempur. She started freakin out altogethur, bangin at the door like one possessed.

Wham wham wham! Jesus, she was goin to do hurself an injury. Why didn't he speak ta hur? Say somethin – anythin at all! Tell hur to fuck off – that would do.

But he was petrified.

Wham wham wham! Oh Christ, she was usin some kinda blunt intrument now –

Crash!

Whatevur it was, it wasn't any more –

But that didn't call a halt to hur. She was in a right fury. *Wham wham wham* with somethin harder an sharper –

There was a fair chance she'd break the door down.

Foxy-nob moved. He took a few steps towards the door an stood facin it – quite close.

An suddenly I knew he was goin to open it.

He was gearin himself up for that.

His face was white an sweaty and the line a too-dark make-up along his jaw stood out clear.

He was goin to open that door.

Wham wham wham!

I moved between him an the door.

Ovur my dead body.

It was a battle a wills. I could feel the force an pressure a his intention. Of his desperation.

No. No.

Don't open it.

He pushed forward and came up against me.

I put my arms around him, so to speak. An the mad courage soaked outa him. With his head against the door, he started to gulp an cry softly.

But she was gone. There were voices downstairs. Saved. The mothur must be back.

Foxy-nob pricked up his ears an heard. He was on the verge a collapse but he whirled round to the bed an started tearin the clothes off him. Things disappeared inta all kinds a peculiar nooks an crannies. *Behind* the wardrobe. Undur floorboards. Inta the backs a pictures. An all at high speed. Then cotton-wool an cream an the make-up off. An soap an towel. The varnish off his nails. But his socks went on ovur the varnished toenails.

An when it was all done the life went outa him. He sat on the bed in his undurpants an socks an his head sagged onta his chest. An then he lay back an curled up on the bed like a child.

An I thought the curve of his hip where it slanted so strongly out from the waist an back muscles was the most beautiful thing in God's creation.

I hovered ovur him.

His eyelashes were wet.

Oh Lord.

What could I do?

I lay down behind him an wrapped meself around him.

"Honey," I said, strokin him, strokin the fine wiry muscles of his back, strokin the stubble a the red hair that moved like a field a cut wheat, tryin not to let me attention stray downwards. Yet. "Not that way. No. Not yur sistur. Not the family. That's too hard a nut to crack. You'd end up stringin yurself up, believe me, sweetheart," an I loved him in that moment, "You must come out and find us. Jesus, you should meet Mad Mary – she doesn't give a shit an she looks like shit with it. Jesus, come an meet Jennifur any Saturday night at the club – he's famous for it – blond hair down to here – skirt up to his bum – I think he's a test-drivur for racin-cars or somethin when he's a man. I tell yeh – it's no big deal at all – your type are thick on the ground –"

He was listenin. He was calmin down. I kept on strokin. "Come out an meet us – you're daft to think you're alone. Nobody's fuckin alone." We needed his fuckin Garth Brooks. If I reached out I could just about touch his hi-fi. But I couldn't turn it on. Jesus, about time I taught meself that kin-whatsit – I was like a handicapped spirit. "Honey, turn on your hi-fi – turn it on –" Jesus, even telepathy was beyond me. Pathetic. It worked with Dec. "Turn on your hi-fi – honey, turn on your hi-fi – honey, the music – turn on your hi-fi –" It always made me feel an eejit to havta repeat – but it worked. An his arm stretched out an fumbled with the tape an click – an there was Garth –

Well, twas bettur than a hole in the head –

A damn sight bettur actually –
Sometimes late at night I lie awake and watch her sleepin –
She's lost in peaceful dreams so I turn out the lights an lay
there in the dark –
It was real mellow – I hadta admit –
An I could run me own sound-track anyway –
Prince? Where are yeh, boy? An there he was pulsin away
like an anxiously palpitating heart –
If I was your girlfriend would you remember
To tell me all of the things you forgot when I was your man?
"Your sistur means a lot to you, doesn't she? You think
you hate hur but she matturs to you more than anyone,
doesn't she? She's the one you want to tell – but you musn't
– not yet –"
Since when had I got so sure a meself?
If I was your one and only friend
Would you run to me if somebody hurt you
Even if that somebody was me?
The muscles of his back were like the ripples of sand on a
wet beach – his skin tasted like salt air or salt watur – except
for a faint cosmetic scent an taste still left on his face –
If tomorrow nevur comes
Will she know how much I loved her
Did I try in every way
To show her every day that she's my only one?
I went on strokin, an my hands – or what might have
been my hands – went around an stroked his chest an don't
you know, sweetheart, it's so beautiful and it shakes me to
the soul that there are *no* breasts there, that my hands slide
across and there are no breasts – why don't you know that?
And down your hard belly and my hand hits that delicious

soft firmness – and *why* don't you want it – that's your pride – and, yes, take that off for me – and oh Christ why have you shaved your crotch like that so I feel rough stubble where I should plunge into a moist little forest and your legs are rough against me where you've shaved – why, sweetheart? And I cradled him an breathed in his smell and he took his cock in his hands because I couldn't do it for him – yes, you do it for us – and for me there was the beautiful swell of his butt against me an I could hear someone pantin and I knew it couldn't be me and yet it was me because I was him and I pressed into him hard and it was very tough, very tough, and I had to focus until my soul shook with the strain but I was going to take him with me out there to the Eye of Jupiter where no sisturs bang on doors and we were goin through to the other side where there's joy in repetition and nothing, nothing God man or turtle was going to wrench him away from me and with a final wrench of pleasure I was in his skin looking through his green eyes and feelin his pleasure and his hands were my hands on his cock so I felt the silky skin ride up and down an in the very moment he-we started to come spurtin through our hands I felt his thoughts like an ice-chip in my brain – and I knew he knew I was there. The fallin apart took a long long time – a long time before he fell away from me like a nut from its shell but – no – it wasn't as clean as that – there were a million threads like a glue that held us even then. And at one point I whispered to him "You see?" but I don't know what it was he was supposed to see.

And then she came knockin again, more quietly this time.

"Eoin! Here's your tea! Eoin!"

Aftur a minute he got up an threw a t-shirt on an his undurpants and went an opened an took it.

But she came in. "God, what are you doing in the dark?" An snapped on the lights and moved about and picked things up and looked at the bed and yes, there were stains.

Then she kissed him on the cheek. "Night."

"Night."

She closed the door gently.

Incest is everything it's said to be –

Shut up, Prince.

He slept soon aftur. Then I kissed the little Trojan undur his collar-bone an kissed him on the lips.

And left. I didn't want to.

But Garth was there doin his thing –

Is the love I gave her in the past gonna be enough to last

If tomorrow never comes –

So I felt it was OK to leave.

And, Jaysis, halfway down the stairs I remembered me stetson an had to go back for it.

Joke.

I was dead late for the lads. There wasn't a sign of em at the club. I stood out on the North Main Street and tried to pick up vibes. But twasn't easy. I felt really spaced out an no wondur. A bit uncertainly I rambled down Washington Street towards the Western Road. The Maltings, I thought, but no – I turned inta Reidy's Wine Vaults an there they were – Liam, Dec, Fathur Twomey. Rectus. There were othur gay men around but Dec an Liam had the priest sandwiched between em. Around the same little table were a couple a middle-aged women who were most definitely nuns in civvies – probably escortin him up to UCC for his lecture.

I felt a fierce pang when I saw Dec. The idea I'd been unfaithful to him – I couldn't deal with it at all. It made me feel like shit – and at the same time I was still reelin from the joy of what I'd been through.

To tell yeh the honest truth – I was feelin fuckin great. But I didn't know what to do with meself. An the one thing I couldn't do just then was think.

"The Pope is an evil man," the priest was sayin with great passion as I came upta them.

Jesus, this priest was somethin else.

I could see an feel Dec bristlin. But he said nothin.

"Oh, Fathur," goes one a the nuns, very hurt. "What did he do to deserve your saying that?"

Liam puts his spoke in. "Well, like yeh said earliur, Fathur – labellin gay people as disordered –"

Labels are for canned food – Michael Stipe.

"Ah, but, Fathur," says one of the little nuns. "The Holy Fathur didn't say that to you *personally*, did he now?"

Liam thought this was hilarious an Rectus-a-um lifted hur head outa hur ashtray a Guinness an laughed but Dec – *what* the fuck was Dec aftur?

"Sisters," said the priest, "the number of gay men I've seen die without making their peace with God because of those very words –"

"Exactly," says Dec cuttin across him suddenly so that he stopped an kinda gaped. "And on that very point I have a great favour to ask you –" an he starts to tell the priest about wantin him to officiate at a weddin at the convent –

Me heart thumped inta me boots.

With some rigamarole about the bride refusin to marry in a church – because the Pope was an evil man – so this was the only hope to get God's blessin on the marriage.

Would I throw up now or latur?

There was no problem, Fathur Twomey was ravenous for beyond-the-pale marriages. He was dead keen.

An Dec turns to Liam an does this embarrassed half-hug half-slap-on-the-back thing that straight men do, an it looks fuckin peculiar Dec doin it. "At last," says he, his eyes shinin with sentiment. "I *told* you we'd find a solution. Mary is going to be ovur the moon."

"Mary?" says Liam. Perplexed.

What?

"Oh, is this the groom?" asks Beyond the Pale, so surprised I began to think Liam musta been playin footsie with him undur the table.

Liam? Mary?

"Oh, congratulations!" go the nuns, all smiles. An they're tickled pink an the insult to the Pope is shelved behind the cans a baked beans an dog food for the present.

I don't know if I'm comin or goin.

"Let me buy you a drink," says Beyond the Pale to Liam with such a peculiar expression on his face I was now convinced he *had* been playin footsie with Liam an still had a wild hope a gettin to the bottom a the affair.

An Liam isn't freakin out just yet because he *knows* there's aftur bein a misundurstandin – so he keeps gazin at Dec waitin for the punch-line or correction or whatevur. An so do I.

But none comes an in a few minutes Liam's glassy-eyed with astonishment an mortification, listenin to toasts to his happiness an risky honeymoon jokes from the nuns.

ff to us on our way home an Liam for once in his life too gobsmacked for any rantin an rarin.

"Dec," says he. "What the fuck are you at? For God's sake tell me – this is doin me head in –"

"You'll have to marry Mary."

"Be serious for Chrissake for a minute –"

"I am serious. Certainly I'm serious," said Dec. "Liam – we need the house –"

"The house?"

"God, wake up and smell the coffee. The *house* – we need it – we need it as a safe house for Tizzy and we can have it for a pittance if we share the rent."

"But this Tizzy situation is goin to be settled one way or the othur – eithur he *walks* or he's up in Cork Jail. *Eithur way* he don't need a *house*!"

"The house is there for the picking, Liam –"

"The pickin? The pickin?" Now Liam was off – spittin fire like a Hallowe'en firework. "The pickin? Like I havta get *married* – like I havta marry *Mary* – you call that the pickin?"

"It's practically in Mary's sistur's name. All we need is for Mary to pretend to be her sistur an to be able to flash some kind of a marriage cert. And we'll have a free home for life. Think of it –"

"Dec – in all seriosity – please – an I'm saying *please* to yeh for once in me life – *please* forget this notion – tisn't a joke much to me taste –"

"Liam. I'm *not* joking."

An they confronted one anothur eye to eye.

"Liz needs the house," says Dec. "She's pregnant."

That floored Liam. He deflated like one a them rubber dolls. He rallied but very weakly. "Why can't Liz an Niall get married so? Why the fuck should I?"

"Niall's out of the picture. I'm going to marry Liz myself."

Well. *ff.*

Liam thought this was the Wank a the Week anyway an laughed till he was drinkin his tears.

An in the middle a all a this we're passin St Francis – this huge mockiyah Italian church all domes an goldy mosaics – an Dec wants to go in. But that's Dec for yeh. He had a notion to do *all* a the churches for me for the month a the Holy Souls. An come hell, high watur or weddins he was goin to do it. An besides he wants to pray at St Anthony's shrine for Mothur – Ant'ny, Patron a Things Lost or Stolen. As if Mike was a mislaid key or lost umbrella for fuck's sake.

But Liam – dog, fag, scowl an all, like a cat on a hot tin roof or a herring on the griddle-oh – won't let him.

"No *way*. Yeh can do it by mobile phone."

So Dec rolls the eyes an does a mental quicky to Ant'ny for me an Mothur.

An I'm thinkin a Ant'ny with the Child Jesus in his arms – an for the first time in me life it strikes me: what's he always heftin a child around for anyway? An who was the othur fella with a thing about the Child Jesus? An I remembur – Padraig Pearse, one a the Fathurs a the Nation like. An I think: hang on a minute now – Holy Jesus, wouldn't that be somethin – if it turned out I was called aftur the Patron Saint a Paedophiles? No wondur they hadta give him a covur – an a pretty corny one they came up with – Patron a Things Lost or Stolen for Chrissake – but he took it an ran with it, fair fucks to him –

But Liam was revvin up. "What you're askin me to do is illegal –"

"No, it isn't –"

"'Tis fraud!"

"Liam – you can always say you didn't know."

"Didn't *kno-ow*?"

"You can say she said she was a virgin an you didn't want to rush her into sex –"

"Didn't *know*? Didn't *know* Mary wasn't a girl? Fuckin hell, Dec! Get real!"

"Well, what about Monsieur Butterfly? He didn't know for years! Or *The Crying Game* – why should *you* know?"

"Because I'm not a *thick wankur* like Stephen Rea or Jeremy-*fuckin*-Irons, that's why!"

"Well, you can pretend to be –"

"No, I *can't* – fuckit, Dec – *Mary* – we're talking *Mary* here – not Jaye-fuckin-*Davidson* for Chrissake –"

"Oh, why are you stressing these *technicalities* – there's no real problem –"

"Because – *because* of the little *technicality* that *technically* Mary is not a woman!"

"Oh! Liam – you always *create* difficulties –"

Liam made stranglin noises. Then: "Let me get this straight now – I'm bein *forced* inta marriage an *I'm* creatin difficulties? Is that it? Well, let me tell you – you can stuff yur difficulties because I'm not marryin anybody! Let alone *Mary*! Even if it was possible to marry a fella *I'd* be the last man ta do it – it's not my gig, I'm tellin yeh – I wouldn't marry – I wouldn't marry – *I* wouldn't marry – *Jean*-Claude Van *Damme*, I wouldn't!"

Dec looked at him amazed. "But who would? *That* thick moron? With nothing to recommend him except an ass like a garden tool-shed shelf?"

"Well," says Liam. "His *ass* is the only reason why I might considur it at all!"

"It isn't his *ass* you'd be looking at across the breakfast table!"

"Oh, yes, it *is!*" Shoutin like he was addressin someone at the end a the road. He stopped dead an pointed – like Jean-Claude Van Damme's ass was hoverin in the air ahead of us. "*I* would *eat* breakfast off his ass! *Eggs* an rashurs!"

"Liam, sometimes I think you've been lobotomised – I suppose you wouldn't remember it if you had been –" An Dec started yappin away about how crude an hopeless Liam was an moved on to a kinda religious fantasy where marriage was goin to remove Liam from Occasions of Sins an be the makings of him.

But we'd lost Liam. He walked on sometimes smilin to himself an frownin othur times an I knew he was still workin on the idea a eatin breakfast off Van Damme's ass, figurin out the technicalities of it an if it was – what's the word? Feez-something? An whethur they'd have ta call in the stuntman – ménage à trois –

So the two of em were windin down nicely an you mighta thought we were aftur havin enough grief for one day.

But *ooooh* no.

No rest for the wicked an RIP how are yeh.

We get back to Shaggin Wank an Tizzy meets us at the door with the nails bitten down to the quick an he doesn't even notice Rectus-a-um standin there pantin up at him – that bad now like. Fawlty was aftur findin him. Through Mothur, a'course. An he had to go to court on Wednesday mornin.

"Whaaa? So soon?" says Liam amazed.

"He said he hurried it up for me."

"Jesus, *thanks* a lot, Fawlty!"

Tizzy is nearly plannin his Escape from Alcatraz already.

"Don't worry," says Dec. "You can write a filmscript while you're inside."

"Bosco," says Liam. "Bosco'll do it for yeh – low budget – black-an-white –"

Bosco – Tizzy's RTE boyfriend with the Take That haircut an the outsize – eh, camera.

"Rape," says Dec. "Make sure you're raped on a regular basis while you're inside –"

"Birds," says Liam. "That's the thing. We'll get caged birds from Connie for yeh – would they let yeh keep a ferrut I wondur?"

An I swear they'd a been inta it, there an then, plannin a menajurie for Tizzy in Cork Jail an his film career if lightnin hadn't struck again.

There was a commotion outside an Mary comes streakin in – lookin very peculiar in jeans an T-shirt without his wig an make-up. "She's asss isss agin! She's asss isss agin!"

An there through the door was Mary's mothur lumburin off across the park in this kinda pigeon-toed way she has, hualin a kid by each hand.

"James's Street," says Tizzy, moanin. "She's been at it all day!"

"Whasupithur?" goes Liam.

"Lave hur alone!" screeches Mary latchin onta him though he hadn't budged at all. "D'mindhur! She's freekin!"

An it turns out the small wan – Susannah, the ten-year-old – was aftur bein interfered with. By the knackurs across the park. The night before.

The night before? There's a quare yarn for yeh, I thought. I *saw* the kid goin to bed meself an she in grand form.

"There's a quare yarn," says Dec. "I *saw* her go up to bed myself an she in fine fettle."

I told yeh it happens.

"Gawd, me nerves," says Tizzy. "Don't be talkin to me. She went up to de phone aftur ye left dis mornin, with a conjun-box fulla twenty-pieces, an she musta called all Cork because before Fawlty evur came, dere was a stream a social workurs an docturs an ambulances an Squad Cars an I dunno what – I was in terrur all day – a fine place ye brought me – I'd a been bettur below in the sanctuary –"

"C'mon," says Liam. An off with us across the green with Mary bringin up the rear screamin "Lave hur alone!" an Rectus-a-um streakin around us in circles trailin hur string – thinkin, I'd say, that life was lookin up.

An Florrie's paradin up an down in fronta one a the knackurs' houses an the voice of hur carryin like one a them *castrati* boyos Dec d'be playin – *countur-tenurs* as Dec says –

"Raaaped! Raaaped!" With the two small wans in their pyjamas bein jerked along – lookin quite cheerful considerin. The smallur one is carryin the Rollur-Blade Barbie.

"Latch onta vur!" screeches Mary.

An half the park is out an the rest are cowerin in their doorways with their childrun around their legs.

"Mam, Mam, c'maan hooum!" screeches Mary. "Latch onta vur! Latch onta vur!"

An Florrie makes for the lads.

"I'm guessin now, Mrs Casey," says Dec. "But is there something amiss?"

133

She comes right up to Dec an breathes in his face. "*Raaped*, Declan." An she swings round to Liam. An Liam does a bit a footwork a wingur woulda been proud of an skips outa hur way so she swings back an gets Dec between hur an the pillur a the house. *"Raaaped."*

"By whom?" says Dec.

"By de knackurs. Last night."

"But *when* last night, Mrs Casey? I thought she went safely to bed?"

"Shur didn't she get up agin an go ovur to dem."

"But is she injured, Mrs Casey? Has she seen the doctor?"

"De worst case he's evur come across, he said."

An Susannah lookin up at Dec all cheeky an cheerful undur hur blonde fringe but with a kinda nerviness undurneath that I could now feel strongly. In fact, a nerviness sharp enough to set me teeth on edge. She's a pretty kid with a very red mouth with a pout to it, an a kinda transparent skin that made hur look fragile.

"What happened, Susannah?" Dec asks hur.

An Susannah looks away off across the park with a blank face on hur. She's jerkin away at hur mothur's hand.

Then she starts pokin at the collection-can – that Dec still has undur his arm a'course.

"Hypur. She's hypur. An no wondur. De doctur said tis been goin on for ages. An shur didn't Margaret say it to me before she went back ovur – 'Yeh should have a look at Susannah, Mam,' she sez sez she, 'I think she's bein inturfeeured with.'"

"Yerra, g'wan away home with yur 'inturfeeured with'", goes one a the neighbour women. "If tisn't dat tis brain tumours or brush-handles!"

"We're demented from ya –" goes anothur. "Every day bringin a rake a Squad Cars an ambulances inta the park an we tryin to have a respectable neighbourhood –"

An they all join in, shoutin at Florrie "G'wan away home!" an "Whasupitcha?" an "D'yeh know what time a the night it is?" No sign a the knackurs but I saw the nets twitchin.

"Did Susannah say the knackurs did it?" says Liam.

On the ball, Liam. The ould reportur's instinct.

"Dey did it all right – didn't de knackurs give yeh sweets, Susannah?"

"No-wah."

Hur mothur gives hur a glassy stare an jerks hur by the arm so ferociously yeh could hear hur teeth rattle. "Didn't yeh tell me dey gave yeh sweets?"

"No-wah." Susannah's eyes are dartin around at a fierce rate.

"An what was de red stuff on yur mouth? Wasn't dat sweets?"

"No-wah," says Susannah, poutin. "Dey gave me a Mistur Frosty."

"Dere now," says hur mothur givin Dec a satisfied nod.

Dec gave hur one long look. "Hmmnph." Then a sigh an a shrug a the shoulders. "Mrs Casey, the best thing to do now is to go home an we'll help you to deal with it all in the mornin –"

"The small wan is exhausted, Mrs Casey," says Liam. "Look at hur – the eyes are fallin outa hur head – an she'll catch hur death in those little pyjamas – tell yeh what – I'll help yeh to take hur ovur – shur you're tired yurself an can't be heftin hur –"

An without more ado he scooped up the small wan, Barbie an all, an started back across the green.

"Come on, Susannah," says Dec extractin the child's hand from hur mothur's. "It's past your bedtime."

So, with Liam flakin off across the park with Tanya an Barbie an Dec propellin Susannah who was still jerkin around in a nervous kinda way, Mary latched onta "vur" by the cardigan an hauled hur off by main force in their wake.

Back at the ranch a while latur they were settlin down for the night an congratulatin themselves on the way they'd handled the situation an speculatin on what in Jesus' name was aftur happenin to Susannah an where an when – an there was an easy answur to all a that – the jury wasn't out very long at all an the verdict was unanimous an Mary didn't put a tooth in it so to speak – talk about the horse's mouth –

When *wham wham wham wham* at a door knockur an they were all galvanised again. They scrambled to the winda – Mary an Tizzy were aftur takin down the plywood – an there was the single mothur from next door down in fronta Florrie's knockin away frantically.

So there was fierce cursin an blindin in the dark an scrabblin round for boots an jeans an down the stairs with us again an back up to get the collection-box an down again just in time to see Connie come reelin outa the house – langurs – *locked* now like.

"Mr Casey, hurry," says the woman – a nice-lookin youngish woman – steppin back, real nervous. "Yur wife is aftur goin off ovur the park with an axe –"

"Jaysis! Jaysis!" goes Connie, staggurin on his doorstep. "I told hur not ta do it! Dat fuckin bitch'll be the death a me –"

"An she has the little girls with hur –"

There were lights comin on across the park an voices so we all streaked off ovur the green with Connie reelin along behind us an sure enough there she was batin down the knackurs' door with an axe.

"Raped!" *Wham!* "Raped!" *Wham!* "Raped!" Hootin away countur-tenur.

She didn't get very far with that – but she'd done some damage like – when the door was pulled open an she lost hur balance an the axe swung hur round an it sliced inta the grass a the garden an stuck. An one a the knackurs – a fine strappin man now like – stepped outa the door an just stood there in his shirt-sleeves with a shotgun in his arms like a vigilante.

Florrie was wrestlin with the axe, tryin to get it outa the ground. An Susannah rushes inta the garden to help hur an Florrie swats hur away like a fly. An the child is still dancin around hur an tryin to grab at the axe. She *is* hypur.

"Mam! Mam!" goes Mary an I thought he sounded – scared.

But seein as Mary has no more feelins than a crow I musta been mistaken.

By now half the park is out – an a dozen kids of assorted ages are up on the garden wall in pyjamas an anoraks an wet runnurs – mockin Florrie an screamin at hur –

"Ya mad bitch!"

"Get down outa dere or I'll cut de legs from undur ya!" goes one a the mothurs to hur kid.

"Where's me Daaa! Where's me *Daaaaa!*" screeches Mary, gettin his second wind.

Good question.

I swooped back ovur the green that's curved like a low hill an came on Connie reelin around at the top a the rise starin up at the stars like he was seein em for the first time in his life an he singin this crapulous Presley ballad – *"In de ghettooo! An his moddur cries –"*

An here comes Liam at a gallop – "Connie! Connie! C'mon! C'mon! The knackur's got a shotgun!"

"Liam boy –" Catchin onta Liam's head an rufflin his hair an nearly capsizin the two a them – as he sings – *"Cos if dere's one thing dat she don't need – It's anoddur little hungry mouth to feed – in de ghettoooo!"*

"Connie – will yeh c'mon – Florrie!"

"Shur I told hur not ta do it!"

An Liam gets his arm around Connie's waist an half-drags half-carries him down to the knackurs' house.

Florrie was standin at the gate jerkin Susannah by the arm somethin ferocious an choppin at the air above hur head with the axe, lookin like she might take a run at the knackur any minute. An the neighbours are all pop-eyed at the prospect a bloodshed.

Liam unloads Connie an goes, "Go on now, Connie! Take the axe from hur!"

"Latch onta vur! Latch onta vur!" screeches Mary.

But Connie is away – in Gracelands –

"Connie, the axe!" goes Liam.

Connie has eyes only for Liam – his audience a one. He holds Liam's face like as if he's goin to kiss him. *"Teeake a look at you an me – Are we too blind to see-ee?"*

"Wankurs! Languurs!" go the kids.

"Get down off that wall, you little brat!" goes Dec to one a the childrun who's fistin at him.

That drew em on us – "*Steamurs!* Faggits! An tis not yeer wall – tis the Copor-a-ation's!"

"You brazen huzzy!" goes Dec – now a young wan was showin him the fingur.

An *that* drew the mothurs on us – "Lave our childrun alone – the gall of it – get back ta yeer own side a the park!"

"Ex*cuse* me – we have the right to be treated with respect, I hope, whatevur side of the park we're on!"

"Respect! What are ye but a showur a sluts!"

"An ye're a pack a jades!" goes Dec gettin more camp by the minute. He was at the hand on hip stage now.

"Where're ye goin with yeer c'lection-box?" go the kids lobbin pebbles an ice-loll sticks at Dec. "C'lectin ta buy ca-awndums?"

"Get down off that wall!" goes Dec.

"Tis not yeer wall tis de Copor-a-ation's!"

Liam was kinda wrestlin with Connie.

"Raped!" hoots Florrie swingin hur axe.

"Ya ould flah-bag!" go the kids limpin up an down the wall, mockin Florrie's toed-in walk an hur mad stare.

"Mam! Mam! C'maaan! C'maaan! D'mind um!" goes Mary at a safe distance. "Daaa! Daaa! Latch onta vur!"

"Will yeh take the axe off hur, Connie," goes Liam. Now he's holdin Connie by the two wrists tryin to keep him off him. "Before she runs at the knackur!"

"Buys a gun –"

"Buys a gun –" go the kids, staggurin on the wall.

"Steals a car –"

"Steals a ceear –" scream the kids.

"Tries to run –"

"Tries ta run –"

"But he don't get far –"

"But he don't gesss feear –"

Connie's performance is fierce handicapped – he's tryin to gesticulate for the high drama but he can't with Liam holdin his wrists. *"An his momma cries –"*

"An his momma cries –" The kids are havin a field-day.

Next thing they're throwin sods a grass an empty cans an pieces a chewin-gum at the knackur who stands there without a budge outa him. "Knackuurs! Any cearpets! Where's yur trailur, paaavie!" An one a them goes back home for a frisbee an they start tryin to brain the knackur with it like they've seen happens to that feen's catamite in *Mad Max 2*.

"An we'll be blempt," mutturs Dec to Tizzy, "when the itinerant blasts them with that shotgun. His ire is up by the look of him. A *fine*-looking man – if it weren't for the dirt –"

"Tis a disgrace," goes a mothur. "She don't give a shit about dem kids – puttin em through all a this –"

"Oh, she should be shifted – off hur chuck –"

"Steamuurs! Faggits! Don't bend down now –" go the childrun.

"Them childrun should be taken away from hur –"

"Tis a disgrace – an we tryin to rear our children decent!"

"Wankurs!" go the childrun.

"Tis the kids I feel sorry for –"

"She should be locked up –"

"He has an awful life altogethur with hur –"

"But shur he d'be outa his mind with the drink – an no *won*dur –"

"Liam boy –" Connie is totally inta Liam at this stage – plawmawsin him an slobburin ovur him. "Shur you're a grand fella for our Mary – we wouldn't want anyone else –

we'd only want the best for our Mary – an if ye evur have any problems ye can come to me –" An Liam is grabbed an locked in an embrace – an I mean locked. Talk about *Die Hard.* "Liam boy –" An he kissin him in his earhole.

"Wa-a-ankurs! Fa-a-aggits! Kna-a-ackurs! Whores!" An the kids scatturin matches an sayin to each othur "Bend down theyur, Paawl – bend down an pick dem up an we see what happens –" An they bent double, laughin, gettin a rise outa Dec.

Dec was well an truly on his high horse by this stage – hand on hip, chin up, eyes lightin. "Have ye no control ovur yeer childrun? They're a disgrace to night! Do ye hear that language?"

An he was squarin up to the women an I thought he was goin to claim em when inta the park comes the Squad Car – an everyone knows who called em because there's only one private phone in the park.

"Showury! Showury! The shades! The shades! Tis the bluebottles!"

"Whore-masturs!" screech the childrun at the Squad Car.

They were reachin at this point, language-wise.

Connie has Liam by the shouldurs an Liam is holdin him at arm's length an they're swayin away like Sumo wrestlurs – anorexic ones – an the kids are mockin em an goin "WWF! Razur Ramon versus de Undurtakur!"

But Connie's goin to finish the song or die – *"an angry young man face down in the street with a gun in his hand – in the ghettooo!"* An he breaks Liam's hold an grabs him by the jaw. "I wouldn't want that for you now at all Liam boy," all grawvur, mad about him, squeezin Liam's jaw till his eyes cross. "I'd only want the best for you always!"

An Fawlty Towers unfolds himself outa the drivin-seat, all seven feet a him. Then out gets Lethil Weapon – Sergeant O'Sullivan like – an he stands there like a bull – with the head thrust out – reviewin the situation.

The knackur is aftur meltin away like a chocolate stain aftur an Ultra Daz white wash. He was there one minute an he wasn't the next – just like that. Practice makes perfect.

Sergeant O'Sullivan sizes everythin up an makes a lightnin decision. "Take the axe off hurr," says he to Fawlty.

"E-e-eh –" goes Fawlty, Supurhero.

"*Take* the axe off hurr."

Fawlty makes a bit of a move –

"Come near me an I'll swing for ya," hoots Florrie slashin at the air with the axe.

Fawlty stops.

"Take the axe off hurr," goes Lethil Weapon. A single-minded man.

"Mrs," says Fawlty. "We can't have this now –"

"*Take* the axe!" goes Lethil, hands on hips, standin there like the Rock a Cashel.

"Come on now, Mrs," goes Fawlty movin clear.

"The *axe*!" goes Lethil.

Blind Obedience is a fuckin wondurful thing. It gets the job done when all else fails. Up steps Fawlty an reaches out the hand an takes the axe from Florrie.

An she starts weepin on cue. An Connie lets go a Liam an pitches himself at hur an starts weepin an slobburin ovur hur.

He probably thinks she's cryin for yur man in the ghetto. An, sure enough, he raises his head an launches inta the finale – *"on a cold an grey Chicago mornin* anoddur *little baby*

child is born – in the ghettooo!" An he twists around to Liam
an stretches the arm an wags the head an delivurs the last bit
like a pro – *"An his momma cries . . ."*

Beautifully rendured as they say.

But Liam goes "Oh my Jesus" – seein it comin a mile off
the very minute I see it meself –

An Connie reels away from Florrie an looks up at the
stars – the two arms spread out an he's off – *"As de snow flies
– on a cold an grey Chicago mornin de poor little baby child is
born – in de ghettoo – an his momma cries –"*

"Oh Jesus!" screeches Liam with the whites a his eyes
showin. "He's goin to sing it all ovur *agaaain*!"

So the lads got inta a kinda mass panic an close ranks an
Florrie an Connie are propelled off at high speed – like they
were a couple a those wind-up toys on wheels – by Liam an
Dec an Mary an Tizzy an Susannah an Tanya an Barbie in a
bunch, with Rectus runnin rings around em –

"Ah people won't ya undurstand
A child needs a he-e-elpin hand –"

I stay put – for a breathur.

An so I don't havta listen to *In the Ghetto* all ovur again. An
because tis a while since I've seen the boys in blue in action.

Fawlty throws the axe inta the back a the Squad Car.
Exhibit A.

"Are yeh leavin hur go?" says a neighbour man to Lethil.

An they all start clamourin.

"She should be shifted!"

"She should be certified!"

"Ye can't lave hur heeyur! She's fuckin dangerous!"

Lethil is tryin to get inta the car. But he can't open the
door back with the press a people.

"Sergeant! De knackur's got a shotgun –"

"I didn't see any gun – or itinerrant forr that matterr –"

"Let ye take hur away with ye at least!"

Lethil is stuck half in an half out a the car. "Shurr we can't take hurr away frrom the childrren."

"The kids should be taken from *hur*! What about the young wan bein inturfeeured with?"

"Ah, shurr, the little girrl will be fine now if hurr mothurr's therre to keep an eye on hurr." Tryin to open the door back.

"We'll report ye! What're ye waitin for? For hur ta massacur us all in our beds!"

"Ah, shurr, she's calmed down now, Ma'am," says Lethil. Shovin the door back by main force smilin politely in the face a the man he was shovin it against. "She's harmless most of the time." An in he gets – right nifty for a man of his bulk – an mutturs somethin to Fawlty an the car takes off with no regard at all for the health an safety a the citizens a Shaggin Wank clingin to it.

The party is ovur. The youngur kids start to whinge an cry. The group a neighbours start breakin up an makin for home an there are a dozen conversations scattered out from the scene a the crime in every direction like rings in the watur when yeh drop a stone in.

I moved around in widenin circles listenin to em all.

"I went down ta de Corporation an I said to dem sez I – dere'll be trouble lettin dem knackurs inta de park –"

"I wouldn't be tarrin them all with the same brush but shur the knackurs d'be mad with the drink –"

"Whasupitcha?" A mothur to hur kid who was bawlin. "Will yeh listen to him – Jesus. I couldn't be listenin to that

144

tonight – I'll havta give him somethin – Tina, you'd nevur
have a bit a Triclorul, would yeh?"

"Only Valurgan – dat wan for kids –"

"Oh, that'll do –"

"To say nothin a them faggits squattin ovur in the empty
house – shur no kid's safe from them –"

"An the cut a the place – an the crowd at the othur end a
de block – whores an whore-masturs dat whole family!"

"Wouldn't yeh feel for dat poor misfortunate girl tryin to
rear hur two childrun in between the lot of um – she should
get a transfur from the Corporation – God help hur –"

"Dat whole block should be knocked –"

"I wouldn't mind the itinerants only for the kids – what
do they want havin so many a them? Paawl! Treeacy!
Michelle! An they've no control ovur em – come back
heeyur or I'll be dug outa ye!"

"Did yeh see Princess Di on the telly last night?"

"Oh she's handsome –"

"I'll nevur sleep tonight aftur that –"

"Yerra, two Roche 5 and a drop a whiskey an yeh'll sleep
like a corpse –"

"I'm not a wan to talk but –"

"Jesus, Deneece, s*tap – lickin* – dat knee!"

"I fell –"

"An then the knackurs d'be goin on television an goin on
about how they're 'traavellurs' an we shouldn't be callin em
knackurs an going on about 'our childurs dis' an 'our
childurs dat' like *we* have no childrun an sayin we give our
kids television names an the like –"

"What do dey want us to call em? Paaaddy? Or Biddy?"

"'Tis worse than the knackurs she is –"

"I went down ta the Corporation an I sez sez I: eithur she

goes or the Residents' Association is goin to *burn* down every house in the shaggin park –"

"Me poor mothur God-rest-hur usedta say: breedin – yeh has it or yeh hasn't it –"

An so on.

Back at the ranch an time to hang up me stetson at last for the day.

For once I coulda done with a nice long quiet night. An a *rewind* an *replay* a certain parts a it.

It'd been one helluva day. Christ!

An they're all drowsy an mellow. An Liam an Mary are wound up in each othur like a heap a bones thrown there. An Dec is sharin the mattress with Tizzy, but seein as I don't actually take up any space as such I lie down in me place next to Dec but without touchin him.

"Liam?" comes Dec's voice outa the dark next to me.

"Yeah?"

"We nevur bought the Jackson postur for Mothur –"

"Tomorra –"

"Or saw Mike –"

"Tomorra –"

"Or gave Cliona back the Scout box –"

"Tomorra –"

"Or saw the nuns –"

Silence.

An twas grand for a while with no disturbance at all except some comfortin human noises an Dec on an off sayin somethin like "I trust you're using a dental dam, Mary?" (Fuck aaaafff, baoy!) or "Did you remember to check for the use-by date, Liam?" (Aaaaw, fuckit Dec!)

An all that was grand an aftur a while the flashlight came on an off an then I could see the red glow a Liam's roll-yur-own lightin up in the dark an I was castin a stray thought in Foxy-nob's direction an contemplatin the collection-can on the ground next to the mattress an rememberin me urun days when twould a been me there out in the cold when –

"Your in-laws are something else, Liam –"

"Declan –" An Liam nevur calls him Declan unless he's seriously annoyed.

But Dec was only startin. "You're going to have the classic nightmare axe-wieldin mothur-in-law – *Misury* isn't in it –"

"Shut the fuck up, Dec!"

"We must press on with the arrangements –"

"I'm *not* doin it, Dec."

"Whasssss?" Creak-creak a the bed.

"In Oscur's words 'an engagement should come to a young girl as a surprise' – so we kept it a secret from you till the last moment – but you and Liam are gettin married next week."

"Ooooooh, Leeeem!"

"Mary – no! Dec – tell him –"

"Ooooh Leeeem!" Mary is on Ecstasy. He's sittin up hangin ovur Liam.

"I'm not *doin* it, Dec!"

"Oooooh Leeeem! I'll be able ta wear me sistur's weddin dress!"

"Mary boy, this weddin is just a mad notion a Dec's – I'm tellin yeh now, Mary – listen to me – I'm *not doin it*!"

"Ooooooh, Leeeem! Yeh reeelly like me dat much!"

"No – I *don't* – I *don't* Mary –"

"Ooooooh Leeeem – I nevur knew yeh felss like dass abouss me!"

"I *don't*! I *don't* – honest ta God *I don't* – shit – look what you've done now, *Dec*!"

"Oh for God's sake, Liam," says Dec. "Stop *moaning*! You always have to make a song and dance about everything! I honestly think you just get off on having paroxysms."

"Whaaat!" Liam was goin to choke.

"I don't know why you won't admit it – this idea of mine is an excellent one – and in any case necessary."

"Why's it necessary?" Tizzy pipes up in a voice croakin with tiredness – but for once in his life askin an intelligent question.

"So Mary can pretend to be her sistur – and claim this house from the Corporation – an we all live happily evur aftur . . ."

I heard Mary suck in his breath in delight at this notion.

"Dec – yur a geeenyus!"

"I know," says Dec.

An *that* mighta been a nice note to end on.

But nooo.

Outa the dark an the comfortin little settlin-down rustles an creaks came Liam's voice again –

"Tis all your fuckin fault anyway – *you*'re the one that told him to put it somewhere more *appropriate* than the lettur-box –"

"That wasn't me," says Dec quick as a flash. "That was Sistur Veronica – and *she* didn't understand the implications. *And* she did her bit anyway – ovur and above the call of duty –"

"Oh that's *great*, isn't it?" I could see Liam rearin up in the dark. "That's passin the buck new-style – anytime yeh havta take responsibility yeh just shift it onta one a yur half a dozen characturs – *I* think you're in an advanced state of schizophrenia – "

An so on –

Indo-China – here I come . . .

Back to the Holodeck . . .

CHAPTER FIVE

I slid inta me fantasy. Cautiously. Alert for booby-traps. No grief this time – any grief an I'd E &E –

This time I'd have em singin *I Don't Know How to Love Him* in harmony.

Right – here we go –

"You cold, boy?" The Major's voice came through the dark from where he was lyin against a tree-trunk.

"Yes, sur." Private Tony's teeth were chatterin as he hunched down in his sodden fatigues.

In the jungle? Was it cold in the jungle?

Fuck that.

"It's that cold dank fog, son – chills yeh to the bone – balls – freezes the balls off yuh."

At least he's talkin to me, thought Private Tony, flushin in the dark when he thought of what had happened that day.

"Maybe you should come over here, son – I think maybe we should huddle together. For warmth."

You do?

"Right, sur. Good idea, sur." Crawlin ovur undur the weight of all that kit took a little time.

"A good soldier conserves energy whenever possible – and utilises all resources available. Body heat, I think, falls in that category. Move in closer, soldier – here – let me – that's better –"

"A-are you comfortable, sur?"

"We-e-ell – you don't exactly make a cuddly armful with all that stuff on you. Is that a couple a grenades I feel there?"

"I-I think so, sur."

"Jesus, soldier, I think you'd better take them off! You want to blow us to kingdom come?"

"Bu-but what if we have to E & E, sur?"

"Let me worry about that, soldier – it's my job – just take em off. *Now*."

"Yes, sur."

"Don't leave em where we'll roll over on em –"

"Eh – no, sur –"

"Right – move right in – close quarters – that's better – watch out for my machete –"

"Where is it, sur?"

"In my belt – at the back – watch it – right. Now you grab a little shut-eye an I'll keep watch – uh, it's nice to have you here, son – I can even pretend I'm back in The World in my own bed with –"

"Gloria?"

"How did you know her name's Gloria, boy?" asked the Major with a start of surprise.

Private Tony felt his breath on his face.

Wife and kids household pet
Army green was no safe bet
The bullets scream to me from somewhere . . .

"I-I just guessed, sur."

"Well, you really are full of surprises, Private. Hey, you a doper?"

"Eh –"

"Christ, soldier, don't tense up like that – I'm not asking if you're a junkie – I mean, would you share a joint? Got one in my ass pocket I think. Lao Green but not bad. Put your hand in – right side – and get it – that's right – dig deeper – uh, deeper – no? Try the other one – can you reach? Go right in – yeah?"

"Got it sur. An here's my lightur sur."

In the flare a the lightur Private Tony watched the Major light the joint. Christ, he really was the spit a Clint Eastwood.

Jesus, I love this fuckin man, thought Private Tony.

I'd smothur me mothur for him.

"OK – let's lie back and enjoy this, son – here – got it? Jesus, soldier – one thing the history books ain't goin to say about this war is that the majority of the troops were zonked start to finish – that'll be deleted from the records – that and a damn sight more. Wait a minute – where's your flashlight? Oh I got it – oh! Sorry soldier – I thought – sorry – did I hurt yuh?"

"No, sur," said Private Tony faintly. "Here it is – oh – oh sorry sur!"

"Jesus, boy, get that steel pot off – I think you've knocked some a the caps off my teeth – and dental work in the States costs a fuckin fortune – goddammit!"

"Sorry, sur – it's off, sur. Here's the joint, sur."

"Thanks. Right. That's better – now look –" The flashlight picked out a photograph in his hand.

"That's a picture of your boy –"

"Right again, soldier."

"With your household pet in his arms –"

"It's an armadillo called Pete – the sweetest goddam armadillo you could ever hope to meet –"

"The boy looks just like you, sur – you're lucky, sur."

"Yeah. Take the joint." The flashlight clicked off. A silence. "I could hope he'd turn out just like you, Private – I'd be proud if he did –"

What? "Um – he's a lucky boy – to have a father like you. I nevur had a fathur, sur. He was killed – ah – in – in the Troubles –"

"I'm sorry to hear that, son – oh that's tough – here – move in a bit closer – damn it, soldier! You're a walking ammo-dump! You want to strangle me in those bandoliers – for Chrissake get them off – I don't need a ton a metal against me – yeah – what's that? Oh – thanks –"

"A-are you OK now, sur?"

"We-e-ell – I've been in more comfortable billets – you OK? Want a final toke? No? OK –" The butt-end a the joint spun away from them. "Here – get that arm around my waist – how's that?"

"Fine, sur. Bettur sur."

"Yeah?"

"Eh – yeah."

"You're freezing, son. Bit of a bear-hug is what you need – get the circulation goin – how's this?"

"Uh!"

"Good, huh?"

"Great – great, sur."

"Jeez, these fatigues are really drenched – a couple a warm blankets would be heaven – we could strip off and get really cosy –"

What the fuck does he mean? thought Private Tony. But a drowsiness was takin hold of him. The few drags were hittin him in his exhausted state. He fought it off – this was Heaven an he didn't want to leave. He heard a great sigh – was it him or the Major? He didn't know – he tightened his grip around the Major's waist but then his exhausted muscles automatically relaxed so he just burrowed in closur, breathin deeply, his face against the Major's neck, the smell a jungle rot blocked out by the great human man-smell and the jungle noises drowned out by the heavy thud of the heart.

He couldn't even hear the heavy metal band. But no doubt they were lurkin somewhere around.

Alice in Chains, he remembered, that's what they were called.

I don't care if we're zapped, he thought. Let em come an waste us like this – I wanta die like this – now – like a boy in his father's arms – this is so –

Absolutely – absolute –

Fuck Gloria –

Not.

He spun inta sleep –

And woke to – what? What woke him?

He lay still, heart thudding. The Major? He was still locked tight in the Major's arms.

But whose hand was on his ass?

"Fuck!" He jerked around.

"Shhhh . . . relax, soldier," came the whisper. "You're OK . . ."

And then the night was full of little movements and strokings and breathings. Hands moved up his back and down again to knead his ass – urgently now –

His fly was open – he could feel the roughness a the Major's fatigues against his dick.

I hate to see a good erection go to waste –

Fuck off, Prince.

His breath was stuck in his throat. I'm goin to die, he thought, I can't breathe.

What does he want, he thought wildly, what's he tryin to do?

He's *tryin* to jerk himself off against yeh, yeh eejit – yeh *muppet –*

All right, all right.

An if yeh don't hurry up he'll finish an *that* will be *that,* soldier.

What did yeh do in the war, Daddy?

Well, I *almost* fucked a Major, son, but –

"Wait – wait," said Private Tony, wrestlin with the Major's fly. Let me do this, let me do this an you can – you can fuckin waste me aftur – I don't give a shit –

And there it was – as massive as he knew it hadta be – Jesus.

A fuckin stallion.

Here they come to snuff the rooster
Yeah here come the rooster
You know he ain't gonna die
No-oo, no-oo
You know he ain't gonna die . . .

An now the Major had clicked an was pushin Private Tony's head down where it wanted to go.

An it was strange that so massive a cock should fit so easily inta his mouth but it did, so he was able to suck like a dream, like a baby on a bottle –

"Shur, there d'be no wan in town –"

What?

"I *hates* bakin – I *hates* it – I gets fed-up bakin – an thas the truth –"

What the fuck?

"So I sez to meself, sez I – let yeh go an buy somethin to take – not to go with yur hands hangin to yeh –"

Whaaat!

"Though half the time they don't even ask if you've a mouth on yeh –"

Oh – *fuckin – hell!*

You know he ain't gonna die . . .

"D'yeh think a Barm Brack now?"

No – an armadillo called Pete –

"Excuse me, Mrs Burke – Liam – look – tis Mr Driscoll – call him in – about the greyhound –"

"Mr Driscoll!"

Got my pills gainst mosquito death

My buddy's breathin his dyin breath

Oh God please won't you help me make it through –

An there I was – a Pure Spirit – standin in our Shop Local weepin onta a packet a Rice Krispies.

Oh fuck, oh fuck –

I was really cryin. An like everythin else since I passed ovur I was doin it with me whole soul – cryin down to the very core. Like a shaggin onion.

I couldn't bear it. I was – what – I was in love with this fuckin non-existent Major – this – this *dork* –

"Forr feck's sake, Liam, wherre did ou get the dog?"

"Oh, I bought hur – ah – I'll be tellin yeh –"

"Are yeh on yur own these days, Mr Driscoll?"

"Indadin I am, Mrs Burke. Fightin with meself since that shaggerr went off to England an good rriddance –"

"Ah Mr Driscoll, shur that's no way to talk about your own son –"

"Yerra, boy, lave me alone – I'm nearly gone deminted frrom him. All he's on about is drrink – he wouldn't do a hand's worrk for ou – blasht him!"

Gloria sent me pictures of my boy –

"Will he be home to yeh for Christmas?"

"God blesh yourr soul woman alive – Chrrishmas! Don't be talking to me about Chrrishmas – tis only jusht arround the corrnerr – an I *hates* the living sight of it!"

"Ah, shur, tis only the wan day, Mr Driscoll! We won't take that much notice of it an tis a weekend this year thang-god."

"Yerra, what's the good of it? Tis nathin but a purre washte – you couldn't ayte nathin at aall the next day – you couldn't ayte no dinnerr at aall. Shurr what's the pint a that?"

This was unreal.

But *this* was supposed to be real.

I tried hard to focus on Mr Driscoll – a thin eldurly countryman, active-lookin an bright-eyed, wearin a peaked cap an a navy suit an a shirt open at the neck without a collar.

"But tell me about the dogeen therre – is it a pup?"

"Eh, no –"

Rectus was peerin out from undur Liam's jacket.

Mrs Burke was gone an we were walking towards the bus stop. Goin where? I didn't know. I was aftur losin it – I didn't know where we were headin for or where we were comin from.

Oh God please won't you help me make it through?

"Mr Driscoll, are you a betting man?" Liam.

"Myself? Yerra no. But I won fourr pounds on the rrots ovurr behind Newmarket therre lasht yearr – behind Kanturrk." This was a great joke – the laughtur was nearly breakin through – spillin through his eyes – at this idea. But what in Jesus's name were rots?

We'd reached the bus stop. Mr Driscoll stopped so I figured he was gettin on a bus.

He stood there at his ease with his hands thrust in his pants pockets – all smiles an the eyes bright with divilment.

"The rots?" says Liam.

"The rrots – in the tunnels. They had seven orr eight of them and they had to be pushin them to kape them going."

"Rots, Mr Driscoll?" Dec. "What are rots while they're out?"

"Rrots – *rrots* –"

"Oh –" Light dawned on Liam. "Oh – *rats* –"

"Yes, shurr – the rrots – an twas shcandalous. They had rrabbits an grreyhounds too. They photogrraphed it unbeknowns to them. They had maybe twenty-fourr rrabbits in a crrate – netted wirre it was. They tied a rrabbit to a rrope – maybe from herre to that pole – and let it off and let thrree or fourr grreyhounds off on it. Ah twas shcandalous altogetherr."

Rots! What the fuck were we doin? I had me agenda – if I could remembur what it was – they had *their* agenda – if I knew what it was –

So what were any of us doin standin here talkin about rots?

"But grreyhounds – my niece – she had a trroop of them

157

– eighteen of them. I said feck it, they're like a shwarrm of childrren. But she was brradin them – what could I say? But don't be tellin me you bought one – crripes – for Chrrisht's sake – two hundered poun a pup – eighteen thousand pound a dog!"

"We got hur for a tennur," says Liam mortified.

"A tennerr? Yerra, what kind of a greyhound is that? Put herr down therre and let me take a look at herr."

Liam put Rectus down. She stood there lookin up at Liam with hur tail between hur legs, a picture a misury.

"Oh God bless yourr soul man alive," said Mr Driscoll an kinda champed with his mouth an said nothin else.

"So whacha think?" asked Liam at last with the head down – tail between his legs like.

"You'd want to give her something for the worums. And the way she's shtanding she might have an injurry. They'rre very frrail – if they jumped a ditch like an ould bashtarrd hound theirr legs'd brreak – even on the trrack on the corrnerr."

"Well, anyway," mumbled Liam. "We don't know how to feed hur an that –"

"Fade herr? Shurr that's no prroblem at aall – brread and brrown brread you'd bake yerrself and boiled turrnips with a bit a butterr thrrough it. Or a bit a soup if you have it. Mate makes them sourr. Tis dangerrous."

"So less of the T-bones, Liam," said Dec.

"Tay-bones? Oh verry bad *aal*togetherr."

"An what about exercise?" But the life had gone outa Liam.

"Yerra, an hourr'd be enough exerrcise –"

"An hour?"

"An hourr'd be enough – take herr down to Glanmirre frrom Mayfield – shurr that's a handy walk – a pashtime only – an I'll give yeh a tip now: pocheen –"

"For me?"

"God bless yourr soul man alive, to rub into the dog's legs –"

"Deep Heat like?" says Liam.

Deep Heat. Poteen. *Rrots.*

"That's what I do with my own dog – the wan you do be seeing up on the carrierr of my bike – on the sate I made for him."

"Oh yeh still have him?"

"Indadin I do – shur now when I rrache home he'll be therre to mate me – he do be up againsht me."

"You don't mean to say?" said Dec, archin the eyebrows.

"I do indade. Indadin I do."

An when we'd put Mr Driscoll on his bus Dec turned a big camp stare on Liam. "Jesus," says he. "It's frightening – the things the rurals get up to – incest is only the tip of the iceberg. I'll swear in any court of law he said the dog d'be up against him to mate with him – a confession of bestiality no less!"

Wife and kids – household pet –

"Can't deny it," said Liam. "That's what he said. But what can he do an his son away in England?"

An we headed townwards.

The Club?

I didn't know – or care. I felt like an extra wheel. No – I felt like *they* were *two* extra wheels. I couldn't forgive em about the – armadillo.

"Dec?"

"Mmm?"

"Do you remembur Mothur sayin somethin to us yesterday when we first came in – about trash on the floor?"

"I do – twas a bit odd."

"Yeah! I was just thinkin – it rhymed. Trash on the floor an somethin about weeks before." Liam was frownin an studyin the ground in fronta his feet.

"Well, that's fascinating, Liam – tell me more –"

"No – seriously, Dec – d'yeh know any song that goes like that? Trash on the floor – weeks before?"

"*Liam –*"

"I'll bet yeh a *fivur* – I'll bet yeh a *fivur* tis a song."

"Look – pop into Ladbroke's when we get to Luke's Cross – I'm sure they'd be interested – an put a bet on the *rots* while you have a hammur in your hand –"

But Liam was serious. "D'yeh know what, Dec? I think Denis and Mike are sufferin from that thing – that thing the kings an queens die of in yur Jean Plaidy books – y'know – it means too much a somethin y'know?"

"I *don't* know *what* you're talking about –"

"Y'*know* – something about lamb-fries – a something a lamb-fries?"

"*Lamb-fries – lamb-fries – Liam!* It's a surfeit of *lampreys*! Lamb-fries! Jesus, what's it like to be dirt ignorant?"

"Fuck the fries," said Liam. "Surfeit – that's the word I'm aftur. Mike an Mothur – they're sufferin from a *surfeit* a soul music. *That's* the problem. Mothur's had to give up his Cohen an he's probably sick to death a Michael Jackson mornin noon an night an yeh know he has all this Aretha Franklin an Gladys Knight an that – so my bet is he's been feedin Mike a surfeit a Soul –" He was throwin anxious glances at Dec's face to see how this was goin down. "But there's too much *feelin* in Soul – they're always cryin an meetin each othur at the Dark End a the Street an that – an Mike's too unbalanced for it – that's the problem. D'yeh want to bet me the fivur?"

"No – I don't." An he hesitated an then said, "To be honest I think you may have hit the nail on the head."

Liam nodded. "Right – well, y'know, I have an idea about how to get round him maybe –"

"You have?"

An there we were, drawin level with Mandy L'Amour's house – *St Rita's* – on our right. In with us to me surprise. An there was Mike sittin in fronta the telly playin with a nut-crackur an watchin a *Star-Trek* re-run. Turned out he was stayin with Mandy since he ran out on Mothur.

Mandy L'Amour, I should tell you, was in mufti that day – by which I'm not referrin to his clothes (blue jeans, plaid shirt, leathur belt an bracelet) – what I mean is he wasn't givin vent to his theatrical self – the one with A Licence to Bitch. He was too fuckin busy but what else is new? As it happened, when we got there he was just throwin the ould leathur jacket ovur the innur man – *your black leather jacket that tells of firm hands that have stroked it, rushed it off, to love you* (he was always quotin this Cherry Smyth AIDS poem) – and was rushin off to a rehearsal for *Josuph an his Amazin Technicolour Dreamcoat* ("They offered me the lead but I wouldn't have him"). And no, he wouldn't be back until late, because he was holdin auditions for *Edward the Second* that he was directin – an he says to Dec "*Mind* ye don't miss the performance at the Club – my *Ghoul Lash* will take up most of the time – but I'm counting on you and Denis for one of the supporting acts – I can sing the aria from *Madame Butterfly* myself for one spot but I can't do them all."

"Oh we've rehearsed," says Dec. "But we were a bit afraid it might be a case of *I brought me harp to a party and nobody asked me to play –*"

"Can you sing that?" Mandy wanted to know. "Gracie Fields – that would go down nicely –"

"You're asking me if I can sing Gracie Fields? Can Boyzone lipsync?"

"Or – I'm putting together an adult alternative panto for Christmas and I could work in a role for you –"

So off went Mandy – "Look, if ye're standing there idle ye could be putting the finishing touches to the paint-job I'm doing in the kitchen – it's draggin a bit since I took on that Drama Class for the kids – or if ye could blow up those balloons there an stick them up for me – I'll nevur get a chance to do it myself and La Traviata there isn't much help –" Meanin Mike.

I'm tellin ya, as Garth would say. Mandy L'Amour was enough to make anyone feel like an empty pint glass – or a flat pint. But don't get me wrong now – there was nothin frantic about all this activity – the man managed to keep a laid-back air no mattur what an I've seen him wrestle a young fella who was tryin to cut himself to the ground in the Club (fierce strong though he looks as lean as a whippet) an hold him down an have a conversation about the Abortion Referendum while waitin for an ambulance to come – aftur refusin help from me – "They'll be a while, Tony – let you go an have a pint and come back –"

Anyway – off he went leavin us with Mike who was, as I said, watchin a *Star Trek* re-run on Sky – sittin there playin with a nut-crackur.

Mike wasn't lookin half-bad – dressed simply as they say in black trousurs an a loose fawny sweatur-type thing with a wide neck. In fact he was lookin quite eye-catchin if yeh like dark-skinned an slendur – because he'd left off his Jackson make-up an his hair-gel so his own goldy skin colour could be seen an his crinkly hair – and of course he has a great butt an all that because he's a dansur. An really when all's said an done it can't be denied Mothur has an eye for a good arse an could spot form like the pro he is under all the Jackson gear an make-up. Come to think of it I once actually heard him say Mike has beautiful bones – bones are the last thing now yur average feen would be spottin but that's Mothur's eye for yeh. Tell yeh one thing – he'd nevur a bought Rectus-a-um.

Anyway this was disastrous – that Mike was lookin good I mean. If he wasn't lookin hideous in all his Jackson crap he was crackin up.

So anyway – there he was watchin *Star Trek* an I knew that the lads should sit down an shut up until the end an the line "We rule that Commandur Data has the right to choose." But Dec – well twas nothin but "Jesus, they must be usin those cheap batteries for him – they'd want to switch to long-life" – Data's an android if yeh remembur. But yeh had to put up with this from Dec.

An Mike took no notice anyway – he's good at that – an when the line came "This court rules Commandur Data has the right to choose" he sobbed like he always does. An – well, I think, in fairness to Mike – well, y'see, I dunno why but I think it's important for me to say that I'm not really scoffin at Mike for this. Y'see – well, I always cry meself at that point – I dunno why but it seems to me a *fuckin* beautiful thing – the idea of anybody havin the right to choose – even an android.

So let me *rewind* an say: Mike an me sobbed like we always do.

An Dec: "Well, I'm glad to hear it – let's hope he chooses to change his brand of batteries – those are crap – and he could do with a good servicing. I'd say that Klingon could take that in his stride no bothur – or would that be one of Captain Picard's duties – perhaps they take turns –"

So Liam grabs the nut-crackur an starts snappin em at Mike's balls but Mike doesn't laugh so Liam goes out to the kitchen to forage for Rectus an comes back with mugs a tea an a few chunks a Barm Brack an half an apple tart. An they start fiddlin around with the Barm Brack because they can see that one a the slices has the goldy ring in it an they want Mike to take it – but he won't take any. MJ doesn't eat.

An the next thing they start up this thing about apple tarts an rhubarb tarts.

Jesus.

Brace yurself.

It started out as a conversation – an ordinary conversation – but what chance does an ordinary innocent conversation have with that lot?

"I *love* a tart," says Liam. "Especially rhubarb now –"

"Oh, I find rhubarb very tart –" says Dec squinchin his mouth.

"But I love a tart tart –" says Liam, smackin the lips.

Dec smirked. "I love a tart with a tart tart –" says he.

Liam looks at him. "*I* love a tart tart with a tart tart –"

"*I* love a tarted-*up* tart tart tarting up a tart tart!"

Liam, lookin dangerous. "Bate *that* in two throws!"

"I love a tarted-up tart tart tarting up a tart tart, said the tart tart tartly!" Dec not to be outdone.

"Foul!" shouts Liam, givin Dec a dalk with a knife.

An I dunno where this marathon would a taken em if Mike hadn't put his oar in –

"I'm afraid a rhubarb," says he.

Me boyos were halted in full flow.

"Are yeh?" says Liam.

"I'm a bit afraid of it myself," says Dec real chatty. "It gives me a bit of wind sometimes."

"No," says Mike. "That's not why."

"Why what?" Liam asks him.

"Why I'm afraid a rhubarb."

"What then?" says Dec. "Does it give you the runs?"

"No," says Mike. "It doesn't – or I dunno if it does."

"Well, does it or doesn't it?" says Liam.

"I dunno," says Mike. "I nevur tasted it."

"You nevur tasted it?" asks Dec amazed. "So why are you afraid of it?"

"Well, that's why I nevur tasted it – because I'm afraid of it –"

"Wait a minute," says Liam. "This is gettin – look – *why* are you afraid of it?"

"Well . . . yeh know Fraggle Rock?" He said "Fraggle Rock" – or somethin like that.

Dec an Liam didn't know Fraggle Rock.

"It usedta be on telly –"

"Oh yeah – years ago –" Liam remembered.

"Well, I usedta watch Fraggle Rock when I was a kid an – y'know the Gorgees?" Somethin like "Gorgees."

"Yeah?"

"Well, they usedta have this garden with rhubarb in it an they usedta chase the Fraggles through the rhubarb – in an out the rhubarb –"

165

Silence from the lads.

"An that's why I'm afraid a rhubarb."

Freeze-frame from the lads, starin at him. Then Liam looked at Dec with a peculiar kinda expression on his face an then gave a little jerk a the head that said "fuck this."

At this Dec looked alarmed. But he just looked at Liam an said nothin.

I know exactly what they were thinkin – twas comin through loud an clear. An it went somethin like this: Jesus *Christ! What* in the name a God can we hope to do with this kinda muppet?

An, really, that mighta been that – they mighta thrown the towel in just like that an left. Poor Denis.

But then Liam's expression changed an he said: "Wait a minute now – would yeh be afraida a rhubarb *tart* now? Or would it havta be a *stalk* a rhubarb? An how would yeh feel about things *shaped* like rhubarb? That *reminded* yeh of rhubarb like?"

Saved. The old reportur's streak comin inta play. Twould carry us, I knew. He always hadta get it straight. He settled back in his chair an started rollin-his-own. We were in for the long haul.

"Oh – I'd be afraid of a tart all right – twould remind me y'see of a stalk a rhubarb – but I'd be more afraid of somethin that *looked* like a stalk a rhubarb. Twould remind me a the Fraggles climbin up an down the rhubarb – slidin up an down the rhubarb – bein chased –"

Liam was pokin at his tobacca. "An what of somethin that had the colour a rhubarb now like?"

"Oh yeah – that purply colour yeah – not the colour on its own like – but the shape an the colour togethur – that would make me flesh crawl – honest ta God – I can't help it –"

Liam stopped in the act a lickin his tobacca papur an stared at Mike from undur his quiff. "An have yeh told Denis about this problem?"

"I dunno – I don't think so – well, no, I thought he might think twas silly –"

"Not at all," said Dec. "He'd be fascinated. I'd tell him immediately – without more ado – if I were you –"

"D'yeh think so?"

"Definitely. I think he should know."

Mike's face clouded ovur. "I forgot – I'm not talkin to him. I'm aftur leavin him."

"Well, that's a shame – think of it – there ye could be tonight – all snug in bed – talkin about rhubarb –"

"Yeah," goes Mike with a sigh. No idea Dec was razzin him.

"Talkin of which –" goes Liam with a meaningful look at Dec. An he changes gear – right outa neutral an inta third. "Mothur is pinin away. We can't do a thing with him. You've *got* to give him anothur chance."

Mike immediately got that stubborn look fixed on his face. He didn't bothur to answur. But that's normal for Mike – the chattiness about the rhubarb was completely outa charactur for him.

Liam lit up – at last. "Look –" says he inhalin, an he squinted at the fag – nervous that twould go out. "That Jackson business – yeh'll just *havta* forgive him – *he* didn't know he was *able* to put a curse on anybody – to say nothin a someone in L.A. for God's sake – half a world away –"

"And he had *my* knees worn out praying for that Space

Cadet," said Dec. "It went against the grain let me tell you. But he did pay well." Dec had done dozens a novenas on Mothur's behalf to get Jackson off the hook – Mothur was terrified that if it came to a court case Mike would crack up altogethur.

"I know," says Mike. "It's not that. I get very angry about that but I know he didn't mean him any harm – that twas just that he – he wanted me –"

"So?"

Silence from Mike.

Dec did the chin-in eyebrows-raised thing at Liam, as if to say "Well? Do yur stuff."

An Liam made a kinda "Right – watch me now" face an pulled back his jacket sleeves like a card sharp goin to deal a pack a cards. A drag a the fag an exhale. "Look – that train – he told us – he's dyin to take yeh –"

"No he's not."

"He *is*, Mike –"

"Why did he say he wouldn't, so?"

"Look at it this way –" an Liam sat back an levelled his fag at Mike an his eye at Dec. "Look at it this way – right – so he said he wouldn't take yeh – but put yurself in his position. I mean there he is – I mean – well I mean –" Liam put himself on *pause* an kinda goggled an wavered a bit before pressin *play*. "Eh – L.A. proved too much for the man – he couldn't take it – so he's leavin the life – eh – he's come to know. I mean, think of his state a mind – he said he's goin back to find what's left of his world – ah –" Now he had the look of a man that knows he's goin to dry up. "To a simpler place in time – eh –" Lookin kinda wildly at Dec for help.

"He kept dreamin –" Dec with the lips pursed.

"He kept dreamin that – that some day he'd be a star – a *sup*urstar – but he didn't get far. But he soon found out the hard way that dreams don't always come true –"

"Oh no-ah-ah-no-no-ah-ah!" said Dec. Which I think was a bit ovur the top.

"I mean – don't yeh feel for the poor bastard?" Liam pressed *pause*, eyebrow up, fag extended.

Silence from Mike but his head was aftur tiltin a bit an his lips weren't pressed togethur like before.

I thought that looked hopeful.

The lads mighta thought so too. Dec made an encouragin face at Liam.

Liam looked very relieved an pressed *play*. "I mean – yeh have to – yeh have to –" He snapped his fingurs at Dec.

"What's the word, Dec? The thing that Mothur said we havta do with King Kong?"

"Empathise. Frankenstein actually."

"Empetise. Empetise – like put yurself in his place. I mean there he is – humiliated, destitute – on the dole I suppose –"

Mike's dark eyes were now lookin sideways at Liam.

"Havin sold his old car –"

"*So-ho-hold* it even," said Dec.

Liam glared at Dec. *Pause.* He focused on Mike again. "So all he's got is this one-way ticket back. Now look at the man's position. He's goin back to his mothur penniless an he's made a total eejit of himself in fronta all his friends an neighbours. I mean the shit has really hit the fan for this man – he's crackin up. An right at that moment you start demandin he takes you with him – home to his family mind. In othur words you're askin him, in the middle a all a this shit, to come out an tell his old granny – his *fathur* even but God *grant* he didn't have one a *them* – that he picked you up in one a the bars in L.A. –"

Mike looked hurt.

"Where you're a famous Jackson impersonator in the cabaret a'course –" in a brilliant save.

Mike cheered up.

"An he's in love with you an he's goin to spend the rest of his life with you an he thinks the sun shines outa yur ass – but *you* want it all an yeh want it now. Don't yeh think that's askin a bit much a him?" He raised the fag an waited for Mike to answur.

L.A. Law wasn't in it.

Mike lowered his lashes.

Liam decided that was an answur.

"An besides – you know tis just a mattur a time. He's got to sort things out an get his act togethur – an then he's goin to send for you – right?"

The lads waited. Peerin at Mike's face.

Mike looked up.

Liam raised an eyebrow.

Confident, like. He'd swung it.

"But," said Mike. "Yur wan in the song – how come he took *hur*?"

"Oh *Jesus*!" The fag actually went flyin backwards ovur Liam's head an Rectus made a dive for it.

"That floozy?" said Dec quick as a shot. "He didn't! He nevur took hur!"

Liam opened the eyes wide at Dec an rallied. "Yeah – what makes you think he took hur?"

"She – she says she's gonna be with him on that midnight train –"

170

"Just because she's standin there on the platform makin a lot a noise about *'My world, his world, our world, I gotta go, I gotta go!'* doesn't mean he took hur!" says Liam.

"That was *hur* story," said Dec. "An as long as I've known hur she's always been a rampant liar! An all belongin to hur! He probably didn't even know hur!"

Mike's face crumpled up a bit. "Ye're havin me on – ye're just razzin me –"

"Ah, no, seriously," said Liam. "Seriously. Tis hur side a the story – *'I'd rathur live in his world than live without him in mine – I gotta go, I gotta go'* – but yeh have to admit she's tryin to make decisions for him there – she's rushin him – she's – she's –" Snappin the fingurs at Dec.

Dec was at a loss.

"Powur – powur," said Liam. "That thing Fathur Twomey was goin on about –"

Dec got it. "Disempowering –"

"She's disempowerin him –"

"And you're as bad as hur," said Dec. "Standin there on the platform shrieking away like Whitney Houston – an *embarrassment* to the man let's face it – in your one glove an your Bad leathur suit with the forty-one chains and forty-seven buckles –"

"I wasn't goin to wear that," said Mike shyly, bitin the lip.

Dec stopped an did a big camp stare. "No? I'm *amazed*! Are you *sure*?"

Liam was in like a shot. "So *what* were yeh goin to wear?"

"Um," bitin the lip again. "One a them raincoats – the long ones –"

"De bag, de good bag, de wan with the handles –" said Dec.

Liam waved at Dec to shut up an scooped up his fag from the floor where Rectus was aftur manglin it – all without shiftin his eyes off Mike's face.

"One a them fawny ones – with a belt – but I'd wear it open like – ovur a dark suit – an a beret – or maybe me black Jackson fedora – I dunno –"

Liam opened the eyes very wide at Dec.

Dec clicked. "Well," said he. "Well. There you are! There you have it! That's the only problem. You didn't have the gear right. No wondur he wouldn't take you."

"That's it!" says Liam. "You didn't have the gear right. An the first thing in life when yeh plan anything is – yeh gotta get the gear right. A weddin now –" He winced. "Or – like Wacko Jacko now – what's the first thing he does when he's goin to make a new video? He plans the gear. What did Scarlett O'Hara do when she was goin to see Rhett Butlur? She took down the curtains an made a crinoline out of um. I mean would Mothur Teresa now be Mothur Teresa an would everyone be givin hur millions if she took to wearin bovvur boots an tattoos? No – she's got the gear right."

"You've got to get yourself the raincoat immediately," said Dec very firmly.

"They have um in Marks an Sparks," says Mike in a breathless voice.

"I presume you have a nest-egg?" said Dec, a bit tart (Jesus, let me keep away from that word). It pissed him off that Mike always had money now – as Denis's consort like.

"Oh yeah . . . d'yeh – d'yeh think the beret?"

"I think the fedora is fine," said Dec. "I think that would look very stylish."

"Jesus but we're very stupid," said Liam shakin the head in a way that reminded me of Connie drunk. "Tis amazin how the solution to a problem can be lookin yeh right in the face. Chalk it down –" an the arm with the mangled fag goes out like it's supposed to. "Chalk it down – when he sees yeh in that gear he won't rest till he has yeh on the *Orient Express* an *fuck* the Midnight Train to Georgia – Jesus, Dec, d'yeh think that's what he was doin when we spotted him down in the travel agent's today?"

"I wouldn't be at all surprised. He *was* clutching a bunch of brochures. Though I thought they looked a bit like those Cruise up the Nile ones – but I may have been mistaken."

"God, Mike! You're off!"

"Hoo-Hoo! As the song says." Dec – very dry.

"Off you go now an get the gear," says Liam catchin Mike by the elbow an draggin him to his feet. "C'mon – let's go –"

"Hoo! Hoo!" says Dec.

Glare from Liam.

But nothin will do Mike – now he's perkin up – but to change an put his make-up on an when he comes down he's wearin this God-awful red leathur jacket familiur to all MTV viewurs (to say nothin a Beatbox fans) like somethin designed for *Star Trek* aliens – with the sleeves pushed up to the elbows – an red drain-pipe pants. His *Thrillur* gear. Well, it is Hallowe'en aftur all.

So they take Mike inta town.

An Marks an Sparks is closed. For the Bank Holiday.

Ho-oly Jesus.

Action Stations.

They zoom around town with bright optimistic looks

fixed on their faces with Supurglue. An Mike goin to pieces by the minute.

Everythin's closed.

"Mothur of Good Counsel," said Dec.

"What about Ant'ny?" says Liam. "He finds things, doesn't he?"

An Dec looks at him, grateful for this unusual fit a piety.

"You do Anthony – I'll do Our Lady."

"Right – meet yeh back here on North Main-ah – five minutes."

"Ten."

An they meet on North Main-ah an lo an behold the Cerebral Palsy shop is open – they're re-stockin. An there's the raincoat in the winda. As good as new. Shop-soiled or somethin. Seven quid.

Except that the stuff in the window display can't be touched until the followin week, the women say. An they're not open for sales that day anyway.

So Dec suddenly had an uncle in the Sacred Heart Missions with acute cerebral palsy – who was leavin for Africa that very day because of a heroic desire to die in the saddle an his only an dearest wish is for a raincoat exactly like the one in the winda. For the tropical rainstorms.

They gave it to us for a fivur.

The icin on the cake: in a Marks an Sparks bag.

So, when they staggur back onta Pana an put Mike on a bus, all Liam says is "Jesus *Christ*! Dec, I need a jar –"

"Not until we get the postur for Mothur."

"You're – *not* – *serious*!"

So they seach town for *hours* lookin for open sweet-shops that might have posturs an by a fluke they find some in a

video shop on Barrack-ah. An the choice is between Wacko
an Naomi Campbell flauntin their egos (to say nothin a
boobs an butt) in the Arizona desert – "I don't think so,"
says Dec – and one a Wacko all soulful in a crimson Romeo
costume. They took Romeo – Mothur would cringe – but
Mike would love it an twas cheapur anyway.

An that left em enough money for a pint. An the bus fare
back to the ranch. So Liam shoved Dec on a Numbur 8 by
main force – before they were tempted to spend the bus
money. Dec wanted to vamp – the waistline, like.

So the next dispute in life was about whethur to have the
jar in The Cow (that was called The Blackhills before an
The Cow before that again – aftur those hills an cows
around Mayfield I told yeh about earliur) or The Cotton
Ball.

Y'see, Dec was barred from The Cotton Ball for callin the
ownur a jumped-up millionaire.

So naturally they end up in The Cotton Ball.

Liam was tryin to rally. Like an ovurtired child that's past
its bedtime. He had a notion he wanted to play darts. An
find some othur ould fella to talk greyhounds to. An chat up
the barmen. An play pool. But what he actually did was: he
collapsed on a bench in fronta the coal-fire – sprawled ovur
the table exhausted with his chin on the collection-can,
gazin at the pint in fronta his nose, the MJ postur between
his two outstretched hands an Rectus between his knees.
"What d'yeh think? We've got him in the bag, haven't we?"

"Hook, line and sinkur. Mothur will be ecstatic. He'll
probably be able to ovurlook the expense of a trip up the
Nile – a small price to pay for True Love surely –"

"Jesus," said Liam with his chin workin against the top a

the collection-box. "He'd probably get away with a trip down to Cobh stoppin off at Fota Zoo – maybe with a visit to MacDonalds an somethin like *Batman Returns* thrown in –"

An he squints one eye upwards an stops. Cliona an The Bonny Boy – Niall Ryan to you – are standin there with pint glasses in their hands.

"Trick or treat?" goes Cliona an does a witch's cackle. God – me worst nightmare: Cliona on Hallowe'en.

The Bonny Boy is totally stressed out. His face is pale an hollow an his black hair needs a wash. His hands on his pint glass are quiverin. An it's not just because he's doin undurage drinkin though that doesn't help – he has the tie off an Cliona's jumpur on ovur his school uniform an Cliona is carryin his tatty old school-bag – the usual.

An Cliona doesn't help – no soonur is she sittin down than the head goes back an the horse's mouth opens an tis –

"Oh the bonny boy is young but he's growing!" in hur fine carryin voice an the whole pub stares.

"At the age of sixteen years he was a married man
An at the age of seventeen the fathur of a son!"

A prize bitch.

Dec didn't help eithur. "I believe you're shelvin your responsibilities, Ryan?" He could be a prize bitch too – the bitch pose with the back straight an the knees crossed. Cliona was givin vent:

"Oh fathur, dear fathur, I fear you've done me wrong
To go and get married to one who is so young!"

"Why don't you stand outside altogethur with yur collection-box?" says Liam raisin his head from where he was pourin Guinness inta an ash-tray for Rectus an givin Cliona a black look.

"Well?" goes Dec to The Bonny Boy, refusin to be distracted. An Niall looks like he wants to dive inta his pint-glass an end it all. "There's not much I can do," says he with a tremor in the voice.

"You've *done* enough!"

"I know shur —"

"I *warned* hur."

"I'm goin to stand by her," says he gazin at Dec with his nice greenish-hazelly eyes. "It's just that — that m-marriage is outa the question." An the last bit is said in a rush like he doesn't believe it.

"Oh in *Kilcrea* Park it would be!" Kilcrea Park being Dec's idea a yur middle-class stronghold — for no good reason except that Niall lived there.

An Dec would a *gutted* Niall by slow degrees if Liam hadn't cut across him. Liam's yur man when it comes to mercy killing. "Dec says he's goin to marry Liz himself."

"Oh," goes The Bonny Boy an he looks sick. But maybe twas the pint goin to his head.

An Cliona exercised hur wit on Dec an Liz for the next half-hour. But I'm aftur blankin all that out so I couldn't tell yeh about it even if I wanted to.

Anyway, we went down to the house an Liz an Mike (with his big green-an-gold Marks an Sparks bag) were there before us — with Tiz an Mary.

So Cliona wanted to go on a battur but the trouble was, they were all skint — except for hurself an Mike an we all agreed twouldn't be "fay-yur" to hit them for it all.

"If we were kids we could go trick or treating," said Dec.

"Peanuts," said Liam. "We'd only get peanuts."

So Dec goes upstairs sayin, "Well, that's that. I don't believe in living beyond my means. Roll on Dole Day."

An Sistur Veronica comes down sayin "Trust in Providence. God will provide. Let us away, children."

An they set off inta town.

An – as chance would have it – we were ploddin away when we passed a coupla women an one a them looked aftur us an laughed an said "God, isn't that very good all the same? Did yeh see the witch?"

Cliona.

That was enough an more than enough for them.

Ten minutes latur they hit their first house.

Cliona, in hur relic-a-the-seventies black cloak, had a branch of a tree to ride on an a condom on hur nose. Liam's quiff was standin up stiff with KY an he had a sign made outa a bit of an ould Cornflakes box hangin round his neck sayin 90210. Liz's hair was tied up with Rectus's string an she was stripped off to hur bra with hur sweat-shirt tied round hur waist an *Papa Don't Preach* (I'm gonna keep my baby) on hur – Madonna like. She was frozen. An they put Mike's fedora on The Bonny Boy an wound his blue school-tie around it – *and all around his college hat I'll wind a ribbon blue* – an wrote *The Bonny Boy* on him. An he was mortified an would nevur have done it in a million years except that he wasn't in a strong position or any position at all to say no to anythin. An he was paralatic anyway – the one pint had him plastered, not bein usedta it.

"What about me?" says Mike in full regalia, the eyes glowin outa the Thrillur ghoul make-up.

An Dec gave him a witherin look.

"An whasss about meee? Whass about meee?" screeches

Mary in his black lace mantilla, black gloves up to the scrawny elbows an leopardskin leggins that showed off his prick to the best advantage.

So that left Tizzy.

To me Tizzy was lookin like a Goldy Anjul doin undurcovur work in civvies. But none a the othurs saw that.

He wanted to be Vivien Leigh.

Tough.

But they were stumped. They didn't know what to do with him.

There was nothin for it in the end – though he fought hard against it – "I'd be mortified, Dec!" – they made him a priest's collar outa a bit a the Cornflakes box an hung a sign sayin *saggart* round his neck. This was to do with the joke goin round at the time: What's the Irish for "child molestur"? Answer: *Saggart* – meanin priest.

So with Liz petrified an Tizzy mortified an The Bonny Boy ossified, they started to do the houses all the way down ta town.

An nothin would do Liam but to sing the Wran Song.

"The *Wran* song? You can't sing that! That's a Christmas song –"

"Tis for collectin money," says Liam. "An we don't want peanuts."

He had a point.

So:

"The Wran the Wran the king of all birds
St Stephen's Day got caught in the furze
Up in the holly an ivy tree
Da da da da da da-da-da dee!" (Because they couldn't remember the words.)

The first door opened an a woman with a bowl a nuts an sweets in hur hands looked out astonished –

"C'mere, Mam! Breeda!" And an oldur woman an a young wan came out an they all started laughin. "Isn't that a scream! Will yeh look at Michael Jackson!"

We were a success.

Pity they couldn't see me.

I was yur authentic ghost.

"Knock at the knockur ring at the bell
Please give us a coppur for singin so well
Singin so well! Singin so well!"

An people got the message no bothur – that we didn't want peanuts – especially with Liam rattlin the collection-box in their faces –

"I have a little box undur me arum
Tuppence or thruppence will do it no harum –"

Tizzy had the job a keepin count a the takins – so they'd know how much to take back outa the box – yeh could see his mouth movin all the time an he nevur took his eyes offa the box. He'd get migraine, sure as God. He did that sometimes.

An aftur a while we varied it a bit an gave em a blast a –

Christy Ring
Hurls the ball
We love Christy
Balls an all –
Here's up um all says the Boys a Fair Hill!

Which is the Cork National Anthem.

In the end we paid the price a success an hadta beat a hasty retreat – at St Luke's Cross the local kids ganged up on us an pelted us with eggs an flour all the way down Summurhill.

But we were on a roll that night. Twas magic. We hit Pana an there, at Cudmore's cornur at the entrance to Winthrop Street is that feen that does the pavement paintin an performs. An like a gift from the gods with knobs on he's doin Jackson's *Thrillur* – what else? Tis Hallowe'en. So he has a light rigged up an a big pavement paintin – chalk like – an the *Thrillur* ghouls risin from their graves an *Thrillur* playin on his ghetto-blastur an he's wearin his Jackson mask an fedora an he has a stuffed Bubbles the Chimp (an he can't a been a *National Enquirur* readur or he'd a known that Wacko an Bubbles were aftur splittin up). But *we've* got the Real Thing – Mike. Yur genuine Jackson impersonatur. In yur genuine *Thrillur* red leathur jacket purchased mail-ordur from England.

So Mike dances his ass off an we make a fortune. People are *showerin* us with money – an, true for Liam, people have like a *compulsion* to throw away their money any ould chance at all they get. Course tis all goin inta yur man's basket but in the end, fair fucks to him, he splits it with us.

Then we have a problem with Cliona who can't tear herself away from the limelight because she's taken to lyin down on the chalk-paintin an actin out a ghoul risin from a tomb – ovur an ovur an ovur – an ovur – an ovur – an ovur again – like a one-night-stand with a bunjee-jumpur. An I'm hopin she'll stay there an marry yur man altogethur an have a rake a little pavement-painturs an Bubbles impersonators an child-ghouls – all delivered dramatically in public in a delivery room chalked out by yur man to great applause an a showur a pound coins. With every priest an guard in Cork in attendance.

But no such luck.

She was comin with us.

Then we do Pana an when we're passin Petur an Paul Street Dec notices the church is open. An he thinks a me. An the Petition Mrs Burke is aftur givin them.

"Wait for us," said Dec to the gang. "Come on, Liam."

Down the little side street an inta the church porch.

"Perfect timing," says Dec – it bein All Souls' Night like.

"Where's the Petition, Liam?"

"Tis heeyur."

"Whey-yur?" says Dec mockin him.

"In the collection-box."

Dec goggles at him.

"I wanted ta put it somewhere safe."

"Safe? And how do you intend to get it out? Without breaking the seal?"

Shrug from Liam.

"Would I be right in saying you're not taking this very seriously?" says Dec with the eyes sparkin.

"Takin what?"

"Doing what we can for Tony."

"Oh for God's sake –"

"I don't know how you can be like that about your own brothur!"

"Be like *what*?" Liam's eyes were startin to spark too.

Oh, leave it out, lads –

"Well, you don't seem concerned."

"Concerned? About *what*?"

"About Tony."

Liam was furious. "And you *are*?" The chest startin to heave. An Rectus in his arms – undur the influence – lookin worried.

"I am. He's wallowing this moment in the flames of Purgatory – that is, if I can believe that he confessed before he died –"

"Oh fuck you an yur flames!" White-faced, with the voice tremblin. "You – you – you're insultin my brothur with yur fuckin flames – why should he be in any fuckin flames –"

"If he didn't die in a state of grace –"

Holy Jesus. Here we were on the Midnight Train to Georgia again. I mean neithur of em had the faintest shaggin idea *where* the fuck I was.

"Anyway, I *told* you he saw a priest –"

"A fella from Brazil in a t-shirt!"

"He was a *priest*, Dec!"

"Huh!"

An there they were daggurs drawn an I don't know where that mighta ended if Cliona hadn't come gallopin up – shriekin away pretendin to be chasin ghosts – high as a kite an demented an gigglin – an she swept the two theolojuns an their dog before hur inta the church. SS Petur an Paul's (they write it SS on the street signs) is a very old church an that night twas enough to give yeh the creeps because tis darkish at the best a times an the only light was comin from the candles before the shrines an from lamps carried by all these rows a anjuls with big pointy wings carved outa blackish wood. An there're carvins in black wood all ovur the place.

"Gaawd between us an aall harum!" goes Mary an scoots back out the door. Twas that bad now like.

So we're peerin around an Cliona disappears inta one a the black-carved confession boxes. An Liam takes one a his mad turns an goes inta the priest's part a the box. You'd havta pay me. An we can hear them foolin around with the slide, pullin it back an forth. An then Cliona bein a banshee an wailin an twould put the fear a God in yeh, she did it so well. Realistically like.

Can a banshee wail realistically? That's like *do androids dream of electric sheep*?

An I'm wondurin about this when Dec touches me on the arm – yes, he does – an says, starin up ahead a him, all heartfelt: "A conversion!"

An lo an behold up at the top a the church on the left-hand side kneelin in fronta the altar to the Mothur a Perpetual Succour is Denis – our Mothur. In a long dark coat with the collar turned up.

Mike goes inta a kind of a spasm but they're all gobsmacked – Denis bein a Protestant.

"What's he doin heeyur?" says Tizzy.

"Lookin at the architecture?" goes Liz.

"In the *dark*?" says Dec. "No! It's a conversion! At *last*! I just *knew* it had to happen!" The eyes shinin.

So they troop up quietly an then Dec decides to go for broke an shoves Mike ahead an signs to him to kneel next to Denis. An he does, green-an-gold Marks an Sparks an all. An Denis turns his head away from the goldy picture of Mothur an Child all gleamin in the candlelight an looks at Mike an then turns away again because he thinks that he's hallucinatin. An this happens a couple a times. But then his head turns with a jerk an he stares at the Marks an Sparks bag an tis clear it dawns on him that Marks an Sparks doesn't belong in his hallucination an that Mike is really there.

An aftur a long long heart-felt stare, he reaches his hand out an touches the red leathur, checkin the reality factur out.

An Mike kinda shuffles closur on his red drain-pipe knees. An Denis's hand goes up an it's shakin a bit but it slides undur the hair at the neckline the way I'd seen it do so many times. An Mike closes his eyes an kinda lies inta the caress the way a horse or a dog does when yeh stroke its head.

Denis keeps strokin.

An behind them Liz and Dec, bein Liz an Dec, are clutchin each othur in the throes a sentiment – religious in Dec's case – four blue eyes undur bits a blond fringe fixed on Romeo an Juliet an sparklin in the candlelight. Those two – their bladdurs were always very close to their eyes.

An The Bonny Boy is standin there in the shadows. An I can't see his face.

So Dec an Liz, aftur havin their moment, take off ovur to the othur side a the church, still clutchin each othur. An they nearly capsize in fronta the main altar – where the Host is sittin there in the big gold monstrance like a sunburst – because Dec tries to genuflect an Liz isn't inta that kinda thing so they almost wrestle each othur to the ground.

Ovur on the othur side Dec goes all devout in fronta the shrine to the Holy Souls. But this isn't Liz's gig eithur an she stands there lookin – well, as cynical as Liz could evur look.

An no wondur. There are the chalky Holy Souls all willowy an androg-whatsit, flounderin in the chalky red flames a Purgatory – full technicolour now like – with Yur Wan above holdin the Infant Jesus. Him again. An Yur Wan is lookin straight ahead again like she's sayin "This has nothin to do with me – Jesus, what can I do?" an the Infant has a wreath a roses in his hands an he's leanin ovur tryin to choose a Holy Soul to rescue from the flames an his eyes are fixed on one Soul but not *exactly* – the ultimate tease like – an there are two androg-whatsit anjuls on eithur side, one holdin up a fingur sayin "Only *one,* boys!" an the othur is kinda shovin one Soul forward an sayin, "How about yur mano here?"

This is where I'm supposed to be, havin the sins burned outa me.

An I almost wish I was. There, I mean. Then I'd *know.* All I'd have ta do would be to lie back an think a Iceland an wait me turn. An have people pray to me. Yeah, people do that – that's legit, technically like.

Purgatory wasn't Liz's gig but lightin candles was. Now she was lightin away like blazes, hur face all bright in the glow. Coins clunked inta the brassy slots.

Dec was havin the horrors imaginin me bein eaten alive by evurlastin flames.

Well, whatevur turns yeh on.

An then I noticed all these scraps a paper strewn all ovur the statues, stuck in between the flames an even in the Holy Souls' hands. It looked for all the world as if someone had torn up a whole bunch a waste papur like five years' fucked Lottery tickets an flung em up on the thing. But there was writin on the scraps. So I hovered. Lookin for a piece that lay face up, that I could read. An when I found it, it read "Holy Souls, please make my blood count and my cell count be normal tomorrow 19/11/94. Dolores". An it all came back to me. All the counts. All the tests. All the results. All the prayurs.

An then all the pieces a papur were shriekin at me an I

could read them without seein them an it was "spare me for my family" an "don't let him drink it all" an "please let him die now" an one – I knew which one – "don't let it be AIDS".

An I couldn't bear it.

I blundered down to the back a the church – away from all the voices – with the candlelight swimmin like twas underwatur so I could hardly see my way. I stood at the end near the Crucifixion tryin to blank out those voices an me eyes cleared a bit an I looked back an saw the red glow of a jacket – Romeo and Juliet still above, makin their vows with their hands joined an their foreheads leanin togethur. An Yur Wan in the picture was starin straight out above their heads, very serene, with a knowin little smile on hur face.

An she still hasn't tied the child's sandal.

An I turn an there she is again an now he has no sandal to tie – he's dyin on a cross – there she is – there she is –

Standin there for all the mothurs an all their pain. An Jesus for all sufferin humanity. An Magdalen for all the sufferin women who evur loved a man. An John – the Beloved Disciple – *the disciple whom Jesus loved* – standin there for us gay men.

It was perfect.

Right down to the Disposable Fathur. Josuph. Who wasn't there.

Talk about marketing. The Church couldn't a done a bettur job if it was makin a Take That video. No wondur they had us hooked for centuries. Before TV commercials like.

An hoverin ovur the whole shebang, not actually *there*, but makin his presence felt just enough to sour every shaggurs's existence, was God the Fathur – yur classic Absentee. Probably workin on a buildin site ovur in Manchestur. Hairdressur, how are yeh! I shoulda been a theolojun. An next thing I felt this gigantic laugh forcin its way up from me guts an I made for the door an the open air but it caught me in the porch in an explosion a white light like a nuclear fission an I staggered outa the church weak as a baby, gigglin.

RIP how are yeh. Fuck-all peace about the aftur-life.

Up an down like a yo-yo.

Shaggin unstable. Must be me hormones.

Then they all came troopin out with Mothur an Mike like Siamese twins an the beginnins of an aura flutturin round em like one a the candles Liz had lit an I felt like puttin me hands around them to sheltur the little flame from the wind.

"I knew you'd eventually see the light," says Dec to Mothur all breathless.

"What light is that, daahling?" Mothur wanted to know.

"He thinks you're converted," says Liam rollin the eyes.

"Oh!" Mothur looked startled. "Well, not exactly, daahlings – it's just that I was willing to try anything – and I'd heard you say so often that the Mother of Good Counsel works wonders an that she has been in charge of my case, so to speak, from the start –"

"Buss dass noss de – *ow! Leem!*" Mary clutched at his ribs an glared at Liam – perplexed. "Wacha do dass far? I wuz oonly sayin *dass* noss de – *uh*!"

An for all the world like a robot with a signal goin off in his brain – *Manchurian Candidate* like – Liam slammed

Mary inta a doorway an flung himself at hur in an all-out sexual assault. Frenzied like.

"Good Lord," said Denis, lookin back at them worried. "That looks very violent –"

"Oh, Denis – you haven't *heard*! They're getting married next week," said Dec.

"Good *Lord*," said Denis, the eyebrows sky-high – he could beat Liam at that any day. "Tell me more . . ."

An that's how we glossed ovur the fact that Denis in his ignorance had been playin on the wrong team – in the wrong church – at the wrong shrine – prayin to the Mothur a Perpetual Succour an *not* the Mothur a Good Counsel. He'd had his miracle an no one wanted to spoil it for him. No one with half a brain.

So – minus Liam an Mary – we all trooped ovur to Loafurs.

"Try to blend in, children," said Dec, doin the Reverend Mothur in *Sistur Act.* An that was easy. In fact, no one took a tack a notice of us. An eventually Liam an Mary arrived lookin like two people who had just shagged someone in a doorway but not necessarily each othur.

Mothur was buyin. An twas all very friendly an the usual – Body Heat like.

An then the definitely *unusual* took ovur.

Instead a tearin off to one a the Hallowe'en parties round town they decided on *a quid a man an back to my house.*

So the trick-or-treat takins stretched to apples an Barm Brack (yeh shoulda been there when they were tryin to get the money outa the can with a knife an the Petition envelope blockin the slot) an nuts an string an six-packs an cidur an a few fireworks – sparklurs like – an candles an even a few hollowed-out pumpkins.

An we went back – home.

Maybe that was when it became important – the house.

Suddenly we were family (I'm not countin Cliona in mindya).

We had a house.

We had a dog.

We had a *baby*.

We had a collection-box.

An a Jackson postur. To say nothin of an Elvis postur.

An a mothur-in-law.

An a dash a incest.

We were in business.

Twas great.

The kids were aftur lightin a bonfire in the back garden so we spent a bit a time standin shiverin around it – twas dyin down at that stage – an Mothur in fine fettle with Mike clutched to him an he holdin forth about bonfires bein *bone*-fires because the Druids usedta burn bones in sacrifice for the New Year on Hallowe'en an how pumpkins are Death's Heads an how Samhain was the Lord of Death – like Hallowe'en in Irish is *Oiche Samhna* – the Night of Samhain – an how Samhain calls togethur all the evil souls condemned to inhabit the bodies a animals – *fastened to a dyin animal* –

At this stage I was "Jesus, leave it out, Denis!" an experiencin a nasty crawlin feelin all ovur the body I don't have because this was all a bit too close to the burnt bone for me in me un-dead state.

I wasn't upta bein reminded just then about that particular bit a shape-shiftin (Mothur's word) – even the look a the ash in the fire was makin me feel queasy –

Been there.

Done that.

Got the T-shirt.

The Bone-fire was dyin so we lit our sparklurs an let them sizzle an Mike an Mothur with a sparklur each lightin up their faces, lookin like an ad for bein secure with Abbey National or somethin.

Then we went into the house an set up the candles an the pumpkins an decorated the place with blown-up black condums – aren't they *fuckin* useful things?

So they ducked an they bobbed for apples an got soaked an frozen an invented new versions a Burn the Biscuit to do with hidin nuts in undurpants – that went too far by far aftur a while. Dec an Liam cut up the Barm Brack an made sure that Mike got the goldy ring an Mary got the matchstick for beatin hur husband an Cliona got the rag for bein an Old Maid – I enjoyed that last bit I tell ya. Tizzy got the bean (or is it the pea?) for wealth an good fortune – the bean – I think. An the pea (or is it the bean?) for poverty went to The Bonny Boy – Dec made sure a that – an the poor creature went white to the gills. I don't deny it – Dec's a bitch.

They played musical chairs with imaginary chairs to imaginary music an then danced to real music on Mary's ghetto-blastur – Madonna an more Madonna –

I was watchin The Bonny Boy like a hawk. Prayin for him to scoop Liz up on the white steed, y'know – but he didn't have a white steed because he was still at school an couldn't afford to keep one. Where would yeh put one anyway in Kilcrea Park?

It came to me in the end with that sinkin feelin like an

elevatur goin down – he was goin to let it happen. The idea a Dec as proxy made some kinda sense to him, too. An all of a sudden I was angry. This fuckin age thing – what was it about? This was the root a all our troubles – The Bonny Boy – Tizzy. Shur all our grandmothurs were married at fourteen an had *kids* an no one said they were too young, for Chrissake, or called it abuse. An everyone usedta be on about Our Lady bein fourteen an that. Mindya, she had it off with the Holy Ghost – I suppose that's different. Mindya, I have me suspicions about the Anjul Gabriel – havin it off with the postman like? I mean what would you do confronted unexpectedly in the privacy a yur own bed-chambur by Michael Bolton with wings? But that's neithur here nor there –

Not that I wanted to go back to the good ould days an thirteen-year-old pregnancies. Now we had family plannin an cut-price condums that burst. An, meself, I call that Progress.

But, havin said that, it's still like we're all sufferin from some kinda national *amnesia* or somethin. Like someone blows a whistle an everyone blanks out on anythin before 1990.

It hadta be somethin to do with De Valera an those crossroads. Everythin else was.

Right on cue they switched to Irish music an we had jigs an reels an Cliona showin off sickeninly because *naturally* it turns out she's an expert Irish dansur so we had hur leppin an rockin hur ankles an batturin the floor an showin off hur knickurs except that she wasn't wearin any – an then we had the Walls a Limerick an the Siege a Ennis with a dozen imaginary dansurs (tricky, that) an that was the greatest craic in the world so I joined in at one point – unbeknowns to em like – because they were a man short. We laughed ourselves sick an Tizzy kept gettin it wrong an messin up the sequence an he'd be goin when we were comin – an it turned out, would yeh believe, that *Mary* was a dab hand – or foot – at this céilí stuff – she really had it to a fine art. So it could have been me worst nightmare with Mary screechin like a mad cat at Tizzy an Cliona doin Joan De-Knees Moriarty (the wan who founded the Ballet Company in Cork) but I was havin too much fun to care.

An I got to thinkin: wouldn't Dev – that's De Valera to you – wouldn't he be proud a us? This was it – the ideal Ireland that he dreamed of – to a tee. Here we were – satisfied with frugal comfort just like he wanted an devotin our leisure time to things a the spirit – here we were in our cosy homestead filled with the laughtur a comely youths an the contests of athletic maidens to say nothin a the wisdom a serene old age (Mothur at a pinch) – with the rompin a sturdy childrun on the way – an really the man was a prophet in his time to be able to foresee it all so clearly way back in nineteen-nought-splash or whenevur it was – the thirties – the forties – I dunno. There we were dancin away at those crossroads like blazes. A credit to him an the Fathurs a the Nation.

Hairdressur? I shoulda done Ant-whatsit – that thing they do in Papua New Guinea. Or maybe not. Tis amazin how a touch a death sharpens the wits.

Anyway – I danced meself to a standstill on a right old high an as soon as I stopped I boomeranged back to me responsibilities.

The Bonny Boy. Christ. What was I to do?

Drag him down to Fathur Twomey for a lecture on that Empowurment crack?

I couldn't drag. All I could do was whispur in people's left earholes. So I applied meself to doin that – with a vengeance.

I did the rounds.

But I turned meself inside out an cross-eyed tryin to get through to The Bonny Boy. Luckily he hadta get the last bus home before I spontaneously combusted altogethur with the effort.

An a while latur I noticed Dec an Liz were gone an me heart missed a beat an I swooped around only to find em at long last out Connie's back in The Shed. There they were surrounded by the finches an canaries in their little wooden cages – an bird-feed an bird-droppins an mouse-traps with massacurred mice in em – with the ferruts outside barin their teeth an twistin an turnin in their cages like the Mighty Morphin Powur Ranjurs.

Well done, Dec, says I, yeh really have a feelin for atmosphere. Haven't yeh got yur wires crossed, boy? Tis Paddy Garibaldi's an candlelight an red wine an waxy tablecloths for this one. The caged birds an ferruts an mousetraps are for givin Connie a blow-job.

"Remember Orla in Dublin that I was livin with for a while? It was *all right*. She loved dick. So did I. I usedta manage like – but I dunno – to me a man's body is much more exciting than a woman's. I can't see what is exciting about a woman's body at all!"

"Dec, I keep telling you that doesn't mattur – I really wouldn't be lookin to you for my sex-life. But it's true that time we spent togethur in Dublin was like marriage. And

like I said to you before you're the husband every woman
wants an nobody has –"

An I swear I didn't invite Prince in but he came in
anyway, with his pulsin anxiously beatin heart –

If I were your best friend
Would you let me – take care of you?
Do all the things that only a best friend can –
Only best friends can –

"Liz, there's nothin I'd like bettur than to take care of you
– I'd be everything a best friend could evur be –"

"I know that – you'd have me spoiled rotten –"

Sometimes I trip on how happy we could be –
Pulee-he-he-he-hease!

"Please, Liz – *please*!"

Oh, Christ!

Would yeh let me wash your hair?
Could I make yeh breakfast some time?

"The idea a being pampered is a bit tempting at the
moment, I must say." She was smilin a bit. "And I'd nevur
have to wash your socks –"

An Prince was movin on to a seduction aftur all, the
crafty buggur –

Is it really necessary for me to go out of the room
Just because you want to undress?
We don't have to make children to make love
And we don't have to make love to have an orgasm –

"I suppose there's love and love – we *do* love each othur –
an who knows what might develop?" says she.

It was high time for me an Prince to get outa that shed an
stop puttin words inta their mouths but I had this
nightmare feelin a not bein able to move.

195

An finally all these dark emotions got me by the throat an I had this fierce attack a vertigo. The bird-cages an the mousetraps an the sacks a feed an the whole universe went spinnin round me an I thought – this is Hell now, this is it – an it's goin to go on forevur for all Eternity like the Brothurs told us an they were right all the time – an when Lucifur fell from Heaven he went inta a tail-spin that he nevur came out of an the poor bastard's been spinnin without the singin evur since – an Hell is nothin but the nausea a bein out a sync with the rest a the Universe – Eternal Vertigo – an really God or the Turtles can do nothin about it if we spin outa sync – an it's not, an it's not – I was reachin an I knew it was spinnin outa me grasp even as I was reachin – it's nuthin to do with *punishment* no more than a plane tail-spinnin outa the sky –

Then I was outside an it was the night-sky that was spinnin around me head in huge wheelin circles an I thought I was dyin all ovur again –

An twas just like the last time – just when yeh thought you were kickin outa existence – suddenly it righted – an the calm was keen an clear –

An yeh sat up an felt yeh'd kill for a fag.

An I started laughin me head off thinkin a that Gary Larson cartoon about "The real reason dinosaurs became extinct" with yur three or four dinosaurs lightin up an draggin away at fags –

I was so glad to be alive. And not in Hell.

Only in Mayfield.

If Connie had come out, I'd sung *In the Ghetto* with him. No bothur.

An I swore I'd nevur touch anothur drop a Begrudgery again in me life.

I was allurgic to it.

An right then I got the notion that what those turtles wanted was for me to set up Happy Families in the house for Liz and Dec an Liam an Mary an whoevur else was along for the ride.

It would be tough. But I could grit me teeth an do it.

True Grit – that was me. I even had a stetson.

I did me cowboy walk back home.

They were handin around joints an tellin ghost stories an singin songs an I settled down to listen but me head was buzzin with Things To Be Done.

An the peculiar thing was: what really started pressin in on me was me two brave buckos out in the jungle. I got to thinkin, who knows what them shaggin turtles had rigged up? Maybe it tickled their fancy to have a real Private Tony somewhere in the universe in some kinda *virtual reality* or somethin who was totally *dependent* on me? Or it could be that *karma* thing. His. Or mine. Maybe I had to work through this fantasy before I could be released into the Great Blue Yondur an meet Derek Jarman.

Point was – I didn't know.

Judgin from the evidence I had to go on – any fuckin thing was possible.

Jesus – maybe *I* was *his* fantasy. Maybe that explained why I was fartin around Cork when I was supposed to be dead? Right – I put that idea on the back burnur.

Anyway, *he* was my fantasy. An maybe when I worked it through I'd get Major O'Hara as a bonus prize.

That settled it – I couldn't abandon Private Tony. I hadta see him through.

But I was fuckin *afraid* at this point to go back inta that shaggin jungle. Fuck, what if I changed the scene? What if they were marooned on a desert island instead – like one a those Shortland Islands Mothur was on about – they wouldn't need any equipment an they could frolic in the surf – ride dolphins an things – Bali Hai an that –

If you try you'll find me

Where the sky meets the sea or-somethin-like-that –

waturfalls even – an that rope bridge where he runs to meet the girl Mothur thinks is really a boy –

But there are waturfalls in the jungle too an plenty a rope bridges –

But the idea a Major O'Hara runnin to meet Private Tony an scoopin him up an givin vent to –

Youngur than Springtime are you

Gayur than laughtur are you –

just wasn't goin to work, was it? No way.

Besides, he'd nevur lift him with all that equipment.

I was rattlin on like this all light-headed an windin down grand when Dec an Liz came in holdin hands.

It cost me – but I just tipped me stetson to them.

An started inta a decade a the Rosary pronto: rope-bridges, waturfalls, Youngur than Springtime, armadillos, rots, Doh a deer, a female deer –

"And at the age of eighteen on his grave the grass was green –"

"Oh *don't* Cliona – makes me think of Tony –" Dec.

Oh –

"Cru-uel death put an end to his growin!"

"*Cliona!* Please!" Liz this time.

"All right so – we'll lay The Bonny Boy to rest –" God, she was wicked. She folded the hands on hur knee an got hur Joan Baez look on – all serious an traditional – an I saw a little gleam in the depths a hur eyes that no one else woulda spotted –

"O-oh my young love said to me – my mothur won't mind –"

Jesus, this was worse than the Wild West – those cowboys musta all been Irish –

I dunno if yeh know the song – tis a fierce mournful soulful thing altogether – beautiful now like – about a girl who dies before her marriage – Number One in the All-Time Greats for Spirits –

An the last fuckin thing she shoulda been singin an well she knew it –

"La-ast night she came to me, my true love came in –
So-o softly she came that her feet made no din . . ."

The point being – she's dead like.

Well, they were all maudlin at this stage – snifflin to a man – Tizzy flickin away the tears with his fingers – Mary baawlin.

All of em except Mothur an Mike who was straddlin him on a chair ovur in a cornur, lost to the world, an twould kinda spoil the mood if I told yeh what was goin on there . . .

"And she laid her hand on me and this she did say
It will not be long lo-o-ove till our wedding day –"

An Liz lookin miserable.

An so the evenin ended with us all drownin in nost-whatsit – floundurin around in it up to our earholes – except for Denis an Mike who were floundurin in somethin else.

All we needed was Connie all maudlin an retro.

I'd got ovur me moment a generosity towards him so I was fuckin glad we were spared that.

CHAPTER SIX

"I don't get it," said Liam.

I didn't get it eithur.

"I mean this Fathur Twomey's certs would probably be a grand job for Nevur-nevurland or Somewhere Ovur the Rainbow – but – the *Corporation*? It's not goin to be *registered*, Dec. An we're goin to have the parish priest on the rampage when he finds out Fathur Twomey did a foxur."

An Dec with a martyred expression listenin to all this.

With just the odd sigh now an then.

"An why can't we just *pretend* to be married? I'll do that for yeh – for a while. Maybe we can swing it with the Corporation – maybe they won't *ask* for a cert!"

We'd left the ladies haulin a rake a bridal dresses around an set off for the Good Shepherd's – the convent where I had me funeral – to make the weddin arrangements. With Rectus an the collection-box (for safe keepin) an the MJ postur (that we'd told Mike was Manchestur United). An flowurs for me grave – well, Little Nellie's grave where I'd been scattered.

"Liam – we've been through all that –"

"What if he cops on –"

"I'll deal with it –"

"You'll deal with it! Yeh know what! I think you're sufferin from delusions a grandeur or somethin – like Hitlur – an yeh know what happened to him –"

"Look, could you just save your breath for the climb? We're pressed for time as it is – what with havin to squeeze the stag-night in tonight now –"

"Stag-night?"

"Well, of *course* we have to have a stag, Liam – if we're to do it properly –"

I didn't think "properly" entered inta it – twas the most half-assed capur I'd evur come across in all a me born days. An I'd had some experience a half-ass – I'd been *buried* by this lot. So to speak.

Beyond the Pale was leavin Cork the very next afternoon so he was doin a rushed job on the weddin. In the mornin. An then there was the little mattur a Tizzy havin to appear in court. When? In the mornin.

This was an Express package arrivin from the Ninja Turtles with D-E-C stamped all ovur it. Postage Unpaid.

"Who's payin for the stag?" Liam wanted to know.

"Mothur."

"Does he know?"

"Not yet."

An we climbed that hill past those huge old prayurful trees an arrived at the Good Shepherd's. An Liam lookin like he's on Death Row.

An there was nothin but scaffoldin an workmen all ovur the place – all ovur the place.

The lads were aghast.

We bate our way through the scaffoldin not even

201

distracted by the workmens' butts – an some of em were Even Bettur than the Real Thing though their faces were chronic but yeh could get ovur that.

An we found The Bride a Frankenstein an Mothur Ursula in Little Nellie's Room with the tin bugle an the bunny-rabbit an the Infant a Prague undur his glass covur an the little white bed where she died.

Last Stand at Papago Wells.

It turned out that UCC – the University – was aftur buyin the whole convent. An nothin was bein left intact except Little Nellie's room an the chapel an the graveyard where I was scattered. The graveyard where Dec first got the notion a bein a nun, when he was a little boy.

Education was takin ovur from Fallen Women an Orphans. I hadta admit twas Progress.

But there was one huge fuckin lump in me throat.

The Bride a Frankenstein was lookin grim, as well she might. She twirled hur denture an spat inta hur handkurchief an looked savage all a the time we were there an there was no hearty back-slappin at all. An Mothur Ursula was blubburin half the time with the plump red face nearly purple. She'd wanta watch the blood-pressure.

"So, Declan," went the Bride through hur big mannish nose. "There's not much we can do for you this time. We're almost lodgers here ourselves at this stage," moppin at hur nose with the big white handkurchief in hur big white hand.

"Tis a pity," goes Ursula with hur heart in hur eyes, lookin only at Liam like she always does – she had him by the hands, it goes without sayin. "Shur we'd love to see ye on yeer big day! And Mary? Is she excited, Liam?"

Because they knew Mary, a'course – she'd worked with the Magdalens (the Fallen Women) in the laundry for a while aftur me funeral until she got fed up of it.

So they went to put the flowurs on the grave at the foot a the othur Infant a Prague guardin the grave with his ball an crown. Him again. An me two boyos imaginin somehow that I was lingerin around there.

Loiterin Without Intent.

A stupid notion when yeh come to think of it – I mean why would any Free Spirit want to hang around a graveyard? With a bunch a nuns? An how Dec squared it off with his notion that I was wallowin in the flames a Purgatory is beyond me.

That Astral Projection crack maybe.

Anyway. A terrible thing happened before we left. We were just sayin goodbye to them an the Bride was doin hur thing with the handkurchief – an suddenly she started to cry. The cold fishy eyes filled up an the hooked nose went red. It was a terrible thing to see. Dec started sayin things about trustin in God an His Will an that, an the Bride gripped him by the arm an squeezed with hur big white hand whit the silvur bridal ring on it – Bride a Christ aftur all not Bride a Frankenstein –

An we left them an they wavin to us an they standin outside that huge red-brick buildin that usedta be like an outsize Wheelie Bin for Cork for generations – where you'd chuck yur pregnant daughturs an yur unwanted childrun an yur delinquent sons – satisfied that they were in the tendur hands a the clergy an you could get on with the really important things in life like goin to Sunday Mass.

It *was* Progress, I thought, savage like.

Dec was lookin watury-eyed now – because a the nuns – an the visit to the graveyard had upset him anyway – an I felt a great rush a love for him rememberin the first day I'd swooped down that drive with him an tried to have an out-a-the-body experience – an the last day when he'd turned an said "Come on so." The last first day. Or the first last day.

For bettur, for worse.

So down we go an Dec an Liam not really talkin – Dec lookin grim an Liam tryin not to look relieved for fear a startin Dec off.

"C'man an we go by the Tea House," says I to Dec. Thinkin to cheer him up – because if yeh remembur he fancied the straight guy runnin it.

So he took me up on it an down with us across the Shaky Bridge an along through Fitzgerald's Park – retracin our steps that first day togethur when I was so delighted with life an content with me lot. An their steps quickened, lookin forward to a cuppa an the slaggin that would go on about yur man.

An when we got there the shaggin thing was gone.

Burnt to the ground. Nothin left but a shell fulla ash an blackened timburs. An old fire, a cold fire.

They stood an stared an I could hear Dec thinkin: a bad omen if evur there was one.

Then Liam an Rectus started pokin around – lookin for bones? But Dec just stood there starin.

They came back boneless an Dec rallied. A huge sigh outa him an then: "Well, that's one fantasy laid to rest." An he turned an walked away.

Liam an Rectus put on a turn a speed aftur him. "What fantasy exactly?"

"Oh, the one about him raping me one night across the freezur."

"Oh, *that* fantasy!"

An they livened up ("Shur I suppose they'll get the insurance an open it again?"). But it kept comin back to me – that sickenin smell a ash – an I couldn't shake it off. I was polluted with it.

So we walked all the way back home an the day rushin by for want a the price a the bus-fare. Dec'd put an embargo on the Scout box.

With Dec deep in thought all the way. An Liam rattlin on about where he might get poteen to rub inta Rectus-a-um's legs an suchlike. An no soonur did we get home but he went AWOL.

Dec was septic. "The usual! Leave everything to Declan! If *I* didn't put in the effort nothing would evur happen. You'd imagine I was doing this for myself." An he turns on the misfortunate Tizzy who was sittin next to him at the kitchen table jigglin tea-bags. "*You're* doing a lot to help!" says he outa spite.

"Me? Me?" says Tiz. "Don't *you* start at me now. Tis all very fine an salty for you! But I'm up in court tomarra an it'll be all ovur de papurs an I'll lose me job even if I walk an I'm aftur *wreckin* me nails an dey'll make a dog's dinnur a me in prison an Bosco'll *nevur* visit me for fear a losin his job in RTE an I'll havta miss de weddin an me roots are showin – I'm nearly off me game – an d'yeh know what Florrie had me doin today? Spongin de walls inside in hur place to make dem damp because the Social Welfare was comin –"

"Oh – what's she aftur now?" says Dec changin his tune – whethur outa pity for Tiz or curiosity about Florrie.

"She's aftur a transfur now – since she heard about de new houses – shur she went off down to de Corporation dis mornin with two rats in a black bag that Connie was aftur catchin out back –"

"Huh! She doesn't know when she's well off – I mean she knows how to work the system to a fine art – with her Home Help an her Free Turf and all the rest!"

"Well, she got no satisfaction from de Corporation anyway – she came back like de Anti-Christ –"

An at this point there's a rap on the door an they pull faces thinkin tis Florrie. In comes Liz.

"Brilliant!" says Dec an the face lights up. "Right on cue."

Whatevur cue that was. "What cue?" says Liz.

"No – don't sit down – we're going ovur to Ennismore."

The Dominican place down the road.

"Oh great! But I thought I told yeh – you don't have to sign on for the class – you can just turn up at The Hermitage on the night –"

"Breeda's yoga class? No, it's not that – look, c'mon, we've got to talk –"

I let them go. An stayed an held Tizzy's hand. To stop him bitin his nails.

Liam came back aftur a couple a hours with a flush in his cheeks – poteen or exercise now I don't know. But Rectus was reelin an reekin.

Dec an Liz came back aftur an age with Dec lookin like the cat that had got the cream.

"We're on."

Right.

An Liz with secrets behind hur eyes.

206

An before yeh could say *"Quark! Quark!"* it was tenna past seven an we were all in town – all the men that is – gatherin forces an gatherin steam for the stag-night. Feelin very peculiar an macho. An not sure we could carry it off.

An wonderin whethur twas compulsory to tie the groom butt-naked to a street-lamp. Or optional like.

An Dec was headin down Winthorp Street when I stopped to look in at the winda a Golden Disc. An next thing I couldn't find him. I buzzed around the area gettin very agitated because I still hadn't shaken off the feelins of loomin gloom an doom that'd got hold a me that day.

Well, it couldn't have been more than ten minutes max since we'd split up when I walked inta Halpins an there he was, sittin with an entire Dutch basketball team – two of em black – orderin a meal. I was just *amazed* at how he done it. I'm *still* amazed. There just wasn't time.

Goin for Gold wasn't in it.

An I had the wild thought: great, Dec gets gang-banged by the whole team an Liz will have nothin more to do with him an that'll put the kybosh on the weddin – aaahh – I slapped that thought down.

So when they'd stoked up on food – an *man* were they able to put it away – we shifted em to The Long Valley an Liam's eyes nearly fell outa his head when he saw what was comin in the door to him.

An this mutterin started up.

"I'm glad you're here to take the strain off me," mutturs Dec. "There can be too much of a good thing."

"Crippled for life!" Liam behind the hand.

"Have you ever tried to do it with a seven-and-a-half foot basketball player with a foot-long erection? No?" Mutterin behind a clenched smile. "Have you ever tried to do it with a half-dozen seven-and-a-half foot basketball players all with foot-long erections? No? I thought not."

The Dutch were buyin drinks all round.

"But I exaggerate – there probably aren't more than three of them gay and two in it for the craic and the erections might only be eight inches."

"Jay, I don't know if I could handle one a these feens –"

"Easy – the usual method – start at the top and work down –"

"Me only claim to fame in this field is a bunch a Chinese here for the Filum Festival –"

"Chinese!" Dec looked at Liam pityinly. He held up a hand with the thumb an forefinger about an inch apart. "God help us! But you know what they say about the blacks – and it's all true – I'm going for the two black guys – first."

Next thing Tizzy an Mike arrive – an Tizzy rivets his eyes on one blond guy the spit a his RTE Bosco an twas love at first sight. It took his mind right off his criminal status.

An they're all called things like Bim an Bas an Jos an Joos an Pim an Bram an Wim an Wham – but they keep shoutin "Hey Yogi!" so the lads start callin em all Yogi to simplify things – like Rock Hudson y'know – all the blondes Steve an all the brunettes Bruce. Or vice versa. An the funny thing is they all answered to this Yogi name no problem. An at some point The Bonny Boy arrives in civvies. "How's it goin, lads?" with a tight little smile of amusement at the sight a the Yogis but othurwise lookin like death warmed up.

So out with us to hit the Jazz an Blues Trail – the *free* Jazz Trail, that is – the pubs with no entrance charges – an somewhere between Hourihan's an –

Oh, hang on now – I'll havta look at me Guinness Action Map to refresh me memory about this (we'd a great night – we don't remembur a thing) –

An let you turn the pages for me –

Somewhere between Hourihan's Detonators – hang on a minute – yeah, *biting blues and all-action jump-an-jive* an Elroy's Honkin Hepcats – *a trail-blazing outfit that tears audiences apart* – they start tryin to explain to the Yogis that this is a stag-night for Liam. An the Yogis are perplexed. An instead a just tellin em simply that Liam is gettin married those prize-airheads start sayin "No women! No women!" an puttin their elbows up to the sides a their heads an wavin their hands around like stags' antlurs an yeh could see the poor foreignurs thinkin "What the *fuck* are they on about?" But they're good sports an they start stickin their elbows up to their heads too to humour us an sayin "No women! No women!" – an they have a kinda dead serious way a bein funny that kills me.

An somewhere between Nestor's Spice – hold it – *funk with a sharp, hot, biting taste* an The Rob Roy's Harmonious Wail – eh, can't find that one – light dawns on the Yogis an they click that Liam is gettin married an they're goin "Ah, yah, yah, no women!" An "Hail good!" an "Good so!" Because it all makes sense to them now. They think. Poor fuckurs.

An they start sayin somethin like *"have-a-lick"* which mighta meant stag-night or weddin or somethin in Dutch but it meant only the one thing to me boyos an they go on red alert. An actually the Yogis are goin *"lick-hur"* all the time anyway – tis *"lick-hur"* at every turn. Like when they like somethin.

So on we go with our pub crawl an the Yogis payin all the way, amazin the jazz freaks with our antlurs an our "No women! No women!" an Liam an Tizzy forget to worry an think they've died an gone to Heaven an –

An they've forgotten the performance at the Club.

Dec nearly has a stroke. Mandy L'Amour'll be dug outa him. So they race off high as kites goin *"danti-dan, danti-dan!"* like young fellas playin cowboys an the Yogis thinkin this is all part of an Irish stag-night but a bit shy about goin *"danti-dan"* too. Antlurs are more their thing. More dignified like.

We get there an Mothur's on a short fuse in his military jacket with the costume ready for Dec – a longish skirt with a leather belt an boots an a check shirt an a red scarf for round his neck. An right onta the stage with them without let or pause as the Golden Couple with their strangled baritone an daft soprano an Dec sang it so as yeh couldn't understand a flamin word an that was a scream an kinda amazin. With Denis elocutin very pound-note-ish – all the rolled Rs an all:

Aaaaaaah! Sweet mystery of life at last I've found thee!
Aaaaaaah! At last I know the secret of it all!
Aaaaaaaaaaah! The longing seeking striving waiting yearning!
The idle hopes the joy the burning tears that fall!
Aaaaaaaaaaaaaaaaaah!

An in the middle there's a big stretch a syrupy music where the two of em threw shapes around the stage an went inta really camp clinches an they managed to make all the poses look so unnatural twas unreal. An then approachin the finishin-line with a kinda lollopin rhythm like a heavy horse canterin along:

Fooooooooor tis love and love alone the world is seeking
Aaaaaaaand tis love and love alone I waited for . . .

With everyone goin "Dowtchaa, Regina!" an "G'wan,
girel!"

An Dec tried for the high last note an got it:

For tis love that rules for-ev-er moooooooooore!

Laugh comin home on the bus! We were drinkin our
tears! Then Mothur comes down kinda cock-a-the-walk –
still in his military jacket – an Mike starts givin him all these
real langurous looks an runnin his fingurs ovur the lines on
his face. So Mothur moves inta a clinch that leaves his stage
efforts standin – an Mike slides like an automatic child-lock
into the straddle-on-a-chair position – maybe they *always*
did it on a chair. Second honeymoon. But the lads are scared
shitless a the Yogis gettin the wind up. If that happens
they're fucked. Or not fucked.

An Mandy L'Amour is in full spate backstage givin a last-
minute pep-talk an he has his work cut out for him because
they're a right bunch a wasturs with outsize egos an they
have that witty bitchy thing to perfection or think they have,
an at least one of um is drunk an has to be slapped around
the face by Mandy to sobur him up. An it turns out that
while the cast were down in Dan Lowry's for a pre-
performance drink one of em met a fella an fell in love and
didn't come back –

An Mandy is fit to be tied but you'd only know it from a
tightenin of the mouth because Mandy is nothin if not a
professional an he knows if he can hold em togethur they'll
probably go out there an pull it off an be brilliant. That's
how it always goes.

Denis an Mike are blind with passion by this time –

Denis is still in the chair but Mike is climbin all ovur him an he sure ain't thinkin rhubarb.

The Yogis don't seem to have noticed this carry-on yet.

An they're goin *"hotfa dumma!"* an *"preema!"*

An *"gi'us-a-lick!"* Red alert.

Next thing Tizzy is tryin to explain to his guy what Ghoul Lash means – sayin no, it's not Hungarian, tis Irish an lash means a sexy girl – like "she's a lash" – an the Yogi is smilin away but tis obvious he's all at sea because what foreignur would undurstand Tizzy's accent anyway? An Tizzy addles the poor buggur even more by tellin him that a lash can mean a belt too –

"A belt?" says yur man makin a tyin-the-belt movement with his free hand.

An I can give yeh Tizzy's answer verbatim (not) omittin the poor Yogi's struggles to hook onta any kinda meanin in it – he's a man ovurboard at this point an goin down fast –

So Tizzy goes: "Aahh no! Not a belt like round yur waist like, but like a blow like – no, not a blow like when yeh blow somethin like – or like when yeh blow someone's cock like – cock like – ah no, not a cock like in the farmyard like but like yur dick like – but not a dick like a Private Eye like – ah no, not an eye like the eye in yur head like – yur head like – but not head like when yeh're givin a blow-job like –"

Fuckin hell, twas chronic. Yeh shoulda been there.

An the misfortunate Yogi is so fuckin addled by this time he keeps confusin French with English an sayin "Comment?" an Tizzy thinks he's sayin "Come on" an thinks he's made an he thinks he wants him to go outside or down to the jacks an I hear him sayin: "Latur" all coy. So tis "Comment?" "Latur!" "Comment?" "Latur!" an on they go like that.

Jesus.

An I turn away with me own brain addled from this only to see Mike's black leathur Bad pants comin down – *Jesus* – surely they can't be goin to fuck each othur right then an there – *what* – so I spin away from that only to hear Tizzy, aftur failin massively to explain what a lash means, headin inta explainin what "the lash with the gash" means. This is too much for flesh an blood to stand so I spin outa hearin range.

In time to see Liam prisin Mike away from Denis by dint a actually placin his foot against Denis's thigh an usin it as a levur. A thing I nevur seen before or since.

Holy Jesus.

But the Yogis are distracted anyway – *Ghoul Lash* is on. A Historic Drama set in the early eighties.

Entur Ghost in S-an-M gear an begins decoratin the Grand Parade loo for Hallowe'en: "*Oh woe is me condemned to trawl eternally!* Alas, if a spirit does not trawl in life, it is condemned to do so aftur death. Doo-oomed to wander around the loo-oos and witness trade it cannot have . . . oooooohhh!"

Me?

I don't think so.

"But, lo! Here comes a Chorus of the Unemployed and the redeeming Social Value of the play . . ."

Entur Chickun Chorus led by Social Value – singin about the terrible blow to the economy caused by the closin down a most a the Public Loos in Cork – to the tune a Connie's *Heartbreak Hotel* would yeh believe –

Oh since they closed the loos down
We have no place to dwell

We're trawlin in the dole queues
An not doin very well
Gi'us our night-job back
Gi'us our night-job
Gi'us our job back or we'll die!"
An what the Yogis are makin a this is anybody's guess.

So we're all highly relieved when we're back on the Free Jazz Trail.

"No women! No women!"

"Danti-dan! Danti-dan!"

"Gi'us-a-lick!"

An the antlurs wavin.

So we're in the Grande Parade Streets bar with US blues legend Henry "Swampman" Gray and the Side Track Band –

Turn the page –

Turn me Guinness Action page –

Thanks.

The Side Track Bank – *steamy, spine-tinglin boogie and blues* – an we're boogie-in fit to tingle an armadillo's spine (an fuck-it, I *am* goin back to that jungle aftur all) an Mike's spinnin an singin like he's gone to heaven an joined the Baptist Choir there but for Denis an Dec tis time to do a bit a serious drinkin.

Dec is holdin forth, pitchin the voice against Henry "Swampman" Gray: "Well, I *have* heard Maynooth is runnin a course on how to sue your parish priest for sexual abuse – there's a money-back guarantee – I'm thinking of taking it. If nothing else, what bettur place than our great theological centre to pick up some tips – you never know what might turn a parish priest on – we haven't read *Forbidden Fruit* yet and that would only inform us about bishops anyway – erect nipples I gather can go a long way."

An a couple a the Yogis start grinnin ear-to-ear at this an Mothur realises that their English must be *really* good so next thing he's off at a gallop an I shuttle between the dance-floor an the table hearin things like: "Oh, *Basic Instinct*! My dear! A film to make Muslim Fundamentalism seem perhaps a good idea after all!" An "I would consider myself a post-modernist feminist – a Camille Paglia woman, daahling – though I draw the line at considering *Madonna* and Princess *Di* as later-day goddesses – but *certainly* testosterone is the most creative cultural force in history –" An "The odd thing is – that horn-thing you're all doing – the Celtic Cernunnos, Lord of the Animals, is *stag*-horned –" An "Homosexuality? Oh it's not *natural*, daahling – but neither is French cuisine –"

Oh, he was away.

He Felt Like Chickun Tonight.

An the aura gatherin strength by the minute. Then he gets inta talkin about Ages a Consent an Tizzy an Liam are called ovur an it turns out the age a consent in Holland is *twelve* – an twenty othur European countries with an Age of Consent undur fifteen – an this creates a grand splash with –

"There now, Tizzy!"

"Yeh should emigrate, Tizzy!"

"We all should emigrate!"

"Oh, no need, daahlings!" goes Denis. "We're all Europeans now you know – we shall bring the mountain to Mohomed in due time." Whatevur that meant.

An the misfortunate Scout Collection-box on the table bein mistaken for an ashtray. Jesus, I knew how it felt. Shades a me own short career as ashes in an urun when I was hauled through every pub in Cork. An suddenly me mouth is full a ashes again. But I shake the feelin off.

So sometime latur we're in The Black Bush with President – *acid jazz and funk* – groovin an boogie-in our way through *razor-sharp sessions with frontman Cecil and his sensational crew* – *"gi'us-a-lick!"* – an next thing Dec is teachin the Yogis "a quid a man an back to my house" an they're goin *"vroom-vroom"* to each othur (a thing they're much given to) an Dec is explainin that it's an Irish stag-night custom an it means everyone should put a couple a pounds in the collection-can an then they'd be invited back to the bridegroom's house latur. So they caught on real quick an started fishin around for pound coins all cheerful, an stickin them in the can. *"Have-a-lick –"*

An in comes Mad Mary bra-less in his black leathur punk gear with his nose-rings an ear-rings an his own black hair spiked an streaked red an the lads take one look at him an to a man they shout "No women! No women!" an Mary gets thrown out bodily inta the street by Liam an The Bonny Boy. The Yogis go *"vroom-vroom"* an Mothur explains that Mary is the bride an that it's very bad luck to have hur there on a stag-night.

So the Yogis twig an go "Aaah, the bride – but she's a punk!" an then tis "Yah, yah – no women! No women!" to us an *"have-a-lick"* to each othur.

An the lads all waitin with their tongues hangin out –

At this point The Bonny Boy has to get the last bus home. So we're in Mojo's, the bikurs' pub, in the dark an the smoke, rubbin shouldurs so to speak with a bunch a people that look like a mixture a extras from *Mad Max* an *Midnight Cowboy* – batin our way through leathur an hair an endin up with joints in our hands that we didn't know how they got there – an thankin God Tizzy was safely shackled to his

Bosco look-alike an wasn't goin to be picked up by any a them because we'd all be out to the Regional (hospital like – the Hilton in Wilton) or down to the Bridewell again tomorrow. So we're mesmerised by TW Henderson an his Bigtime blues band from Louisiana – *a major Festival attraction* – an *big's* the operative word – these fuckin *humungus* long-haired men with these *massive* guts on em an yeh couldn't help but be fascinated wonderin how in Jesus' name yeh could evur get at their dicks – given the opportunity like. An they sound fuckin terrific so we stay up front undur the ovurhang a their bellies. I was feelin high as a kite an I figured, not for the first time, dead an all as I was, I was still a passive smokur. An the nasty smell a ash that'd followed me all day was blocked out by the sweet smell a hash an all me troubles seemed a bone-fire away.

Next thing Tizzy comes batin his way down from the bar all flustered an joins our boppin group.

"Whasupitcha, girel?" screams Liam at him.

An Tizzy shouts in Liam's ear "I'm aftur scorin with yur man!"

So they crowd round all agog at this – there's hope for all yet like – an shove their heads in close to Tizzy's so we're like a rugby scrum for all the world. Grand an macho like. I'm right in the middle. I ain't got no butt to shove in the air like.

"Where?" yells Liam. "Out on the street?"

"No!" goes Tizzy. "I told him latur! I don't wanta rush it like."

"Ya lucky buggur!" goes Liam an he turns to the expert. "Mothur? D'yeh think any a the rest of um are gay?"

"Oh, I'm quite sure they'd all help us out if we were busy!"

"God, I dunno –"

"Children, don't fret! I've yet to find a man who wouldn't bend ovur given certain conditions."

"What did yur man actually say to you, Tizzy?" Dec wanted to know. "Just so we know what to expect."

"Well," says Tizzy blushin. "He just pointed at himself an said 'fuckur'."

"Whaaaaaa!"

An they fell around laughin, bangin inta each othur like skittles an sloppin drinks all ovur the shop because they'd relaxed the scrum-hold an the Yogis were boppin against their bums.

"Seems a mite direct," said Denis when they'd formed the scrum again tightur than before.

"Are you *sure*?" says Liam. "Are you *sure* that's what he said? *Fuckur?* Just like that?"

"I am," says Tiz, hurt at bein doubted.

"You musta got it wrong!"

"What kind of a fool d'yeh think I am?" goes Tiz. "He said it! What's more he kept *on* sayin it an pointin at himself an then pointin at me. An *I* repeated it an he nodded like mad!"

"Heavens!" says Dec. "How crude – but what can one expect from a pagan country."

"It's Protestant, Declan," says Denis.

"Same thing," says Dec.

An I thought they'd lock horns – antlurs – then an there in the scrum but Mothur was feelin generous an Ovur the Rainbow with his arm around Heal-the-World an he was moylow anyway so when he opened his mouth – to answur we thought – this is what came out:

"There was a young vicar of Birmingham
Who –
No, no – yes –
There was a young vicar of Birmingham
Who buggered young boys while confirmin em –"
"Vicars don't confirm, Denis," said Dec.
"Oh, you're quite right –"
"An old bishop?"
"Right: this is the Protestant tradition now, children –
listen attentively –
There was a old bishop of Birmingham
Who buggered young boys while confirmin em –
As they – as they – eh – oh blast – what rhymes with
'confirmin em'? Oh *bugger*!"

"Hey! Yogi!" go the Yogis an start slappin our bums so we
break up the scrum an go back to boppin.

An somewhere along the line I hear one a the Yogis callin
across to Tizzy's fancy – *"Fuckur! Fuckur!"* An it dawns on
me that's his *name*. The fuckur's *called* "Fuckur" – an I've no
one to share the joke with, an that's agony an gives me a
moment's loneliness.

But just then I get a little ghost-gift. They play Rory
Gallagher's *Ghost Blues* – Rory bein a Corkman like. The
perennial Rory Gallagher TW Henderson calls him – an
Denis tells us that means lastin a long time like or recurrin
all the time.

Rory an me, both.

I thought: I'm perennial an this *Ghost Blues* is for me.

An I was dead pleased at this.

So a quid a man an back to my house.

An the place didn't look half bad. They'd brought in gas-

219

lamps an Supersurs an bits a furniture borrowed from Florrie an the single mothur next door an Mary had curtains an nets up an a bit a carpet on the floor.

Anyway the Yogis were all *wasted* with the drink so they wouldn't a noticed anythin odd in any case.

The remains a our Hallowe'en candles an pumpkins were lightin an the black condom balloons bravely flyin again. An all the bridal gear belongin to Mary's sistur – includin the monkey-suits for groom an best man – was strewn right left an centur –

Jesus, what the fuck had sent yur wan off inta orbit like that leavin all this stuff behind? She coulda hocked it or whatevur. A row with Connie, Liam'd said . . . yeah.

"There was an old bishop of Birmingham," goes Mother, *"Who buggered young boys while confirmin em As he knelt on the hassock –* oh dear – hassock –"

"Hassock – cassock," said Liam.

"Oh, *thank* you, Liam! Yes – *as he knelt on the hassock –* no – " An he broke off.

An there, like two inches from his face, nose to nose, is this peculiar-lookin young fella in an outsize fawny jumpur with his shouldurs stooped like an ould fella's an his hand on his hip. An he starts holdin forth. "Nine to five! I ask yeh! An me here longur than any a them! Well, I went down to the office an I said to hur sez I: *I'm* not doin weekend work whatevur you thinks – an me here longur than any a them? I ask yeh! *You* put me down for Tuesday late – an me here longur than any a them! I mean to say –"

"Good Heavens!" said Mother amused. "This must be one of Liz's young friends. He seems to have a problem of sorts."

"You might call it that," goes Dec furious. An he turns on Liz who's comin in from the kitchen. "*Well!* You nevur lost it, Liz! I don't understand how you can *do* this! You did the same for the funeral! We're tryin to run a *wedding* for God's sake –"

"I'm sorry!" goes Liz shamefaced, haulin the kid outa Mothur's personal space an he churnin on with his nine to five I ask yeh. "I forgot it'd been arranged –"

"For God's sake! Typical!"

"Y'see, his parents wouldn't take him for Hallowe'en –"

"Couldn't you have made an excuse?"

"He'd a been very disappointed –"

"Well!"

Liz if yeh remembur does a bit a part-time work at the Home for retarded kids. Remembur *One Flew Ovur* at me funeral? Eatin handfuls a me ashes?

OK – this one was the Cuckoo's Nest.

"He seems to have a problem about nine to five," said Mothur. "What –?"

"Oh, it's just that he thinks he's one of us below – one of the staff y'see –"

"Aaahh, shu' God help him!" goes Liam.

An yur man churnin on like a broken record. "Nine to five! I ask yeh! Did yeh hear the rumour? They're closin the whole unit. An me here longur than any a them! I ask yeh –"

"Where's yur Male Covur, Liz?" goes Liam, razzin hur.

An this is always a great bit a craic – about the Male Covur – the fella the women are supposed to have for support in case the kids get violent – when I say "kids" now I mean some of em are adults actually – physically – like Nine-to-Five who was sidlin up to Mothur again.

"Did yeh hear the news?" 007.

"No," says Mothur.

"About Dracula?"

"No – do tell me –" All interest. Like Prince Charles is just goin to confide in him about Camilla Whatsit's favourite brand a bloomurs.

An there's a heavy knock on the door –

They all freeze.

An then Mary goes: "Tis aall right! Tis only de Hoodies!"

The Hoodies bein a gang a young fellas in sweat-shirts with hoods given to terrorisin the neighbourhood.

But twas Lethil Weapon an Fawlty Towurs. What the fuck did they want? At such a time a night? Tizzy?

Everybody freaks – snappin the joints away from the Yogis. But Mothur has the whole wo-orld in his hand. There's no stoppin him. He's flyin a kite. "Come *in*, come *in*, my *dear* Sergeant! Oh, I *do* hope you're off duty and can join us in a celebratory drink!" He puts his arm around Liam. "Our dear Liam is getting married in the morning! I'm afraid you've crashed on the tail-end of our stag-night!"

An Lethil an Fawlty gawk around an see all the basketball playurs an the wind is taken outa their sails – whatevur they're aftur.

Lethil rocks from foot to foot. "We had a call frrom one of yourr neighbourrs herre who thought someone had brroken into his house – we knew of courrse twas you –"

"*Such* a stroke of luck for a young couple! To get a house so quickly! You know how it is these days, Sergeant."

Lethil nods the head – glad not to have to press it. "Well, Mr Harrte," in his heavy way an he sniffs at the air like a bloodhound. "We won't disturrb ye furrtherr. But we wanted to see ye about anotherr matterr and I'm verry glad now that you yourrself arre herre – I hope you can ensurre that the lad'll be at the courrt in the morrning – we hurried the prrocess up as much as we could forr you and twould be an embarrassment to us if he didn't turrn up –" An he stops. "But the wedding's on, you say?"

"Oh ye-es, Sergeant!" goes Mothur all airy-fairy. "But – not to worry! We'll put the wedding time back a little and take in the court-case on our way!"

An Lethil looks a bit startled.

"I'm sure it won't delay us very much," goes Mothur more or less pressin Lethil inta a chair and pressin a glass inta his hand.

"I don't know about that at all, Mr Harrte –" An he raises his nose an starts sniffin again –

Then he swings his bulk around an spots Liz settin up one a them watur incense-burnurs right behind his chair.

"Oh, our Liz is *so* New Age!" goes Mothur gaily. "Herbal remedies! Aromatherapy! Reflexology! The lot!"

An Nine-to-Five is shoved back into the room reekin a Spiritual Sky Cannabis – perfume that is – that someone has lobbed ovur him an he obliges by hangin ovur Lethil all agog at the uniform. "Garda? Garda Patrol? Did yeh hear the news about Dracula?"

Mothur is on a roll.

"Sergeant, do tell me," says he settlin down on a chair overright Lethil. "How does it affect a man of *your* intelligence and experience to be forced to participate in this kind of witchhunt?"

"Witchhunt?" goes Lethil, as astonished as a man could evur be.

223

"Garda? Garda Patrol? Did yeh hear the rumour?"

"I know, of course, that as a servant of the state you must do your duty – but you must feel the indignity of it very *keenly.*"

"Indignity?" goes Lethil amazed.

"Garda? Did yeh hear the rumour? Taxes – I ask yeh!"

"Oh, Sergeant, I do understand – you must be discreet – and I respect that – but I *know* how you must feel. Alas, we are still in the Dark Ages! Our guests have just been telling us that the legal age of consent in civilised countries – such as Holland for example – is *twelve*! And in some twenty other countries between twelve and fifteen. Heavens, Sergeant, it is so ludicrous – but I daresay there are those who despite our recent disclosures of incest and brutality would have the effrontery to call a country with the most enlightened and rational laws in Europe barbaric!"

"Uh –" goes the Sergeant lookin bewildered at this ferocious spiel. An takes a slug outa his drink. Then he frowns an opens the mouth to say somethin –

"I ask yeh – the whole unit – Tuesdays late –"

"Sergeant, *when* you consider that homosexuality itself aroused the same kind of witchhunt hysteria in the *very* recent past! But such is progress – and we can be proud, I suppose, of our non-discriminatory seventeen years –"

"Well –" goes the Sergeant hesitatin –

"Nine to five, she gave them!" Nine-to-Five was off at a gallop. "An me here longur than any a them! An I went down to the office an I said to hur sez I: if *you* thinks *I'm* going to work late on Tuesdays – an me here longur than any a them – nine to five! Did yeh evur hear the like?"

In Lethil's face.

"I never did," goes Lethil.

"Liiiz!" calls Mothur.

"Nine to five! she gave me. *I'm* not workin nine to five! I'm goin down to the office now an I'm goin to tell hur. An me here longur than any a them – I mean to say! Why should *I* work nights? Why should I –"

"Liiiz!"

An Liz comes trit-trottin in.

"Did yeh hear the rumour? They're closin down the whole unit. I ask yeh! An me here since eighty-two –"

"Liz, forgive me, but if you could remove your young friend for a moment – I'm discussing a matter of the *utmost* importance with Sergeant O'Sullivan –"

"The whole unit! Shur *I've* been here longur than you – *excuse* me now – I came in eighty-seven –"

An Liz hauls Nine-to-Five away. "C'man – there's Coke in the kitchen –"

"Who's the young fella?" asks Lethil.

"Oh Sergeant, he's one of those *unfortunate* youngsters from the Home – apparently he thinks he's one of the staff there – our Liz is *so* good – but *Sergeant* – " an he halts with the hand to the head as if a thought just struck him and how *could* he be so stupid an so on, "You *have* met Detective-Superintendent Harry Haakman?"

Who?

"No, I haven't," goes Lethil.

"From Holland?"

Where else?

Tis a wondur he didn't call him Yogi Fuckman altogethur.

"No, I can't say I have now," shiftin his bulk around an fixin a tryin-to-remembur face on him.

225

"Rest assured – you shall – I shall personally introduce you to him – you *do* know of him?"

"E-eh –" goes Lethil.

"*Excuse* me now! *I* came in eighty-two – nine to five –"

"Oh – perhaps I've been indiscreet – those discussions are unofficial as yet –" An Mothur goes inta all this pantomimin of being discreet an *what-a-blundur-I've-made an I-shouldn't-have-mentioned-it* an finally *but-I-know-I-can-trust-you* – "Sergeant, he told me he's here to discuss reform of our *antiquated* system – just came by Cork on his way to Dublin –"

Oh yeah? What the fuck for?

"*Excuse* me now – *I've* been here since eighty-four – I ask yeh!"

"Took in a little jazz – *fervent* jazz fan – plays saxophone himself – like Bill Clinton – largely involved in the drug scene – he will be discussing that too – you know the Dutch have some very progressive experimental programmes in operation –"

Lethil did know – with drugs he was on home ground – his face cleared at last an he opened his mouth – an snapped it shut again – Nine-to-Five was viewin his tonsils –

"C'mere – did yeh hear the news?" 007, like.

"Eh – no," goes Lethil.

"About Dracula?"

"Eh – what about him?" goes Lethil.

"He's dead." Very confidential.

"Oh is he now?"

"Didn't they tell the Garda Patrol?" Suspicious like.

"Well, they might have told them down at the Bridewell. Was it an accident?"

"Liz killed him."

"Oh did she now?"

"Didn't yeh hear that?" A bit worried now.

"Well, maybe I was off duty at the time. How did she do that?"

"An injection."

"An injection? I thought it should be a stake – a stake thrrough the hearrt –" An he spots Liz behind makin frantic signs to him to shut up. "Or an injection – yes, that'll do it too."

An Liz hauls Nine-to-Five away. "C'man – there's Coke in the kitchen –"

"*Excuse* me now – she can feck off now with hur nine to five – taxes – they're takin taxes now – she'd be bettur off on the dole –"

"Sergeant – it's the big thing in Dublin now, you know – at Headquarters – it's only a matter of time –" says Mothur.

"Oh, what is, Mrr Harrte? I'm afrraid I'm afterr losin you – the lad therre –"

"Radical reform – keep your ear to the ground, Sergeant – that's the way to advancement –"

Lethil looked canny at this point. The discussion was tunin in to his wavelength. "Well, Mrr Harrte, I'd like to meet this Detective –"

"Haakman. Harry Haakman. A *charming* man. Rest assured, rest assured – *you* shall meet him – I shall personally see to it – *you* would find it fascinating to talk shop with him. Oh yes, radical reform, Sergeant. Meanwhile we must struggle through the system as it stands – but I'm sure justice will prevail – after all, as you realise, our poor Tizzy can hardly be classified as a criminal!" With an airy laugh. "And doesn't Irish hypocrisy *madden* you, Sergeant?"

Lethil tried to rally. "Well, now, Mrr Harrte, there are cerrtain prractices –"

"Nine to five I ask yeh – *excuse* me now – *I* came in eighty-five – I told hur – you'd be bettur off on the dole I ask yeh –"

"Yes, *indeed*, we all have our peccadillos – *even* the Fathurs of our Nation – *the names that stilled our childish play* etcetera –"

"Oh, you'd be rreferrring to Rrogerr Casement therre, Mrr Harrte –"

"Casement? Oh but you are absolutely right, Sergeant! But actually it wasn't *Casement* I had in mind . . ."

Lethil cocked an eye. "Oh, is that so –" An he waited, interested now.

"I *told* hur! An me here longur than any a them!"

Mothur put the head back an opened the mouth an twas clear he was goin to proclaim –

Oh Jesus protect us – surely not the old bishop a Birmingham?

Little lad of the tricks –
Raise your comely head
Till I kiss your mouth –"

"Eh, Mrr Harrte," goes Lethil shiftin about uneasily. "I don't think it's apprroprriate forr me to –"

"There is a fragrance in your kiss
That I have not found yet
In the kisses of women
Or in the honey of their bodies –
an he looked slyly at Lethil. "Who would you say wrote that, Sergeant?"

"He'd be bettur off on the dole –"

Lethil considered, risin to the challenge. "Oscurr Wilde, I would say, Mrr Harrte."

"No, Sergeant – Pádraig Pearse – translated from the Irish, you know –"

"Brothur? Did yeh hear the rumour? Would yeh say tis true? They're takin taxes from us now – shur we won't have a bit goin home – we'd be bettur on the dole –"

Mothur carried on regardless.

"Lad of the grey eyes
That flush in thy cheek
Would be white with dread of me
Could you read my secrets –"

An he looks to make sure that Lethil is suitably gobsmacked. Which he is. "Oh yes, oh yes, that was his 'renunciation' I'm afraid, dear Sergeant – you do know the poem?"

"'Renunciation'? Oh yes, indeed, Mrr Harrte – shurr twas always on the school currriculum in my day – I suppose it still is."

"Oh, perhaps you might refresh my memory with a line or two?"

No bettur man.

"I'm goin to sign on altogethur – shur aftur tax we misewell be on the dole – I ask yeh! Nine to five she gave them – she misewell be on the dole –"

"Carry on Sergeant."

Lethil planted the feet an straightened the back the bettur to give vent:

"Naked I saw thee
O beauty of beauty – oh – eh –"

He changed tack.

"I tasted thy mouth,
O sweetness of sweetness – eh –urm – well –"
An he blushed. "Well, the last few verrses –
"I blinded my eyes,
And I closed my earrs
I harrdened my hearrt
And I smotherred my desirre.
I have turrned my face
To this rroad beforre me,
To the deed that I see
And the death I shall die."
"He'd be bettur off on the dole –"

"Ah, *beautifully* rendered, Sergeant – you elicit the *heroic* tone so well – ah, yes, *the delirium of the brave* as Yeats said – he had the death-wish – and no wonder – and how astute of you, Sergeant, to bring in the comparison with Wilde – to think of *poor* Oscar – two years hard labour – an experience which killed him essentially – for no more than writing the *equivalent* of that poem – he was largely convicted on the evidence of some letters – heavens! And Pearse! Well, perhaps you *have* to write the National Proclamation of Independence for one's proclivities to be overlooked – or perhaps it doesn't matter *what* you do if you can do it in Gaelic –"

An Lethil swayin the head in a bewildered way that reminded me of nothin so much as one of them bulls in the bull-ring when the matador has worn em out an the toreadors, isn't it, stick those things in their necks.

An then the final stroke – the final plunge a the sword inta the neck that sevurs the spinal cord: "In any case, in these relatively enlightened days," an somethin about *altar* an *morays* that I didn't catch, "Oscar is soon to be granted a posthumous pardon – another drink, Sergeant?"

But Lethil'd had enough.

Fawlty was AWOL an Lethil couldn't figure out for the life of him where he'd got to. An thought he musta walked down to the Mayfield station for some unknown reason. So he left, takin Liz an Nine-to-Five with him in the Squad Car, promising Mothur he'd get them a taxi an make sure they got back to Douglas safely – an he to Nine-to-Five: "We'll check the strreets now and make surre Liz did a good job and therre's no sign of that blaggarrd Drracula –"

So, with the Law gone, from then on out there was some fierce shenanigans. I was the only one who wasn't outa his skull with drink so I remembur it all – but me, I'm takin the Fifth on it –

I'm goin to draw a veil, as they say, ovur the rest a that night – not just *ff* crudely like – but draw a veil –

Yeah, yeah, I know yeh'd prefer the naked truth –

But a veil, I think, is in ordur – for a stag like. I mean that's traditional, isn't it? No one evur gets to know what the fuck the bridegroom gets up to on a stag.

One thing though – some time durin the night I drifted inta the bathroom an found Fawlty tied to the hot-an-cold taps with his own handcuffs – butt-naked now in the empty bath on his back – with his arms back behind his head an an eye-catchin display a biceps an triceps an his uniform jacket folded up an stuffed between his head an the taps. Every comfort provided. His eyes were closed. In despair I think.

There were some candles set up on top a the loo an I was peerin at his dick checkin it out for size an any forensic evidence when he opened his eyes an went "Aaaaargh!" an

231

there was this shadow against the wall daggin away with a knife – Cliona doin *Psycho* in one a Mary's housecoats. Twas enough to put the heart across yeh.

Next twould be a crowbar an *Misury.*

But it wasn't – twas Mad Mary with a fistful a mugs an a packet a fig-rolls.

An the two settle down on the edge a the bath with Cliona shovin bits a biscuit inta Fawlty's mouth an Mary givin him sips a tea like monsoon-showurs that go streamin down his naked chest – an playin with his dick at the same time pretending tis the gear-stick of a Ferrari.

An Fawlty is goin: "You've gone farr enough now, girrls – I must ask you to let me go." With the fresh face a him flamin. Tis a wondur he didn't ask em to desist or move along now.

But they hadn't gone farr enough for their likin – nowhere near – an Fawlty an his gear-levur still had one helluva rough ride ahead.

Well, twould be a quare stag-night that didn't leave *somebody* tied up butt-naked.

Mindya, tisn't usually yur local bluebottle.

So let me draw a veil ovur the rest a the proceedins –

What? Oh, Tizzy an Fuckur? Oh –they got their wires crossed to the point a carnal knowledge – yeah, sure – aftur Tizzy got Fuckur onta a mattress upstairs an Fuckur outa his skull, with his English desertin him completely, gigglin an cooperatin some a the time an then puttin up a bit a resistance sayin somethin like *"neat doin"* an Tiz thinkin he's tryin to say "well done" – but – judgin from body language – it *musta* meant "stop doin that." So they were goin nowhere fast till yur man started mumblin this "lick-hur,

232

lick-hur" thing – an Tizzy had his i-zip down pronto an was lickin away for dear life.

Yeah, Tizzy waded in where anjuls fear to tread an it went somethin like this – pardon my Dutch:

"Neat doin! Neat doin!" An he tries to stop Tizzy.

"But yeh *said* lick hur!" An poor Tizzy gettin upset an not knowin if he's comin or goin. "*What* d'yeh want? D'yeh want to fuck? Yeh *said* 'fuckur'!"

"Yah, yah – Fuckur – Fuckur –" An he slappin himself on the chest.

"G'wan so –"

An at some point yur man musta thought "What the hell!" if he thought anythin at all – I suppose like Connie he didn't know what to do with it – but Tizzy had a few ideas an none of um involved lettur-boxes.

An Tiz goin "I've only de wan ball" which I think wasn't necessary because yur man was seein double anyway.

Twould make yeh think twice about the EU.

Or maybe not . . .

Anyway – let me draw the veil an just tell yeh that the comin an goin was unreal – the landin upstairs was like a train station – an the Yogis blundurin about in their T-shirts an sugar-all else goin "*Danti-dan!* No women! No women! *Gi'us-a-lick!*" the whole fuckin night –

Well . . .

They thought an Irish stag-night was somethin else. I'm tellin ya, as Garth would say . . .

CHAPTER SEVEN

Private Tony's fingurs were white and wrinkled as he clutched his M16. This monsoon was a buggur. The instant downpour had made a mudslide of the ground undurfoot and his body was chilled to bone. The only good thing was it drowned the rotten smell of dead vegetation and stagnant pools – an his own unwashed body.

He kept close to the Major.

He glanced down at his sodden jungle boots and when he looked up again he was alone. Drippin vegetation swayed around him and ovur his head.

"Major? Major? Major sur?"

His heart hammered against his ribs.

But then the swaying vegetation ahead of him parted an he gasped in relief –

"Major –"

But it was the Faceless Enemy. Who bared his teeth (how could he if he was faceless?) and Private Tony, his skin tinglin with shock, and hampered with all that equipment, swung his rifle in that faceless face and –

It jammed – *it jammed* and in nightmare slow motion he watched the Enemy raise his AK47 –

"Boy!"

He felt a hand on his shouldur an with a fierce start came to himself.

"Christ, Private! How many times have I told you to keep close behind me!"

"The – the enemy, sur – he was right there –"

"There's no one there, Private – you're hallucinating –" The Major looked at Private Tony keenly. "You're exhausted, boy – and no wonder – pity I can't help you with some of that equipment – but if I'm to be pointman I've gotta have my hands free –"

"I know, sur –"

"I'm sorry you had to spend the night with your hand on the detonator for the Claymore mines and your other hand on your weapon – I know it must have disturbed your sleep – but we can't be too vigilant, boy, if we're to survive –"

"It's just all the equipment, sur –"

"We'll be glad of it if we run into an ambush – with no firepower to back us up – we're on our own, soldier –"

"Yes, sur – I'm fine, sur –"

"You're far from fine, son – I can see that. We've got to rest – but where?"

"Maybe we could go into that tunnel complex, sur."

"What tunnel complex? Where?"

"That one there, sur – that nail I see sticking up through the vegetation is probably connected to a wooden trapdoor leading to a narrow shaft leading to a tunnel complex. Sur."

"Oh – *that* tunnel complex – oh, right, soldier –"

Major O'Hara dug in the vegetation with his M16 and flipped ovur a wooden trapdoor. sur enough it led to a narrow shaft probably leading to a tunnel complex.

"We don't know if it's abandoned, soldier – I'd better check it out – you keep watch –"

"Excuse me for saying, sur, but I think I'd better do that. Your shouldurs are too broad, sur – you might get stuck in the narrow shaft or one a the passages."

"True – and if I encounter a rotting corpse I wouldn't be able to navigate it – but, soldier, if you came up against the Faceless Enemy cornered in the complex – can you deal with that?"

Private Tony wasn't at all sure but he said "Yes, sur."

"Well, you'd better take off all that crap you're festooned with in that case – I'll set up the Pig here and keep watch –"

"Yes, sur!"

So Private Tony stripped to the waist and – armed only with a pistol and flashlight – lowered himself into the shaft.

"Private!"

"Yes, sur?"

The Major clasped his forearm. "Take care, son –"

"Yes, sur."

"If the air gets too foul – come back – I've known men to suffocate –"

"Yes, sur."

"Here – you'd better take this bayonet – between your teeth –"

"Wuhs, fuh."

"Be alert for tethered poisonous snakes –"

Private Tony snaked into the tunnel. This was terrifying. He was no tunnel rat. He had nevur been down a tunnel before. But he knew sharpened punji stakes would threaten his every move. He knew that around any cornur of the zig-zag tunnel he could set off a booby trap that would entomb him or a mine that would blow him to kingdom come – or come upon the Faceless Enemy with AK47 cocked to do likewise.

But the thought of the man he loved spurred him on. This was a chance to show the stuff he was made of.

He shuddered. Turned a cornur and came bang up against a laterite wall. A dead-end – imagining the Faceless Enemy behind with a bamboo spear poised to impale him. He reached the turn-off point he had missed and started to wriggle down a slope – Journey to the Centur of the Earth – passing a foot-square entrance to the right – a flash of the light showed it was an ammo dump – and came up against a blank wall. Had he missed anothur entrance? He was retching against the bayonet. His body was slick with sweat and his heart hammering as hard as it had evur done. He was goin to lose his nerve.

And be dragged kicking and screaming from the tunnel by the Major? *Nevur.* He felt about with his hands. Nothing. Think. Think. Yes. Beneath him. He was lying on a trapdoor. He backed up and used the bayonet to lift the covur – wary as hell. No tethered snake. A short tunnel.

A room. A bed.

A bed.

Journey's End.

Home Sweet Home.

Half an hour latur Major O'Hara was lying on the narrow bed reading some dispatches, while Private Tony pedalled the bicycle-operated generator.

"This was probably a First Aid station, Private. I bet there were some gruesome operations performed here – without the benefit of anaesthetic of course."

"Yes, sur," panted Private Tony. It was torture pedalling the bicycle in the close air.

"Don't overtire yourself, soldier – if it gets too much you could take time out and go and investigate whether there's a kitchen somewhere – should be – you might be able to forage some rations – and there should be a well. I can grab some sleep while you're gone so I won't need the light – in fact, I think I'll take a cat-nap right now – carry on, Private –"

An hour later Private Tony's head was startin to swim. Jesus, the indignity of it if he fell off the bicycle in a faint! The Major was restless and kept waking up so Private Tony kept on pedalling. He found it helped to keep repeating "an armadillo called Pete, an armadillo called Pete" in a kind of a rhythm. Finally he staggered off the bicycle an the light wavered an failed as he fell to his knees racked with a dry retching that shook his whole body.

"Boy? You OK?"

"No, sur, I've had it, sur," gasped Private Tony.

"You've done well, son. I'm proud of you."

A silence.

"Come here, boy –"

Private Tony stretched out on his back on the bed next to Major O'Hara. Every muscle ached but he was in bliss. He had done his bit. The Major was proud of him.

He felt totally spaced out. His muscles slowly relaxed in pure exhaustion. He wriggled closur to the Major's naked torso.

Heaven.

There was something missing –

Oh yes – the heavy metal band –

Well – they'd nearly *fit* down here – but, hang on –

unless he was very much mistaken he could now hear the mournful vocals and liquid guitar of *Rooster* somewhere at a distance along the tunnel net-work – aftur all, *Dirt* was the same a their last album – they should feel right at home –

Got my pills against mosquito death
My buddy's breathin his dyin breath
God, won't you help me see it through –

"Sur?"

"Yes, son?"

"What was that armadillo called again?" He remembered of course but he wanted to hear it.

"Oh – Pete?"

He felt the Major's smile through the dark.

And he felt the Major's hand come down on his privates.

"Do you mind if I do this, soldier?"

"No, sur," gasped Private Tony an his voice sounded strangulated like yur wan's – *leave me breathless* – *show me heaven please* – Covur *me* – *o-o-oh* –

"Sur – can I ask yeh to do something?"

"Uh-huh –"

"Could you – like – *covur* me? I mean lie on me? I want to feel your weight on me –"

"Don't mind if I do, son –"

And then he pressed into the bed with the full weight of the man on top of him and he could feel the Major erect against him even through the fatigues so he knew he could go ahead – with impunity – so he tugged at the Major's belt and tugged his fatigues down over his buttocks – the man was one huge muscle – *I want muscles all ovur his body* – and he felt the massive dick probe between his legs –

"Wait – wait – wait, sur –"

And the Major raised his hips and Private Tony dragged frantically at his own fatigues and pushed them down and off and then the Major was doin the same and they were locked together again – naked – with that beautiful weight crushing him – and – and –

It's now or nevur –

Be mine tonight –

Tomorrow will be too late –

he pushed himself free and swung himself astride the Major's back – hearing the Major's gasp of surprise – and he shoved his tongue into the Major's earhole and grasped his own erect cock in his hand – Christ, no lube – he went down and pushed the muscled buttocks apart and spat around the rim and came back and clamped his teeth in the hair at the back of the Major's head and with his hand pushed the head of his cock between the buttocks and – and – and –

And – Christ – fuck – ah – ah –

"Christ – ugh!" His mouth was full of short hairs. "Christ, Major – fuck – Major – *relax* – Jesus – oh –"

"Uh – *Private*!" came the Major's voice but completely muffled. "*Private! Get your hand off the back of my head!* You're smothering me!"

"Oh – *Major*! For Christ's sake *relax – relax,* sir – relax or I can't get in there –"

"*Relax?* How the fuck d'you expect me to *relax* in the circumstances, Private! If you can't *do* it get the fuck out!"

Private Tony was in pain. Oh Jesus. "I can't, sur – I can't get out eithur – Jesus, sur – please – look Major – Major – I'll talk you down – I'll talk you down, OK? Right – now let's take it nice an easy – no hurry – Jesus – just think of something – think of – of Santa Claus – an if you're in pain – wait a minute –" He clasped his left hand ovur the Major's. "Now if you're in pain just make a fist – right? And I'll stop. Like at the dentist's – OK?"

Why the fuck did I evur start this? Uptight bastard. What did I expect? And why didn't I get the condoms an lube out? Unsafe fuckin sex besides –

Wait a minute – this is a fantasy – it doesn't mattur about condoms yeh eejit –

An yeh don't need lube eithur – faith can move mountains – no bothur –

Jay, yeah –

A fantasy, right? So what's your problem? So there's no reason why yeh shouldn't be ridin that tightly muscled back like Boy on a Dolphin . . . or a Turtle . . .

Just Do It. Like Adidas. Or is it Nike? So much for advertisin.

"OK, Major – I'm countin yeh down –
India
Mike –
George –
Oscar –
India –
Novembur –
George –
India –
Novembur!
Yeeeeeees!
And Major – I think we have lift-off . . ."

The liquid guitar was suddenly soundin right in his left earhole –

241

Here come the rooster
You know he ain't gonna die —

This time comin outa the fantasy wasn't like comin up from the depths a the sea. I was suddenly clear, wide awake and alert. In the early morning darkness I felt a weight on me — a warm human weight.

But something hard an cold as an ice-chip was against my temple. Hard and cold as metal.

The voice when it came was that breathy unmistakable voice that's been menacin us from the cinema screen for decades — you've heard it — *Well, do ya feel lucky punk?*

But this time it was goin: "I'll say this once so you listen to me and listen to me good — you tell one soul out there what happened here, *you little fuck*, and I'm goin to spray your fuckin brains all over this country or whatever country you happen to be in at the time — do you hear me, *soldier?*"

An though I knew there was a mistake an he couldn't be talkin to me — I wasn't a soldier — I was a spirit an I didn't have any brains to spray — I answered, me voice rustlin in me throat like dried vegetation: "Yes — sur."

It was the cold grey mornin of the second day of Novembur. The day of the Commemoration of the Dead.

I felt like a walkin hangover.

I felt like the bottom of a parrot's cage.

Everythin was collapsed.

The pumpkins were collapsed in on themselves like so many used condoms an our condum-balloons that had looked so brave the night before were like so many collapsed an pathetic pricks. Mary's weddin-dress was grey in the mornin light collapsed on the floor, sad as a burst balloon.

The beer-cans were caved in an the bonfire outside was a mass of grey ash. Ash everywhere. In the cans, inside the pumpkins, in the Scout can.

Grunge wasn't in it.

Cigarette ash. Pumpkin ash. H-ash. Bonfire ash. Bone-fire ash.

I felt fuckin contaminated.

The air was putrid with the smell a sex an hash an cigarette-smoke – an undur it all I caught the whiff a rottin vegetation.

I was nevur goin back to that jungle again.

Nevur goin to run the risk a zoomin *him* in again.

Tough, Private Tony.

I looked around at the othurs – Christ –

Were we *seriously* supposed to rise again like phoenixes from the ashes?

I was good at that.

No more bothur to me –

But the othurs?

I was seriously tempted to let em sleep it out an fuck the weddin.

But Tizzy's court-case –

I navigated round doin me left-earhole job an some time latur I had em all up an staggurin an blundurin around – legless still an bare-assed –

Mothur an Mike had been spirited away durin the night. Shape-shifted inta – I dunno – turtle-doves maybe. Or just turtles. Or spontaneously combusted in a bone-fire a passion. The possibilities were interestin but my bet was they were spirited away in a Sun cab down ta Mothur's flat.

Fawlty had gone staggerin off into the dawn – a broken man.

All a the stags were desperate for a cure an they voted to get dressed an up to The Cotton Ball like *fast* for a hair a the dog that bit em.

They all forgot about poor Tizzy.

Except me. I watched him gettin ready, shakin like a leaf in a high wind. "So I-I bettur be off," says he at last wringin the hands. "Who's comin with me?"

An a'course no one could. Go with him. Because they were all runnin weddins or gettin married or bein bridesmaids an so on. Or Dutch.

"That does it," says Liam who was climbin inta Mary's sistur's fiance's monkey-suit. "He can't go by himself. I'm goin with him."

"You can't!" goes Dec – climbin inta Mary's sistur's fiance's boyfriend's monkey-suit.

"Leeeeeem!" screeches Mary – in his undurwear fastenin Niall's blue school-tie to his gartur – somethin borrowed an somethin blue at one go.

"Look – Fathur Twomey's comin at half-eleven, right? I'll be back, I swear. I'll get a taxi. Stall him if I'm late."

"*Stall* him! Now I've heard everything!" Dec bare-legged in his tails.

"C'mon, Tizzy. Let's go." Liam grabbed up his bow-tie an strode off an he combin his hair goin out the door. "Hold Rectus or she'll folly me."

An Dec let him go – just like that. An his face an his thoughts were blank to me.

I broke out in a sweat. So to speak. There wasn't a hope in hell that Liam would come back an Dec knew it. Christ. Me worst fears were trundlin ovur the horizon – *Rollin rollin rollin – rawhi-i-i-ide!*

There was goin to be a weddin, yes, But Liam wasn't meant to be the groom.

This weddin had undurstudies in the wings. Doin novenas. Tizzy's poor face flashed in fronta me eyes – the way he looked when he thought he might havta go on his own. An weddin or no weddin I had no choice. I hadta go with him. An suddenly I *was* with him – in the Sun cab with him an Liam. An I thought I'd had a moment of amnesia or somethin because I couldn't remembur locomotin from one place to the othur.

So in no time at all we were in the Classic Cork Position: up on the steps a the Courthouse. An Tizzy lookin up at the huge pillars like they were Jurassic Park loomin ovur him.

Inside an up the stairs past courtrooms lookin like *Olivur Twist* – y'know – where they havta hold up the child in the dock because he's too small an the judge can't see him to sentence him. The Good Old Days – y'know, an what's the world comin to? But Tizzy's courtroom is like The Sidekick's Lounge an tis *jointed*.

The Sidekick's Lounge? Y'know – in *The Tick* – oh, yeh don't – well, nevur mind – tis a very small room an it sure ain't *L.A. Law*. We bate our way in an there's Lethil lookin relieved at the sight a us an the judge at a table an the lawyurs at tables in fronta him an guards an people standin all round the walls three deep an the benches risin up at the back with people an people ramblin round the court an guards haulin fellas handcuffed to em – tis like a kindurgarten for all the world –

An like *Where's Wally* the cropped red head a Foxy-nob in the pack a people in the benches.

An me heart gave a sickenin heave-ho.

An there was Breeda wavin to us discreetly from the front bench – what was *she* doin here?

Some lads vacated the benches an we squeezed in.

An poor Tizzy was pitiful, chompin away at the fingurnails, an a fierce tremor was comin at me in waves from where Foxy-nob was sittin.

"I swear to God that my evidence before the court shall be the truth, the whole truth and nothing but the truth –"

"State your name –"

The judge was a thin grey-haired man with a way a leanin back in his chair, knees crossed, an arm hooked ovur the chair-back – not casual now like but alert like an eagle surveyin the court ovur his glasses.

An twas extraordinary – yeh could tell the solicitors from the guards from the criminals even if they all swapped clothes an haircuts –

They were like *Star Trek* alien nations confrontin each othur. An as time went on, an a dozen cases were run through by the judge like he'd nevur heard a the speed-limit, I realised I hadn't a hope in hell a undurstandin what was goin on –

"Are you suitable?"

"Strike it out –"

"Sergeant, is this going on?"

I stopped listenin an studied the people – an yeh – yeh could see it in their faces an their height an the way they stood – the guards were fine hefty bacon-an-cabbage countrymen, the solicitors were – what – skinny cheese-an-biscuit yuppies an the criminals were poor misfortunates who could only stretch to baked beans on toast.

The Legal System. Cheese-an-Biscuits usin Bacon-an-Cabbage to lock up the Baked Beans.

I thought a this an I said to meself: there's somethin wrong here. There's somethin *seriously* wrong here.

An me thoughts wavered an I tried to concentrate –

"Sign a bond –"

"To substitute community service order for twelve months –"

"Peremptory –"

Twas double Dutch to me.

An a tidal wave a worry swept over me thinkin a Dec an Liz an next thing for some unknown reason I found meself standin at the top a the steps leadin down to Shaggin Wank. Starin ovur at Florrie's house an our house. An I started down the steps. An when I tried to focus on Tizzy again I could see his face but I was still movin down those steps in Mayfield. For all intents an purposes I *was* in Mayfield. The houses were empty or so I first thought. All gone up to Ennismore? Or up in The Cotton Ball? But then I saw movement through Florrie's nets. She was there, all dolled up in a foxy fake fur for the weddin – hat, bag, gloves, the lot. An she was talkin to someone. There was a small woman, very smart – hair styled an all, cleanin away like a robot in the kitchen. In fact movin through the house like a miniature hurricane cleanin all before hur. This hadta be Florrie's Home Help.

"D'yeh see dat bag deyur?" goes Florrie, pointin to a big

Dunnes plastic carry-bag on the floor. "Dat's de wan I told yeh about. With de photos."

"Oh, grand," goes yur wan blazin away with the cleanin in hur rubbur gloves. "No problem. I'll hang onta it for yeh."

"I put de kids' second-best shoes an clothes in too – dey're wearin deir best things today. I'll get dem to change latur aftur de weddin an I'll give you de good wans to mind."

What was she doin? *Runnin away?* Hur? Nevur. Hockin stuff behind Connie's back? Sounded like that. But photos? The frames.

"Grand," says yur wan jugglin away with the Dettol an the Mr Muscle.

"Rise please –"

An *Jesus*! I was back in the courtroom.

Me heart gave a jolt. This was bad. How the fuck could I have started trippin on *Florrie* at such a time? This is what came outa gettin off on Major O'Hara – jerkin off on Indo-China – I knew twould come to this – I couldn't control me mind any more.

Tizzy had his nails bitten down to the elbows.

An then the judge started this crack –

"Anybody else pleadin guilty?" To the benches.

An the guards: "Guilty? Anybody else pleadin guilty?"

An a young fella stood up in the pack a people an put up his hand.

"Guilty?"

"Not guilty, Yur Honour."

An the judge asked him his name an looked it up an read the report an then looked ovur his glasses at Lethil:

"What's a bradawl, Sergeant?"

"It's a tool, Yur Honour, for boring holes."

The judge swings back to the young fella an fixes him.

"For fishin, Yur Honour, for the bait –" says me boyo, smilin a bit.

An the judge fixes Lethil with a look ovur his glasses.

"Ah, now, Sergeant, I don't think we can assume it was used as an offensive weapon –"

"We've had trouble with him beforre, Yurr Honourr."

"Where did you apprehend him, Sergeant?"

"Outside his house, Yurr Honourr. At thrree o'clock in the morrning."

"His *own* house, Sergeant?"

"Yes, yur Honour."

The judge squinches his eyes. "No, no, Sergeant – we have to dismiss this –"

An Lethil shrugs it off.

"Anybody else pleadin guilty?"

"G'wan, g'wan, Tizzy!" Liam was diggin him an dalkin him. But he was petrified like a rabbit caught in the headlights of a car.

An anothur young fella stood up.

"Yes – guilty?"

Yur man just gapes.

"What's your plea?"

"He's pleadin guilty, Yur Honour." A woman in a black fake-leathur jacket.

"And who is this, Sergeant?"

"His motherr, Yurr Honourr."

"Can't the boy speak for himself?"

"No, Yur Honour," says the woman. "Dis is his first time, Yur Honour, an he don't know how."

Big sigh outa the judge.

An it ends up with Breeda testifyin as to his character – or his mothur's charactur – an twelve hours Community Service.

An then there was a rash a mothurs all pleadin guilty.

Mothurs pleadin guilty.

God help them.

An I couldn't help meself. The notion a Florrie got me by the balls again.

The courtroom faded in a kind of a whoosh an I was back in Florrie's kitchen an the cleanur was gone an Florrie was *still* messin around in hur weddin-gear.

I moved outside.

An Florrie comes out an locks hur door an lumburs off makin for the steps – not the steps you know but the othur steps leadin up to the shoppin centur.

An I seem to be rivetted to the place. I want to find Dec but I can't move.

I know I'm really back in the courtroom with Tizzy an that this is a nightmare.

An with a sickenin jolt it comes to me that I'm disintegratin. Like an android who didn't invest in long-life batteries. Give me anothur while an I'd be singin *Daisy, Daisy, give me yur answur do* . . . like Hal the computur bein dismantled in 2001 AD.

Fuck it, the turtles were dismantlin me.

I remembured the armadillo called Pete an the rots in the tunnels an zoomin in Major O'Hara that mornin – Foxy-nob and Breeda in the same court – Florrie with a Home Help hidin photographs – Fawlty in the bath – Liam marryin Mary – Turtles all the way down –

This was *mad – none a this was real* – I was hallucinatin like a fuckin triggur-happy video-projector –

I probably wasn't even dead –

Just insane. Up in the Red Brick maybe.

But if I *was* dead I was a dysfunctional ghost.

An a crap Guardian Anjul.

An turtles were aftur givin me the thumbs down.

"Anybody else pleading guilty?"

I looked – fully expectin to see a *rot* or an armadillo called Pete in a fuckin gown sittin in the judge's chair. But no. Twas still the Legal Eagle lookin ovur the glasses.

"G'wan, Tizzy, g'wan!" But Liam couldn't get a budge outa Tizzy.

An then me poor Foxy-nob – hallucination or not – gets up an pleads guilty. An he's quiverin like – like Rectus-a-um when she's ovurtired.

"What's this, Sergeant?" Addressin one a the othur sergeants. "A bra?"

An me poor Foxy-nob goes scarlet while the whole court sniggurs an grins an guffaws.

"Bradawls – bras – what next?" An he looks ovur the glasses at Foxy-nob. "Why did you steal such an item?"

"F-for my sistur, Your Honour – for her birthday."

The Legal Eagle goes tchuh-tchuh-tchuh. "Has he been here before, Sergeant?"

"No, Yur Honour. But Roches have him on their books before – for small items."

"Pay in future. Three hours Community Service."

An that's that. Foxy-nob collapses back on the bench with a hand ovur his face.

"Anybody else pleading guilty?"

Liam gives Tizzy a vicious dig in the ribs an Tiz gets up with the eyes like saucers. An starts kinda mouthin.

"What's your plea?"

"Not guilty!" says a well-dressed voice in me ear-hole. An tis Mothur with Mike attached.

Well, why not? In fantasy anything goes.

Mothur's pleadin guilty.

"Can he not speak for himself?"

Mothur is on his feet. "No, Your Honour. This is his first court appearance."

"Appearance? This isn't a *pantomime*, Mr Harte." Everybody knows Denis. An his link with the Arts. "Whose report is this?"

"Mine, Yurr Honourr," goes Lethil.

"What's this?" Looking at the report in his hand. "Cakes?"

"A Fathurr Rrock boy was – eh, molested, Yurr Honourr."

With a bashful glance at Mothur.

"Cakes? He stepped on some cakes?"

"Well – therre was a – bit of horrseplay too, Yurr Honourr – ah –"

"Is the Father Rock boy present?"

"I'm here, Yur Honour!" yells a spotty-lookin carrotty young fella an he stands up bold as brass. Cheerful out. The Legal Eagle peers at the kid. "How old are you?"

"Turteen, Yur Honour."

The judge is fierce perplexed. He starts at Lethil. "The boy is under-age – I can't deal with this – Sergeant?"

Lethil goes puce. He clears his throat. "Well, as the lad didn't sustain an injurry and the parrents didn't press charrges, Yurr Honourr, I took it that Fathurr Rrock was the injurred parrty in this case – an that the lad needn't enterr into it at all – he came of his own accord."

"Humm . . ." He swings back to the kid. "Did you sustain an injury?"

"What's that, Yur Honour?" yells the kid.

The judge winces. "Keep your voice down or you'll be fined for contempt. There's no need at all to shout like that. Were you hurt?"

"No, Yur Honour," yells the kid.

"Did you hear what I said just there about keeping your voice down?"

"I did, Yur Honour!" yells the kid with all his might an main.

The Legal Eagle fixes him but the kid just stands there with a comic grin on his face.

Everyone's grinnin. They're delighted with him.

He's a charactur. An he knows it.

Small silence with the Legal Eagle lookin at the report. An the report *can't* be sayin what it's supposed to be sayin.

"I'm surprised at Father Rock – " He's still lookin baffled an irritated. "This is irregular – but I'm reluctant to waste any more time on it – either yours or mine, Sergeant – putting it through the system again –" He's tappin his pen on the report. Silence. Then: "And what if he replaces the cakes? What would be the monetary equivalent?"

"Ten pounds should covurr it, Yurr Honourr."

"Can you pay?" To Tizzy. "Are you working?"

"No, Yur Honour," croaks Tiz. Perjury like.

"How would you like to pay it?"

"F-fifty pence a week, Yur Honour."

Legal Eagle fixes the Fathur Rock boy. "And can we trust you to keep your tray of cakes in your hand and not put it where they can be trampled on?"

The kid grips the bench-back in fronta him. "Yeh can, Yur Honour!" he yells really puttin his back inta it. An then he raises one hand with the palm up pantomimin himself carryin the tray on his shouldur.

An everyone guffaws.

"Your Honour," goes Mothur who is still on his feet. "I'll be happy to make any restitution considered appropriate."

Legal Eagle raises an eyebrow at Lethil an Lethil gives a little nod.

"Mr Harte –"

An that was that.

An Tizzy wasn't destined for a criminal career aftur all. Or a film career eithur.

Or so it seemed in this pilot-programme-for-a-new-series dished out by me disintegratin brain.

An it didn't surprise me in the least when the whole shebang faded in fronta me eyes an I found meself standin on Pana somewhere near HMV.

I'd probably find meself havin a conversation about rots next or the bakin – probably with Major O'Hara holdin a banana in me ear-hole.

An then sure enough (well, I'm callin the shots) there's an unearthly voice grindin in me ear. Verbatim (not): "Every particle has an antiparticle which it can annihilate. There could be whole antiworlds and people made out of antiparticles. However, if you meet your antiself, don't shake hands! You would both vanish in a great flash of light –"

Oh great! The Turtles givin a Press Conference. An I turn

round an find meself starin inta a TV shop with a big bank
of about a dozen TVs in the winda an in every TV there's
me friend Puking in his wheelchair an Holy Jaysus it turns
out the guy is some kinda android – a very inferior model
like – because the voice isn't human at all – it sounds like it's
comin from a tin cannistur.

I waited for the dozen Pukings to sing –

"Daisy! Daisy! Give me your answer do!
I'm half-crazy all for the love of you!
It won't be a stylish marriage – I can't afford a carriage –
But you'll look sweet upon the seat
Of a bicycle made for two!"

But they didn't.

Anjuls speak through dreams, I thought. They're always
at it. So I slammed meself up agin the winda an listened. An
he was talkin about a philosophur called Cunt – I swear –
who wrote a book makin a case against the use a reason.
Think about it.

An a guy called Hubble who proved that twenty
thousand million years ago everythin in the universe existed
at exactly the same place.

I swear.

So I listened to this an then I stood out in the middle a
Pana with the traffic blastin through me – a thing that does
fearful things to me nervous system – an I gave Hubble an
Puking an yur man Cunt a twenty-one-gun salute.

Thanks a million, lads! That clears it all up.

Now we don't havta worry about space that goes on
forevur or time without end – naaw! Because all the mattur
in the universe originally existed *in an area of no dimensions.*
What could be simplur?

An we can all relax an go back to watchin the Movie Channel, confident that Puking Cunt an Co. are goin to sort it all out for us.

As for me – well, twas crystal clear at last: the Turtles were out sweepin the doorstep of the antiparticle dimension an they missed me. An if I didn't meet me anti-self *an shake hands* I could live forevur.

Beam me up, Scotty!

An I'm back on the steps a the court. This is mega. I'm beginnin to enjoy meself. Like usin a remote.

Liam is dolin out money for fags to the Fathur Rock boy.

"There was a young vicar of Birmingham – sorry! Blast.

There was an old bishop of Birmingham

Who buggered young boys while confirmin em

As they knelt on the hassock

He lifted his cassock

An injected – bugger! Liam – what rhymes with 'confirmin em'?"

But the Fathur Rock boy is takin off with a wink an a swaggur an Liam is starin down the street.

"Vroom-vroom-vroom!" An tisn't the Yogis – tis Foxy-nob revvin up.

An Liam is pointin the nose in his direction, remindin me a someone – ? Oh yeah – Rectus.

"Back in a flash –" An next thing he's down on the kerb an tis "What type a engin?" an "Have yeh changed the pipes? Have yeh taken out the baffles?" an tis all about alloy spokes an standard pipes an watur-cooled 2-stroke an Harleys an trademarkin sounds an the Metro-Goldwyn-Meyer lion an potato-potato-potato an potata-potata-potata if yeh're from Idaho (laugh!) an why ride a slice a bacon when yeh can ride the whole hog (laugh, comin home on the bus!) – *and* – while I'm still bitin me nails – Liam gets a leg ovur – *vroom vroom vroom* an they're gone.

An we all stand there an Tizzy goes, "He's aftur forgettin about a helmet!"

Nice one, Tiz.

So we stand – waitin for them to come back round the block or whatevur – aftur their spin . . .

As if.

An aftur a quartur of an hour there's fuck-all trace a Liam an we've lost the groom.

Cut to Mayfield. With no fade-out at all. Some manic film-editor with a giant scissors has taken control. Me? Directur's Cut.

But I *still* get landed at the top a the Shaggin Wank steps. An me mouth is fulla ash again. An for some reason I'm shakin like an autumn leaf just goin to be whipped from its tree in a high wind.

I tell meself to cool it. None a this is real.

An I look ovur to our Rainbow's End an see the black smoke pourin outa Florrie's windas. An our upstairs windas an front door.

An there's no sense a shock at all – tis like I knew it all the time –

More than that, tis like I done it meself with me rantin on about ashes –

Florrie'd done a good job. She musta doused the whole house good an propur. One chip-pan would nevur a devoured the whole place so fast. The roof was goin already. An the roof a our house.

An then I'm in a room fulla smoke an hot ash but no

257

flame an I feel more than hear Rectus cryin ovur the crackle an whoosh a the fire outside the room-door an the crashes a the floors cavin in. She's cowerin in a cornur near the front winda. An I can hold hur hand but I can't break a winda for hur. I'd nevur got me Supurhero badge. Wouldn't even qualify for the Sidekick's Lounge.

I'm sick to the core. Fuck this for a fantasy. I should be able to hit me remote an change channel.

I hit the remote.

An then I'm in two places at the same time an it feels strange – like pullin elastic apart that's goin to snap back at any second – I'm still inside holdin Rectus-a-um but I'm outside too watchin Connie in a suit staggerin down the steps with the arms out.

"I told hur not ta do it! I told hur not ta do it! Dat bitch will be de death a me!"

He comes staggerin up an elbows his way through the neighbours an makes a dive at the house.

They grab him.

"No, no, Connie, yeh can't go in dere!"

"She's out, she's gone up ta Ennismore – she's not in dere!"

"Ya can't gwin deyur. She's out, I'm tellin ya!"

"Elviiis!"

"She's out!"

"Elviiis!"

"Yur wife's all right, Connie!"

Connie is on his knees. "I told hur not ta do it! Dat bitch'll be the death a me! *Elviiis!"*

"Whas he sayin? Whas he sayin?"

"He's callin for one a de childrun," puts in a neighbour woman.

"But shur de childrun are up at the pub – it must be de dog – is it de dog, Connie?"

Yes, *the dog* –

"Christ, de poor animal's burnt ta death –"

"He doesn't *have* a dog!"

"Elviiis!"

"Didn't I see a speckledy greyhound deyur yesturday?"

"Connie! Did yeh get a new dog?"

Yes –

"I told dat bitch not ta do it! I told hur!"

"Jesus, de ferruts!" goes one a the men.

An a few a them race off round the block a houses to get in the back an rescue the ferruts.

An now I can hardly see hur with the black smoke an she's tremblin in me arms an if I'm the Directur I should be able to say "Cut."

I hold hur tight an try "Beam me up, Scotty" but that doesn't work eithur.

I can't believe I'm goin to havta watch me poor dog die – this can't be real – but fuck it for a fantasy – I misewell be watchin Stephen King –

An then I hear the Fire Brigade siren an the glass shatturs an I look out dizzy with smoke an relief expectin to see a Hunk in a Helmet –

But, Jaysis, tis Mad Mary in his weddin-veil chokin an staggerin in the pillur a smoke blastin out from the broken winda.

With me heart soarin sky high I give Rectus a mental funt in the rear an she leaps through the hole an I folly hur just in time to see two great hulkin firemen jump on Mary an bear him screechin to the ground an start rollin him up an down in the muck an the soot.

"Oh dere's de dog!" goes one a the neighbours.

"Fair dues ta yeh, Connie!"

"More powur ta yur elbow!"

Because in the confusion a the Fire Brigade arrivin an Mary bein jumped they think Connie has rescued Rectus.

Cork Family Burnt out of Home by Thugs on Daughter's Wedding Day – Distraught Father heroically saves Family Pet: I'd do it again, says Connie . . .

An Liz is there in hur gold bridesmaid's dress tryin to rescue Mary from the firemen but it takes a while before they realise he isn't on fire aftur all an let him staggur to his feet with the weddin-veil an wig skew-ways an the weddin dress streaked with grass-stains an muck an soot an the whole back a the skirt ripped away exposin the skinny legs an the scrawny butt.

"Me dress! Me dress!"

"Elviiis! Elviiis!"

Me house. Me house.

"Fiyur! Fiyur!" An Florrie arrives hootin fit to bust in hur fake fur with Roberto in tow – *Jesus* – in his raincoat on sedatives – they'd let him out for the day.

An then all we could do was stand there an watch Florrie an Connie's antics while the houses were bein deluged by the Fire Brigade.

And that – was that.

And so: The Weddin.

Because there *was* a weddin aftur all. Against all odds. Dec was waitin in the courtyard a The Hermitage at Ennismore when we traipsed down the boreen (with Mary draped in Roberto's raincoat – *de wan he uses for de odhur business)* – Lucifur in tails breathin smoke an flame.

He took in the news a the fire with a widenin a the eyes an flarin a the nostrils an a tightenin a the lips.

But then: "Fathur Twomey is *waiting* to perform a wedding ceremony and he can't wait any longur. Did ye see any of the othurs?"

"Leeeeeeeeem's noss heeyur!" goes Mary sobbin. "An me dress is fucked!"

"I know! I know! But where's Denis – Tizzy – Niall?"

"They're not here yet," says Liz. "An Connie an Florrie are up at the house –"

"Buss shur Leeem's noss heeyur!"

"Liam or no Liam, there *is* going to be a wedding."

"Buss shur de house is burnss down!" goes Mary sobbin.

"That isn't the point."

I thought it was.

"Liz, you're on." An he shoves hur an Mary into the bunkhouse next to the chapel.

Ah yes.

"Jesus *Christ*!" comes Cliona's voice from inside the bunkhouse. At the sight a Mary.

The Yogis an some Shaggin Wankurs are waitin in the little chapel with its wooden beams an its candles an incense an the heads swivel every time anyone comes in.

Mandy L'Amour is there lookin lean an sharp in a blue grandad shirt – stage-managin like a traffic-cop with Nine-to-Five clung to him copyin his every move.

They've shifted the big altar-table to the far end a the room an arranged the chairs to make an aisle up the middle. The place looks – eh, *festive* all right but fuckin peculiar.

There's autumn leaves all ovur the shop an these big sheaves a wheat standin in all the cornurs an against the altar with shepherd's crooks an things like whips with brass on the handles an big statchas a – *jackals*? Then I notice the weird-lookin candle-whatsits on the altar-table an I click: they've borrowed the set a *Josuph an his Amazin Technicolour Dreamcoat*. An they've a music system set up in a little entrance-hall that's at right angles to the bottom (normally the top) a the room – undur a small artificial palm-tree. All we're short is a flock a shaggin sheep.

Beyond the Pale is in position clutchin his prayur-book givin tight little smiles an lookin at his watch. But not dressed as the Pharaoh thanks be to God.

Me disintegratin brain is launchin its worst nightmare. An I start fumblin around to find me True Grit – an I can't just put me hand on it – I know tis there somewhere or it was the last time I saw it –

An here comes Breeda with a big charismaniac smile on hur – Holy God! What has Dec told *hur* about this – he couldn't a told hur about Liam an Mary –

Aaahh – but he didn't.

Plonk – plonk – plonk: the sound a all the pieces fallin inta place.

I fix a charismaniac smile on me own face rememburin the burnt house an fuckin terrified a touchin any dark feelins again. At the very least I might get vertigo. At worst the whole chapel might self-destruct.

"Rargh-rargh-rargh-rargh-rargh –" Connie is shamblin in.

Mandy tries to ushur him an Florrie to their seats but – "rargh-rargh-rargh-rargh-rargh" – they're daggurs drawn an no way will he sit with hur – "rargh-rargh-rargh-rargh-rargh" – an he shambles off an sits glowerin at hur from the othur side where Susannah an Tanya an Rollur-blade Barbie are already boppin up an down like hypuractive Muppets.

I see Mothur ditherin about the entrance cuggurmuggerin with Dec – an there's Tizzy makin a beeline for Fuckur.

"Thanks be to God – in the name a the Fathur – this is the word a the Lord – an also with you – thanks be to God – the body a Christ – Amen –" Nine-to-Five has his needle stuck in a different groove – he's playin the B-side. He must think it's Sunday – his Day a Rest from Nine-to-Five–I–ask-yeh.

"Rargh-rargh-rargh-rargh-rargh" –

An there's a *fierce* blast a trumpet music from the speakur system that gives everyone a jolt an someone's got it wrong because this sure ain't the Weddin March –

Mandy is down by the hi-fi an he dithurs bitin a fingur but decides to let it run –

Up the chapel Mothur is mouthin at Breeda – "Aaaa – Eeee – Da" an makin a face like he's sucked a lemon. I figure tis his tape. Dowtcha Denis.

So the music works up to a fierce lathur like Fairy Liquid an everyone cranes the neck but no one appears at the back a the church.

Except Rectus-a-um trit-trottin in lookin for Liam.

Oh – an here comes Roberto like a weasel or Dustin Hoffman in his fawny raincoat.

An this music is outa hand – it reaches an all-time hysterical climax with no notion a foreplay whatsoevur an all the necks crane an the eyes gape an the music goes *uh-huh, uh-huh, uh-huh, uh-huh, uh-huh, uh-huh, uh-huh, uh-huh* like someone labourin for an orgasm – an maybe tis just the thing for a weddin aftur all – but not for *this* weddin –

Uh-*haaah*! With great clash a cymbals an God knows what else – an entrance to bate all entrances an everyone's mouth falls open in expectation –

Not a sausage –

The mouths close an the music carries on regardless at an ear-splittin level an now it flings itself inta a wham-wham-thank-yuh-ma'am with its trumpet flourishes an cymbals an a *wham* an a *wham* an a *wham* – an a *wham* – an a *wham* an a *whaam whaam whaaam whaaam* – *wham wham-wham-wham-wham-wham-wham* – *danti-dan.*

Heads swivel.

Fuck all.

An I'm on me way out to see what's goin on when in zooms Jur in his wheelchair an cowboy hat an whirrs right through me like a dentist's drill – Jesus, I *hate* that – with a bottle fulla some colourless liquid cradled on his lap an he's goin too fast to take the turn up the aisle an ends up ploughin into the third last row a chairs an a showur a – *jam*-jars – yeah, *jam-jars* – a showur a jam-jars spills outa this plastic bag he's carryin an hits the floor – an all the Yogis start duckin with their bums in the air to pick em up –

So I head back in –

Meanwhile – as they say – the music settles down inta this mind-bogglingly beautiful trumpet march an surely *that's* what Whacko Jacko means about the march-time Goldy Anjuls an I think he's right an they must be at it all the time – an man, them Yogis have a nice line a butts – an don't butts in general look so fuckin fuckable in sweat-pants – an no one would *know* if I –

But just then me every last atom quivurs an floatin right through me on this golden music comes – *Mike in a Dominican habit*?

What the fuck?

He floats up the aisle like a fantasy on wheels – as if he was born wearin it an his dark skin glowin against the creamy-whiteness of it. An Mothur *melts*.

Mindya, the effect is kinda spoiled by the fact he's carryin his shaggin raincoat.

Definitely one a me bettur holograms, this one.

An I thought: this is the last fling a me disintegratin brain – the last splutters before it short-circuits an maybe everythin that's happened since I – died –

Maybe I haven't even died.

Maybe it's all been an NDE – a Near-Death thing – an I'll go shootin back inta me body again?

An no fuckin way did I want that.

I wanted to go *on*.

Not *back*.

The music is stridin forward anyway with a little *danti-dan* here an there – here comes the cavalry.

Cut – an Rectus is yelpin an I'm outside in the courtyard – an fuckit, she's OK but I'd yelp too if Cliona was chasin me around a courtyard with somethin huge an strange on hur head – somethin with autumn leaves an waxy apples an othur fruit an nuts an stalks a wheat. Oh yeah – I'd seen it earliur decoratin the table in the dinin-room next to the bunkhouse.

I would just *love* to trip the bitch up – Cliona, that is – but I can only glowur an watch till she lassos poor Rectus with somethin like a curtain-cord an then grabs up this

browny thing like a fancy tablecloth an drapes it ovur hur
arms an down ovur the ass a hur goldy bridesmaid's dress.
Then with a triumphant grin fit to make yur blood run cold
she throws back the head an makes hur entrance inta the
chapel with Rectus strainin at arm's length.

The Queen a fuckin-Sheba.

It hadta happen.

No way would that bitch miss out –

No way will I watch – but Fortune smiles an no soonur
does she make the turn up the aisle when the music stops in
mid-stride – Mandy L'Amour is bent ovur the hi-fi like tis
the control-system a the Starship Enterprise in a crisis – a
last-ditch attempt to find the Weddin March – he's *rewin* an
ffin to beat the band – but when he finally hits *play* we're
marchin away with Aida again –

So *danti-dan* –

An *push my button, baby,* here I come – *me darling
brothur Liam* strides through me in the entrance, sweatin as
if he's been runnin, with a shamefaced look on him – but
me atoms kinda cling to him an he sweeps me in with him
an half-way up the aisle an I watch him take his place up in
the front row next to the Queen a Sheba an Rectus yappin
an whinin around his legs an he's kissin hur on the nose an
fondlin hur ears – Rectus, that is – not that bitch. An me
heart starts goin wham wham wham to beat Aida – an
there's a stir in the chapel an I can hardly bear to look
around –

But it is – it is – tis Mad Mary roundin the last bend an
inta the straight –

All cleaned up in Liz's goldy dress with a wreath a yella

roses on hur dark hair an white roses in hur hands an a huge smile fixed on hur face –

An hatchet-nose an all she looks beautiful –

Every woman looks beautiful on hur weddin-day, they say.

An me whole soul turns inside out an me eyes blur – I'm goin to suffocate with the relief of it.

Bad an all as it is – me brothur an Mad Mary – it isn't me worst nightmare when it comes to the crunch.

Twill nevur last anyway . . . an they're bringin in divorce . . .

But – wasn't Mothur goin to give hur away?

Here she comes – but people are expectin to see hur in white an heads are bouncin around like puppets or muppets an mouths openin an shuttin an necks swivellin an eyes squintin in puzzlement an widenin in surprise an no one knows what the fuck is goin on –

Yes, wasn't Mothur goin to give Mary away?

An she shouldn't be sittin down up at the top, should she? She should be goin up to the altar – where Liam should be waitin –

An where's Liz?

She's still outside. With Dec an Mothur.

Oh God.

An The Bonny Boy strays in late in his fathur's shirt an tie, I'd say, an his school blazur an grey trousurs an the hair combed an the shoes polished like he's goin to a Scout meetin – an me heart goes out to him –

An he kinda dithurs around in the aisle an there's no place to sit – an the Yogis start pushin up in the bed tryin to make room for him – an he kinda makes to go in an at the last minute changes his mind an shakes his head an stays ditherin in the aisle an looks as if he's goin to go back out –

An starts to go back out an me heart lifts –

Just *Do It*, Niall, like Adidas – Nike – *go on* – go out an just *stop* this fuckin farce – why don't yeh just take Liz down to see that crapulous *Indecent Proposal* – g'waan! Ye can throw peanuts at the screen an sniggur at Demi Moore tryin to be a femme fatale –

An I give him a mental heave an feel the resistance an tis Dec on the othur side with a hand hooked in Niall's elbow – an for one incredible moment we've a tug-a-war – but he wins an propels Niall up to the front.

An all the muppets bounce.

An there at last is Liz on Mothur's arm.

An she's all dressed up – how did they do that? Ah yes – Mike's MJ Award Ceremony gear – his black trousurs an cumm-whatsit an black boots an short white jacket all covered in white pearls – an it's all too long an too tight in the wrong places but it still manages to look like stylish weddin-gear with a difference – if yeh squint yur eyes.

An I'm standin in the yard sulkin.

But that makes me feel like a jerk.

So I beam meself back inside again.

An The Bonny Boy gives a start an puts one hand in his pocket an one to his Adam's apple – an ducks his head down an does a teenage slouch the few steps closur to the altar an stands there.

Suddenly I'm turnin inside-out like a glove bein pulled offa someone's hand.

An everythin is startin to blur for me –

Maybe I'm on me way out or maybe the fantasy is fadin

but I hang on – I want to see it through. I hadta give up on Private Tony – me best wasn't good enough – but I wasn't givin up on this one – *this one* I was goin to delivur –

Push like they say to the groanin mothurs-to-be –

Push an Mothur hands Liz ovur with a fierce sweet smile an a pat on the hand as if he was born to be Fathur a the Bride – which is far from the case –

Push an Dec an Cliona step forward – an Nine-to-Five.

An the music is somethin else because even though tis bright gold an cheerful as David Letturman it *is* a military or some kinda triumphant march – so tis fierce belligerent at the same time – an the eyes I don't have are very blurred at this stage an when I look at Liz I see hur like a small version a La Stupenda in one a them Valkyrie costumes with a goldy breast-plate an a helmet with horns an a spear – an Niall in a Roman soldier effort all leathur an silvur an scarlet with his helmet undur his arm – an yeah, I've got it right.

Marriage is *War* –

An there they are headin inta battle –

An yeh havta give it to em – it takes guts –

An soonur them than me –

Then the vision fades an me eyes clear an they're back to bein Liz in borrowed MJ gear an The Bonny Boy in a blazur.

An there's a rivettin flourishin an toolin outa the music system an the music stops – with a nice final *danti-dan*. Beyond the Pale is lookin uncertainly at Niall – he *knows* he's got the wrong groom – but he opens his mouth to begin anyway –

Daaan-tidi-dan-tan-taan – uh! Wham!

Daaan-tidi-dan-tan-taan – uh! Wham!

An off goes Aida again –

Mad Mary gives a mad scairt a laughtur an Beyond the Pale hasta pretend he was just clearin his throat or fishin for flies.

An Mandy scoots up the aisle an collars Nine-to-Five an practically *lifts* him back to the seats.

This time *Aida* works itself inta a fierce state a excitement till it gets to a final powurful –

Duh! Duh duh duh duh duuuuuh!

Up at the altar all the shouldurs straighten up an Beyond the Pale takes a deep breath –

Duh-duh-duh-duuh-duuh-duuh
Duh-duh-duh-daaaa-di-da!

Paroxysms outa the music system – Aida was havin the equivalent of an epileptic fit –

Wumph-wumph-wumph wumph-wumph-wumph wumph-wumph-wumph-wumph!

Wumph! Wumph! Wumph! Waaaaaaaaa!

Silence.

"Give us this day – and also with you – Amen – in the name a the Fathur –" Nine-to-Five churnin away down at the back.

"Rargh-rargh-rargh-rargh-rargh –" Connie is launchin a protest – like where's Liam an our Mary? The Shaggin Wankurs don't know what the fuck is going on but they hold Connie down anyway. Outa habit, I suppose.

Beyond the Pale starts lookin for a place in his prayur-book – but he takes too long – tis clear he's bidin his time – afraid a openin his mouth again.

TURTLES ALL THE WAY DOWN

"An of the Son – the body of Christ – Amen – an also with you –"

"Rargh-rargh-rargh –"

An Beyond the Pale looks up – big encouragin smile for the bridal couple that wavurs a bit when he looks at Niall an glances down at Liam.

An I can't swear to it because I'd moved behind Liam an couldn't see – but I *think* Liam winked at him – judgin from the way Beyond the Pale did an eyes-front –

"In Heaven – and also with you – this is the word a the Lord – Amen – go in peace to serve the Lord – the Lord be with you –"

Mandy L'Amour raises a fingur an levels it at Nine-to-Five an he shuts up.

"Dear Children of God –"

Yannnng!

How d'yeh do-ah!

So you've met my faithful handy*man –"*

An Mandy takes off horror-struck down to the hi-fi to turn it off –

But that takes a few minutes –

Don't get thrown out by the way I look

Don't judge a book by its co-over –

Mothur buries his face in his hands –

I'm not much of a man by the light of day

But by night I'm one helluva lover –

I'm just a Sweet Transvestite from

Transsex-

Silence.

Mothur surfaces.

"Amen – nine to five – to love an serve – I ask yeh – the

Fathur the Son an the Holy Spirit – Brothur – you'd be bettur off on the dole –" The strain was tellin on Nine-to-Five – he was gettin his wires crossed.

"Dear Children of God –"

Beyond the Pale is openly lookin at his watch at this stage. He's got a plane to catch. This is goin to be a quickie.

"We are gathered here to witness the marriage of –"

"Nine to five – Amen."

Beyond the Pale is glancin at a scrap a papur in his prayur-book an hesitatin – *knowin* he's got the wrong groom.

"Liam Eamonn O'Rourke –"

"Niall Ryan," says Dec standin there piously with the hand claspin the wrist ovur his balls in the approved fashion. Beyond the Pale plunges on. "Of this – young – man – Niall Ryan –" lookin at Niall –

"Rargh-rargh-rargh-rargh-rargh –"

"Niall Ryan and –"

"Aftur taxes – and also with you –"

"Patrick Joseph O'Casey." An he grabs up his scrap a papur an peers at it real close. Perplexed.

Christ! Who the *fuck* was eeejit enough to give him the names?

Connie.

"Eh – Patricia Joseph O'Casey?"

"Elizabeth Violet Fitzgerald," says Dec.

Beyond the Pale is starin at Dec.

"An error, Fathur. Elizabeth Violet Fitzgerald."

Beyond the Pale is losin it fast. He stares at Dec.

"I ask yeh! *What* d'yeh think I am? Thanks be to God –"

"Of this young man Niall –" He'd forgotten.

"Ryan."

"Niall Ryan – and Elizabeth Rose –"

"Violet."

"Violet Rose."

"Elizabeth."

"Violet Elizabeth –"

"Elizabeth Violet."

"Elizabeth Violet – uh –"

"Fitzgerald."

"Elizabeth Violet Fitzgerald. Of Niall – uh – of Niall and Elizabeth –"

An Mike in his white habit gets to his feet an stalks outa the church trailin his raincoat along the floor behind him – leavin Mothur rivetted to his seat with the shock – an Liam an Rectus starin aftur him ovur the back a their chair.

What the fuck?

I nip outa the chapel an he's out in the courtyard cryin an his raincoat is on the ground.

An here comes Liam with Rectus undur his arm.

An here comes Mothur in a fevur a anxiety. "What *is* it, *dahling*?"

"He took me raincoat!" An he's cryin an his mascara's runnin.

"*Who* took your raincoat? Isn't that your raincoat?"

"Look at it! Look at it! *That's* not me raincoat!"

An here comes Dec breathless an palpitatin. "A ring, a ring, do ye have a ring? We don't have a ring, do you have a ring? Mike – the ring – give me the ring – the ring – gimme the ring – the *ring*!"

Mike is lookin stupid at him till he looks at his own hand an sees he's wearin the Barm Brack ring. An he tears it off an Dec snatches it an dives back inta the chapel.

"Roberto," says Liam to Denis. "Roberto took his raincoat an left the one he uses for the – the Othur Thing –"

Mike is kickin the raincoat an sobbin.

"He was holdin it," says Liam. "An I was sittin in fronta him an I noticed a smell but I thought Rectus had pissed – an then I noticed twas from behind – from the coat – an that twasn't a new coat – but Mike, I'll get it back for yeh – he's inside –"

"I *can't* wear it aftur *him*!"

"Ooh, *daahling*!" Denis goes, foldin Mike to his bosom an gettin his shirt smeared with mascara. "Don't *fret* – we'll replace it *immediately*! Oh daahling, daahling! What a *dreadful* thing to *happen* to my *sweetheart*!"

Leave em to it, Liam, says I.

So we left em to it.

But Liz an Niall were married by the time we got back – yur McDonald-style weddin. Chips on the side.

"And finally – a special request – I've been asked to remember Tony, brother of the groom, on this happy occasion –"

An everyone looks shockin embarrassed.

"Rargh-rargh-rargh-rargh-rargh!"

"Though he cannot be physically present I'm sure he is with us in spirit –"

"He'd be bettur off on the dole –"

"May he rest in peace –"

"Aftur taxes –"

"Amen."

An they all start sniggerin.

An I'm – a bit – ah – hurt maybe? Like now I'm a joke?

But I brush this feelin aside because it's nice someone remembered me anyway. I'm wonderin who –

Liz an Niall are marchin down the aisle to Connie's "rargh-rargh-rargh-rargh-rargh!"

Nobody – nobody – had the nerve to touch the music system again.

An Liz radiant –

An as we didn't have a crowd a shawlies to say it an nobody else thought a fillin in for em I gave hur the Cork marriage blessin meself – with what I hoped was the right mixture a fondness an humour an pity an hard-won experience – "She's laughin God help hur!"

Mandy had out-done himself – mulled wine in the dinin-room – I suppose wavin magic wands was a way of life with him.

An Jur with his bottle a poteen that he insisted we drink outa those fuckin jam-jars. He said twas traditional but I think he was havin us on – *shur what jam-jars did we have?* Anyway twould make a gas memory an Mandy's thought a everthin an was dancin around with a Polaroid camera he'd brought. Mindya, Connie drank the lion's share a the poteen because he was ravin on about why Liam hadn't married our Mary an the only way to shut him up was to keep shovin jam-jars inta his hand – an soon he was toastin the happy couple – Liam an Mary like – an singin the Hawaiian Weddin Song hangin outa Liam's neck.

Beyond the Pale did his papurwork at the speed a light, changed, tossed back his mulled wine, gave his phone-numbur to Liam an left escorted by Breeda.

An soon aftur the gatherin broke up – they were all knackered an the Yogis were leavin Cork that afturnoon an Liz an Niall wanted to start the honeymoon an – well, the main reason was that Mike wanted his raincoat an Mothur was the one financin the celebrations.

"But daaahlings! *Dinner* in Paddy Garibaldi's tonight at my expense!"

An the next thing a *swarm* a Sun cabs comes ovur the horizon – talkin a Valkyries, Apocalypse Now wasn't in it – they musta emptied the base. An there's fierce revvin an lockin an backin-back for the next ten minutes –

The happy couple were sent off on their honeymoon down to Mandy L'Amour's with beer-cans an Nine-to-Five attached – an at the last minute Dec an Liam chucked the Jackson postur an the Scout can (Petition an all) in aftur em for weddin presents. "Nine to five! Nine to five I ask yeh – Liz, Liz do *you* think I should work Tuesdays late an me there longur than any a ye – I ask yeh – Brothur, Brothur – did yeh hear the rumour? We'd be bettur off on the dole . . ."

"Well, I think that all worked out very nicely," said Dec to Liam. "They'll be able to present the parents with a Fait Accompli. Nothin like it – the Fait Accompli. But, tell me – *what* happened to *you*?"

"Oh I got – side-tracked."

"I *know* – I *heard* about Harley Davidson – but what I don't understand is: why did you come *back*?"

"Oh . . ." says Liam with a strange expression on his face. "Yeh've heard a the fryin-pan an the fiyur?"

"Don't mention frying-pans to me!" says Dec with a shuddur.

"Well, I'll tell yeh latur – anyway – it didn't work out. Nice kid though."

Oh. Me poor Foxy-nob.

Mike an Mothur climb into their cab hand in hand – an Mike still in his Dominican habit – the taxi-man nearly put his back out twistin around to gape at em – Jaysis, *he'd* somethin to tell the wife that evenin – an they trippin up ovur the seat-belts because it's very difficult to navigate efficiently if you're handcuffed to someone else an yur eyes an his are locked togethur permanently.

Tis nice for some.

An Mothur's goin: "I *know* it's something to do with *injecting* but I'm *damned* if I can think of a rhyme for 'confirmin em' – *as they knelt on the hassock he lifted his cassock and injected – what*–"

"It's got to be *in em* again – injected somethin-or-othur *in em*," shouts Liam in the winda an the cab movin off.

"Oh, thank you, Liam! *Injected da-da-da-da-da in em*–"

There's no sign a Cliona an the priest is gay. I think. So she must be – yes, she is – a goldy blob crowned with waxy fruit is disappearin round the cornur makin for the Mayfield Garda Station.

Mandy L'Amour has a cab all to himself in solitary splendour with his hi-fi an caterin stuff an camera an sheaves a wheat an shepherd's crooks an whips an jackals an candle-whatsits an palm-trees – he has a rehearsal for *Endgame* in an hour.

An off go two Sun cabs crammed to the gills with Yogis an Dec – bound for the airport via the hotel. Tizzy waves them down an tries desperately to squeeze in but he can't – an Fuckur starts to point to somethin on his lap – his watch on his wrist I suppose – an goes "sept heures sept heures" in

French – tellin Tizzy the time a the plane I suppose. But Tizzy thinks he's sayin "sit there, sit there" like a Corkman – "si'deyur si'deyur" like – so he climbs ovur the othurs an sits on Fuckur's lap an off they go with Tizzy like a blushin bride.

"You'll have a good ten minutes before the plane, Tizzy," says Dec – very dry.

For which rewind.

An I was on the boreen starin aftur them when Jur whizzed right through me with his jam-jars at a rate a knots – an while I was still off balance anothur Sun cab comes sweepin through me in an electrifyin *whoosh* – me nerves – Connie, Florrie an the kids off down to the *Examinur* office with their Story – *Cork Family burned out by Thugs on Daughtur's Wedding-day* . . .

Then Liam took one of his turns an got the notion he needed some fresh air to clear his head an Rectus-a-um needed exercise like *immediately*. So he strode off for Glanmire – inta the sunset if he were headin west which he wasn't – he was goin due east – with Mary limpin behind him (the heels) wearin Roberto's stinkin raincoat ovur the bridesmaid's dress.

That left me.

I stood on the bridge, leanin ovur, starin inta the rivur. Those mullet were there hangin in space – their space.

Facin up the rivur.

Turtles all the way down.

Fuckin Yogis.

He'd be back to me. When they'd left. I only hadta wait the few hours. No big deal.

Was it?

Wait. Like the Goldy Anjul, the smug bastard.

Fuck.

I felt like endin it all. But that wasn't an option like. Anyway, I couldn't go out not knowing who the fuck the Protestant whore was, could I?

But no doubt about it. I was a crap Guardian Anjul.

I'd be bettur off on the dole.

Twas a miracle to God some good had come outa it all.

I threw me head back an stared up inta the cloudy sky an looked God in the eye.

What the *fuck* am I supposed to be doin? I asked again but kinda weary now.

Heart an soul I sent out a message:

India –

Mike –

Lima –

India –

Sierra –

Tango –

Echo –

Novembur –

India –

Novembur –

George –

I *mighta* heard the sizzle a the background radiation but that was all.

Fuck.

The tiled corridor looked extraordinarily long to Private

O'Rourke – stretching ahead of him like something he remembered from *Alice in Wondurland* when he was a kid – with small little doors at the end.

Private Tony swallowed hard. He walked down the endless corridor.

He'd been waiting for it.

He knew – he'd known all along – that O'Hara had to fix him one way or anothur.

And there were lots of ways in the army.

He could feel the sweat inside the bunched fist he raised to knock on the door. The knock was no louder than the beating of his heart in his ears.

"Come in," said Major O'Hara.

This was it.

The end.

What was he goin to say to his mothur?

The Major was alone.

A deal, then.

Go quietly, soldier, or else . . . I'll fuck you outa the army.

O'Hara glanced up and away again, steel-blue eyes grim, and shuffled some papers together.

Private Tony waited. He wished he could stop the tremor in his hands.

"Well, I guess we've survived," said the Major at last with a frog in his throat. No eye contact. He flicked the corner of a page with his fingernail an then looked up. Looked in Private Tony's face with an effort. "Look, soldier – I'm sorry –"

Oh. Soft-soap.

"I'm sorry I didn't manage to get to see you in the

hospital but – there were decisions that had to be made and it was easier to do that – uh, without personal contact – ah –"

Make it easy on yurself, thought Private Tony.

"Don't think this is easy for me – ah – I know you put your best into – ah – I know you performed well, soldier – uh –"

Extra-lubricant.

"Aam – above and beyond the call of duty – no one could demand more – uh –"

Go on – tell me I got balls.

"Ah – I must admit I've had tougher rides with more experienced men – uh –"

Right. But?

"But –" He was lookin ovur Private Tony's left shouldur. "I've considered everything – and I guess it's selfish of me – but I'm gonna have to throw you a curve –"

"I'd prefer you were straight with me, sur," said Private Tony an blushed.

The Major blushed too. "Uh, well – in the circumstances – I know it's not fair but –" Deep breath. "It would mean putting the welfare of the – the group before your own personal interests but – but –"

Cut the bullshit, man.

"Well – I'm goin on a little reconnaisance trip soon and I'm – I'm – uh – lookin for company – an seein as how we operate so well together . . . uh, we make such a good team . . ."

White light.

"Uh – what d'yuh say?"

Private Tony's eyes blurred an the blood started to leap through his veins.

But yeh nevur would have guessed as he said: "*Yes,* sur. Thank you, sur."

The door opened slowly at me knock.

I gave a slow-burnur of a smile and tipped me stetson.

I said: "Honey, I'm home."

Published by Poolbeg

Mind That 'tis My Brother

by

GAYE SHORTLAND

A lethal mixture of sex, religion and MTV, *Mind That* has been described by the author's teenage daughter as "not very healthy but a good laugh" in a conversation between herself and God.

At its most serious it deals with the spiritual dimensions of sexuality and the need for the world to recognise Prince as our one true Hope of Salvation. At a less serious level it is a celebration of Cork, of humour, of gay sex in particular and of life in general.

The plot? Well, it tells how Tony is brought back to Cork in an urn having died of AIDS and how his friends make fitful efforts to fulfil his last wishes and scatter his ashes over the grave of Little Nellie of Hold God in the Good Shepherd Convent.

However, Tony discovers that he isn't so keen on being buried – he's doing fine as a spirit and besides, he's in love. Meanwhile Dec (who's into a bit of cross-dressing), Mother the artist, Mad Mary the transvestite, Tizzy (famed for his one ball) and the rest meander around a city where meandering is a way of life.

There isn't a word of fiction in it.

ISBN: 1-85371-421-6